P9-BJB-474

V. S. NAIPAUL

V. S. Naipaul was born in Trinidad of an Indian family. He came to England to read English at Oxford, and has lived in London since coming down from the University, with intervals of travel in the Caribbean, India and East Africa. In the autumn of 1968 he was awarded the W. H. Smith prize for his novel *The Mimic Men*. He has also won the Hawthornden Prize, the Somerset Maugham Award, the Llewellyn Rhys Memorial Prize and the Phoenix Trust Award. He is equally distinguished as a writer of fiction and of non-fiction, and has recently completed an as yet untitled history of Spanish and British rule in Trinidad.

THE SUFFRAGE OF ELVIRA

Democracy has come to Elvira, Trinidad; and Surujpat ('Pat') Harbans finds that fighting an election is a surprisingly expensive business. Both Chittaranjan, who controls the Hindu vote, and Baksh, who controls the Muslims, must be appeased, while somehow or other the negro vote must be wooed away from his rival candidate, Preacher. Baksh's son Foam is an energetic but over-enthusiastic campaign manager; he is responsible for the stirring slogan, VOTE HARBANS OR DIE! Matters are complicated by the presence of two attractive Jehovah's Witnesses, who persuade the Spanish constituents to abstain, and by Tiger, the mongrel puppy considered in some quarters to be an evil spirit. When polling day finally arrives the destinies of many citizens of Elvira have been affected in unexpected ways. This election is as funny and as fantastic as the one at Eatanswill; it is a perfect subject for the wit, irony and succinct elegance of style which characterize V. S. Naipaul's individual vision of the West Indian scene.

By V. S. Naipaul

★

In the Russell Edition

MIGUEL STREET

THE MYSTIC MASSEUR

THE SUFFRAGE OF ELVIRA

A HOUSE FOR MR BISWAS

★

MR STONE AND THE KNIGHTS COMPANION

THE MIDDLE PASSAGE

AN AREA OF DARKNESS

A FLAG ON THE ISLAND

THE MIMIC MEN

THE SUFFRAGE OF ELVIRA

by

V. S. NAIPAUL

The Russell Edition

ANDRE DEUTSCH

FIRST PUBLISHED APRIL 1958 BY
ANDRE DEUTSCH LIMITED
105 GREAT RUSSELL STREET
LONDON WC1

SECOND IMPRESSION RUSSELL EDITION MAY 1964
THIRD IMPRESSION RUSSELL EDITION NOVEMBER 1968
PRINTED IN GREAT BRITAIN BY
D. R. HILLMAN & SONS LIMITED
EXETER
SBN 233 95558 5

CONTENTS

FOR PAT

ACKNOWLEDGMENTS

The song *My Heart and I* is quoted by permission of Lawrence Wright Music Co. Ltd.

The song *Swinging on a Star* is quoted by permission of Edwin H. Morris & Co. Ltd. and Messrs Burke & Van Heusen Inc.

PROLOGUE: A BAD SIGN

★

That afternoon Mr Surujpat Harbans nearly killed the two white women and the black bitch.

When he saw the women he thought of them only as objects he must try not to hit, and he didn't stop to think how strange it was to see two blonde women forcing red American cycles up Elvira Hill, the highest point in County Naparoni, the smallest, most isolated and most neglected of the nine counties of Trinidad.

The heavy American bicycles with their pudgy tyres didn't make cycling up the hill easier for the women. They rose from their low saddles and pressed down hard on the pedals and the cycles twisted all over the narrow road.

Harbans followed in a nervous low gear. He didn't like driving and didn't feel he was ever in control of the old Dodge lorry banging and rattling on the loose dirt road. Something else about the lorry worried him. It was bright with red posters: *Vote Harbans for Elvira.* There were two on the front bumper; two on the bonnet; one on each wing; the cab-doors were covered except for an oblong patch which was painted HARBANS TRANSPORT SERVICE. The posters, the first of his campaign so far, had arrived only that morning. They made him shy, and a little nervous about the reception he was going to get in Elvira.

Just before the brow of the hill he decided he needed more power and stepped a little harder on the accelerator. At the same time the women wobbled into the middle of the road, decided they couldn't cycle up any further, and dismounted. Harbans stamped on his brakes, his left foot missed the clutch, and the engine stalled.

The bumper covered with two *Vote Harbans for Elvira* posters hit the back mudguard of one cycle and sent the cyclist stumbling forward, her hands still on the handlebars. But she didn't fall.

The women turned to the lorry. They were both young and quite remarkably good-looking. Harbans had seen nothing like it outside the cinema. Perhaps it was the effect of the sun-glasses they both wore. The trays of both cycles were packed with books and magazines, and from the top of each tray a stiff pennant said: AWAKE!

The taller woman, who had been knocked forward, composed herself quickly and smiled. 'Good brakes, mister.' She spoke with an American accent—or it might have been Canadian: Harbans couldn't tell. She sounded unreasonably cheerful.

'Fust time it happen,' Harbans said, almost in a whisper. 'Fust time in more than twenty years.' That wasn't hard to believe. He had the face of the extra-careful driver, thin, timid, dyspeptic. His hair was thin and grey, his nose thin and long.

The shorter woman smiled too. 'Don't look so worried, mister. *We*'re all right.'

In a difficult position Harbans had the knack of suddenly going absent-minded. He would look down at the grey hairs on the back of his hands and get lost studying them.

'Eh?' he said to his hands, and paused. 'Eh? All right?' He paused again. 'You sure?'

'We're *always* all right,' the taller woman said.

'We're Witnesses,' said the other.

'Eh?' But the legal sound of the word made him look up. 'You is . . .' He waved a wrinkled hand. 'Election nonsense.'

He was coy and apologetic; his thin voice became a coo. 'My head a little hot with worries. Election worries.'

The taller woman smiled back. 'We *know* you're worried.'

'We're Witnesses,' said the other.

Harbans saw the AWAKE! pennants for the first time and understood. The women dragged their red bicycles to the verge and waved him on. He managed somehow to move the Dodge off and got it to the top of Elvira Hill, where the black and yellow board of the Trinidad Automobile Association announces the district as 'The Elvira'. This is short for The Elvira Estate, named after the wife of one of the early owners, but everyone who knows the district well says Elvira.

From the top of Elvira Hill you get one of the finest views in Trinidad, better even than the view from Tortuga in South Caroni. Below, the jungly hills and valleys of the Central Range. Beyond, to the south, the sugar-cane fields, the silver tanks of the oil refinery at Pointe-à-Pierre, and the pink and white houses of San Fernando; to the west, the shining rice-fields and swamps of Caroni, and the Gulf of Paria; the Caroni Savannah to the north, and the settlements at the foot of the Northern Range.

Harbans didn't care for the view. All he saw about him was a lot of bush. Indeed, the Elvira Estate had long been broken up and only the tall immortelle trees with their scarlet and orange bird-shaped flowers reminded you that there was once a great cocoa estate here.

It was the roads of Elvira that interested Harbans. Even the election didn't make him forget to count the ruts and trenches and miniature ravines that made it hell to drive to Elvira. So far he had counted seven, and noted the beginnings of what promised to be a good landslide.

This consoled him. For years he had been able to persuade

the chief engineer of County Naparoni to keep his hands off the Elvira roads. Big repairs were never attempted; even asphalt was not laid down, although the Pitch Lake, which supplies the world, is only thirty miles away. Harbans could depend on the hilly dirt roads of Elvira to keep the Harbans Transport Service busy carrying sand and gravel and blue-metal stone. Harbans owned a quarry too. Road works were always in progress in Elvira. That afternoon Harbans had counted three road-gangs—four men to a gang, two filling in the gaps in the road with a hammer and a light pestle, two operating the traffic signals. Respectful boys. When Harbans had passed they had stopped working, taken off their hats and said, 'Good luck, boss.'

At the small Spanish settlement of Cordoba he saw some labourers coming back from the day's work with muddy hoes and forks over their shoulders. They didn't wave or shout. The Spaniards in Cordoba are a reserved lot, more negro than Spanish now, but they keep themselves to themselves.

Even so Harbans expected some small demonstration. But the labourers just stopped and stood at the side of the road and silently considered the decorated lorry. Harbans felt shyer than before, and a little wretched.

From Cordoba the road sloped down sharply to the old cocoa-house, abandoned now and almost buried in tall bush. The cocoa-house stood at a blind corner and it was only as he turned it that Harbans saw the black bitch, limping about idly in the middle of the road. She was a starved mongrel, her ribs stuck out, and not even the clangour of the Dodge quickened her. He was almost on top of her before he stamped on his brakes, stalling the engine once more.

'Haul your arse!'

Only his edginess made Harbans use language like that. Also, he believed he had hit her.

If he had, the dog made no sign. She didn't groan or whine; she didn't collapse, though she looked near it. Then Harbans saw that she had littered not long before. Her udders, raw and deflated, hung in a scalloped pink fringe from her shrunken belly.

Harbans sounded his horn impatiently.

This the dog understood. She looked up, but without great animation, limped to the side of the road with one foot off the ground and disappeared into the bushes in front of the cocoa-house.

It was only when he had driven away that Harbans thought. His first accidents in twenty years. The strange white women. The black bitch. The stalling of the engine on both occasions.

It was clearly a sign.

And not a good sign either. He had done all his bargaining for the election; the political correspondents said he had as good as won already. This afternoon he was going to offer himself formally to Baksh and Chittaranjan, the powers of Elvira. The bargains had only to be formally sealed.

But what did this sign mean?

Agitated, he drove into Elvira proper, where he was to find out. The first person he was going to call on was Baksh.

I

THE BAKSHES

★

Democracy had come to Elvira four years before, in 1946; but it had taken nearly everybody by surprise and it wasn't until 1950, a few months before the second general election under universal adult franchise, that people began to see the possibilities.

Until that time Baksh had only been a tailor and a man of reputed wealth. Now he found himself the leader of the Muslims in Elvira. He said he controlled more than a thousand Muslim votes. There were eight thousand voters in County Naparoni, that is, in Elvira and Cordoba. Baksh was a man of power.

It was a puzzle: how Baksh came to be the Muslim leader. He wasn't a good Muslim. He didn't know all the injunctions of the Prophet and those he did know he broke. For instance, he was a great drinker; when he went to Ramlogan's rumshop he made a point of ordering white puncheon rum, the sort you have to swallow quickly before it turns to vapour in your mouth. He had none of the dignity of the leader. He was a big talker: in Elvira they called him 'the mouther'.

Chittaranjan, now, the other power in Elvira, was aloof and stiff, and whenever he talked to you, you felt he was putting you in your place. Baksh mixed with everybody, drank and quarrelled with everybody. Perhaps it was this that helped to make Baksh the Muslim leader, though the position should have gone in all fairness to Haq, a fierce black little man who wore a bristle of white beard and whiskers and whose eyes flashed behind steel-rimmed spectacles when he spoke of infidels. Haq was orthodox, or so he led people to believe, but Haq was poor. He ran a grubby little stall, just twice the size of a sentry-box, stocked only with cheap sweets and soft drinks.

Baksh made money. It was hard not to feel that for all his conviviality Baksh was a deep man. He was a talker, but he did things. Like that shirt-making business. For months Baksh talked. 'Make two three dozen cheap khaki shirts,' he told them in Ramlogan's rumshop. 'Take them to Princes Town and Rio Claro on market day. A cool seventy dollars. Some damn fool or the other come up to you. You tell him that the shirts not really good enough for him. You say you going to make something especially to fit him pussonal. You pretend you taking his measure, and when you go back the next week you give the damn fool the same shirt. Only, you charge him a little extra.' He talked like that for months. And then one day he actually did it all as he had said. And made money.

He lived in a tumbledown wooden house of two storeys, an elaborate thing with jalousies and fretwork everywhere, built for an overseer in the days of the Elvira Estate; but he used to say that he could put up something bigger than Chittaranjan's any day he chose. 'Only,' he used to say, 'they just ain't have the sort of materials *I* want for my house. This Trinidad backward to hell, you hear.' He kept designs of Californian-style houses from American magazines to show the sort of house he wanted. 'Think they could build like that in Trinidad?' he would ask, and he would answer himself: 'Naah!' And if he were at the door of his tailoring establishment he would spit straight across the ragged little patch of grass into the deep gutter at the roadside.

For a tailor he dressed badly and he said this was so because he was a tailor; anyway, 'only poorer people does like dressing up, to try and pretend that they ain't so poor'. He dressed his children badly because he didn't want them 'running about thinking they is superior to poorer people children'.

In June 1950, when Harbans drove into Elvira to see Baksh, there were seven young Bakshes. The eldest was seventeen; he would be eighteen in August. This boy's name was not generally known but everyone called him Foam, which was short for Foreman.

★

The decorated Dodge lorry came to a stop in a narrow trace opposite Baksh's shop. Harbans saw the sign:

M. BAKSH
London Tailoring Est.
Tailoring and Cutting
Suits Made and Repair at City Prices

A flock of poorer people's children, freed from school that Friday afternoon, had been running after the lorry ever since it entered the Elvira main road. Many of them were half-dressed according to the curious rural prudery which dictated that the top should be covered, not the bottom. They shouted, 'Vote Harbans for Elvira, man!' and made a chant of it. Harbans resented the whole thing as an indignity and was tempted to shoo the children away when he got out of the lorry, but he remembered the election and pretended not to hear.

He wasn't a tall man but looked taller than he was because he was so thin. He walked with a clockwork jerkiness, seeming to move only from the knees down. His white shirt, buttoned at the wrist, was newly ironed, like his trousers.

The only rakish touch in his dress was the tie he used as a trousers-belt. Altogether, there was about him much of the ascetic dignity of the man who has made money.

Foam, Baksh's eldest son, sat at the Singer sewing-machine near the door, tacking a coat; an overgrown bony boy with a slab-like face: you felt that the moment he was born someone had clapped his face together.

Foam said, 'Candidate coming, Pa.'

'Let him come,' Baksh said. If Harbans had heard he would have recognized the casual aggressiveness he had been fearing all afternoon. Baksh stood at a counter with a tape-measure round his neck, consulting a bloated copy-book and making marks with a triangular piece of yellow chalk on some dark blue material. At one end of the counter there was a pile of new material, already cut. A yardstick, its brass tips worn smooth, was screwed down at the other end.

Light came into the shop only through the front door and didn't reach everywhere. Age had given the unpainted wall-boards the barest curve; darkness had made them a dingy russet colour; both had given the shop a moist musty smell. It was this smell, warm and sharp in the late afternoon, not the smell of new cloth, that greeted Harbans when he walked over the shaky plank spanning the gutter and came into the yard.

Foam kept on tacking. Baksh made more marks on his cloth.

Two months, one month ago, they would have jumped up as soon as they saw him coming.

Harbans suffered.

'Aah, Baksh.' He used his lightest coo. '*How* you is?' He flashed his false teeth at Foam and added all at once, 'And how the boy is? He doing well? Ooh, but he looking too well and too nice.'

Foam scowled while Harbans ruffled his hair.

'Foam,' Baksh said, very gently, 'get up like a good boy and give Mr Harbans your bench.'

Baksh left his chalk and cloth and came to the doorway. He had the squat build of the labourer and didn't look like a leader or even like the father of seven children. He seemed no more than thirty. He seated Harbans and spat through the door into the gutter. 'Ain't got much in the way of furnishings, you see,' he said, waving his hands about the dark windowless room with its gloomy walls and high sooty ceiling.

'It matter?' Harbans said.

'It matter when you ain't have.'

Harbans said, 'Aah.' Baksh frightened him a little. He didn't like the solid square face, the thick eyebrows almost meeting at the bridge of a thick nose, the thick black moustache over thick lips. Especially he didn't like Baksh's bloodshot eyes. They made him look too reckless.

Harbans put his hands on his thin knees and looked at them. 'I take my life in my hands today, Baksh, to come to see you. If I tell you how I hate driving!'

'You want some suit and things?'

'Is talk I want to talk with you, Baksh.'

Baksh tried to look surprised.

'Foam,' Harbans said, 'go away a lil bit. It have a few things, pussonal, I want to say to your father.'

Foam didn't move.

Baksh laughed. 'No, man. Foam is a big man now. Eh, in two three years we have to start thinking about marrying him off.'

Foam, leaning against the wall under a large Coca-Cola calendar, said, 'Not me, brother. I ain't in that bacchanal at all. I ain't want to get married.'

Harbans couldn't protest. He said, 'Ooh,' and gave a little chuckle. The room was too dark for him to see Foam's expression. But he saw how tall and wiry the boy was, and he thought his posture a little arrogant. That, and his booming voice, made him almost as frightening as his father. Harbans's hands began to tap on his knees. 'Ooh, ooh. Children, eh, Baksh?' He chuckled again. 'Children. What you going to do?'

Baksh sucked his teeth and went back to his counter. 'Is the modern generation.'

Harbans steadied his hands. 'Is that self I come to talk to you about. The modern world, Baksh. In this modern world everybody is one. Don't make no difference who you is or what you is. You is a Muslim, I is a Hindu. Tell me, that matter?' He had begun to coo again.

'Depending.'

'Yes, as you say, depending. Who you for, Baksh?'

'In the election, you mean?'

Harbans looked ashamed.

Baksh lay down on a low couch in the darkest corner of the dark room and looked up at the ceiling. 'Ain't really think about it yet, you know.'

'Oh. Ooh, who *you* for, Foam?'

'Why for you bothering the boy head with that sort of talk, man?'

Foam said, 'I for you, Mr Harbans.'

'Ooh, ooh. Ain't he a nice boy, Baksh?'

Baksh said, 'The boy answer for me.'

Harbans looked more ashamed.

Baksh sat up. 'You go want a lot of help. Microphone. Loudspeaking van. Fact, you go want a whole campaign manager.'

'Campaign what? Ooh. Nothing so fancy for me, man. You and I, Baksh, we is very simple people. Is the community we have to think about.'

'Thinking about them all the time,' Baksh said.

'Time go come, you know, Baksh, and you too, Foam, time go come when you realize that money ain't everything.'

'But is a damn lot,' Foam boomed, and took up his tacking again.

'True,' Harbans fluted.

'Must have a loudspeaking van,' Baksh said. 'The other man have a loudspeaking van. Come to think of it, you could use *my* loudspeaker.' He looked hard at Harbans. 'And you could use *my* van.'

Harbans looked back hard into the darkness. 'What you saying, Baksh? You ain't got no loudspeaker.'

Baksh stood up. Foam stopped tacking.

'You ain't got no loudspeaker,' Harbans repeated. 'And you ain't got no van.'

Baksh said, 'And you ain't got no Muslim vote.' He went back to his counter and took up the yellow chalk in a businesslike way.

'Haa!' Harbans chuckled. 'I was only fooling you. Haa! I was only making joke, Baksh.'

'Damn funny sorta joke,' Foam said.

'You going to get your van,' Harbans said. 'And you going to get your loudspeaker. You sure we *want* loudspeaker?'

'Bound to have one, man. For the boy.'

'Boy?'

'Who else?' Foam asked. 'I did always want to take up loudspeaking. A lot of people tell me I have the voice for it.'

'Hundred per cent better than that Lorkhoor,' Baksh said.

Lorkhoor was the brightest young man in Elvira and Foam's natural rival. He was only two-and-a-half years older than Foam but he was already making his mark on the world. He ran about the remoter districts of Central Trinidad with a loudspeaker van, advertising for the cinemas in Caroni.

'Lorkhoor is only a big show-offer,' Foam said. 'Ever hear him, Mr Harbans? "This is the voice of the ever popular Lorkhoor," he does say, "begging you and imploring you and entreating you and beseeching you to go to the New Theatre." Is just those three big words he know, you know. Talk about a show-offer!'

'The family is like that,' Baksh said.

'We want another stand-pipe in Elvira,' Harbans said. 'Elvira is a big place and it only have one school. And the roads!'

Foam said, 'Mr Harbans, Lorkhoor start loudspeaking against you, you know.'

'What! But I ain't do the boy or the boy family nothing at all. Why he turning against a old man like me?'

Neither Baksh nor Foam could help him there. Lorkhoor had said so often he didn't care for politics that it had come as a surprise to all Elvira when he suddenly declared for the other candidate, the man they called Preacher. Even Preacher's supporters were surprised.

'But I is a Hindu,' Harbans cried. 'Lorkhoor is a Hindu. Preacher is negro.'

Baksh saw an opening. 'Preacher giving out money hands down. Lorkhoor managing Preacher campaign. Hundred dollars a month.'

'Where Preacher getting that sort of money?'

Baksh began to invent. 'Preacher tell me pussonal'—the word had enormous vogue in Elvira in 1950—'that ever since he was a boy, even before this democracy and universal suffrage business, he had a ambition to go up to the Legislative Council. He say God send him this chance.' Baksh paused for inspiration. It didn't come. 'He been saving up,'

Baksh went on lamely. 'Saving up for a long long time.' He shifted the subject. 'To be frank with you, Mr Harbans, Preacher have me a little worried. He acting too funny. He ain't making no big noise or nothing. He just walking about quiet quiet and brisk brisk from house to house. He ain't stick up no posters or nothing.'

'House-to-house campaign,' Harbans said gloomily.

'And Lorkhoor,' Foam said. 'He winning over a lot of stupid people with his big talk.'

Harbans remembered the sign he had had that afternoon: the women, the dog, the engine stalling twice. And he hadn't been half an hour in Elvira before so many unexpected things had happened. Baksh wasn't sticking to the original bargain. He was demanding a loudspeaker van; he had brought Foam in and Harbans felt that Foam was almost certain to make trouble. And there was this news about Lorkhoor.

'Traitor!' Harbans exclaimed. 'This Lorkhoor is a damn traitor!'

'The family is like that,' Baksh said, as though it were a consolation.

'I ain't even start my campaign proper yet and already I spend more than two thousand dollars. Don't ask me what on, because I ain't know.'

Baksh laughed. 'You talking like Foam mother.'

'Don't worry, Mr Harbans,' Foam said. 'When we put you in the Leg. Co. you going to make it back. Don't worry too much with Lorkhoor. He ain't even got a vote. He too young.'

'But he making a hundred dollars a month,' Baksh said.

'Baksh, we really *want* a loudspeaker van?'

'To be frank, boss, I ain't want it so much for the elections as for afterwards. Announcing at all sort of things. Sports. Weddings. Funerals. It have a lot of money in that nowadays, boss, especially for a poor man'—Baksh waved his hands about the room again—'who ain't got much in the way of furnishings, as you see. And Foam here could manage your whole campaign for eighty dollars a month. No hardship.'

Harbans accepted the loudspeaker van sorrowfully. He tried again. 'But, Baksh, I ain't want no campaign manager.'

Foam said, 'You ain't want no Muslim vote.'

Harbans looked at Foam in surprise. Foam was tacking slowly, steadily, drawing out his needle high.

Baksh said, 'I promise you the boy going to work night and day for you.' And the Muslim leader kissed his crossed index fingers.

'Seventy dollars a month.'

'All right, boss.'

Foam said, 'Eh, I could talk for myself, you hear. Seventy-five.'

'Ooh. Children, Baksh.'

'They is like that, boss. But the boy have a point. Make it seventy-five.'

Harbans hung his head.

The formal negotiations were over.

Baksh said, 'Foam, cut across to Haq and bring some sweet drink and cake for the boss.'

Baksh led Harbans through the dark shop, up the dark stairs, through a cluttered bedroom into the veranda where Mrs Baksh and six little Bakshes—dressed for the occasion in their school clothes—were introduced to him.

Mrs Baksh was combing out her thick black hair that went down to her hips. She nodded to Harbans, cleared her comb of loose hair, rolled the hair into a ball, spat on it and threw it into a corner. Then she began to comb again. She was fresh, young, as well-built as her husband, and Harbans thought there was a little of her husband's recklessness about her as well. Perhaps this was because of her modern skirt, the hem of which fell only just below the knee.

Harbans was at once intimidated by Mrs Baksh. He didn't like the little Bakshes either. The family insolence seemed to run through them all.

If it puzzled Harbans how a burly couple like Mr and Mrs Baksh could have a son like Foam, elongated and angular, he could see the stages Foam must have gone through when he looked at the other Baksh boys: Iqbal, Herbert, Rafiq and Charles. (It was a concession the Bakshes made to their environment: they chose alternate Christian and Muslim names for their children.) The boys were small-boned and slight and looked as though they had been stretched on the rack. Their bellies were barely swollen. This physique better became the girls, Carol and Zilla; they looked slim and delicate.

Baksh cleared a cane-bottomed chair of a pile of clothes and invited Harbans to sit down.

Before Harbans could do so, Mrs Baksh said, 'But what happen to the man at all? That is my ironing.'

Baksh said, 'Carol, take your mother ironing inside.'

Carol took the clothes away.

Harbans sat down and studied the back of his hands.

Mrs Baksh valued the status of her family and felt it deserved watching. She saw threats everywhere; this election was the greatest. She couldn't afford new enemies; too many people were already jealous of her and she suspected nearly everybody of looking at her with the evil eye, the *mal yeux* of the local patois. Harbans, with his thin face and thin nose, she suspected in particular.

Harbans, looking down at the grey hairs and ridge-like veins of his hands and worrying about the loudspeaker van and the seventy-five dollars a month, didn't know how suspect he was.

Foam came back with two bottles of coloured aerated water and a paper bag with two rock cakes.

'Zilla, go and get a glass,' Baksh ordered.

'Don't worry with glass and thing,' Harbans said appeasingly. 'I ain't all that fussy.' He was troubled. The aerated water and the rock cakes were sure not to agree with him.

The little Bakshes, bored up till then, began to look at Harbans with interest now that he was going to eat.

Zilla brought a glass. Foam opened a bottle and poured the bright red stuff. Zilla held the paper bag with the rock cakes towards Harbans. Foam and Zilla, the eldest Baksh children, behaved as though they had got to the stage where food was something to be handled, not eaten.

The little Bakshes hadn't reached that stage.

Baksh left the veranda and came back with a cellophane-wrapped tin of Huntley and Palmer's biscuits. He felt Mrs Baksh's disapproval and avoided her eye.

'Biscuit, Mr Harbans?'

The little Bakshes concentrated.

'Nice biscuits,' Baksh tempted, stubbornly. 'Have them here since Christmas.'

Harbans said, 'Give it to the children, eh?' He broke off a large piece of the rock cake and handed it to Herbert who had edged closest to him.

'Herbert!' Mrs Baksh exclaimed. 'Your eyes longer than your mouth, eh!'

'Let the poor boy have it,' Harbans cooed, and showed his false teeth.

She ignored Harbans's plea and faced Herbert. 'You don't care how much you shame me in front of strangers. You making him believe I does starve you.'

Herbert had already put the cake in his mouth. He chewed slowly, to show that he knew he had done wrong.

'You ain't shame?' Mrs Baksh pointed. 'Look how your belly puff out.'

Herbert stopped chewing and mumbled, 'Is only the gas, Ma.'

The other little Bakshes had their interest divided between their mother's anger and Harbans's food.

Harbans said, 'Ooh, ooh,' and smiled nervously at everybody.

Mrs Baksh turned to him. 'You eat those cakes up and drink the sweet drink and don't give a thing to any of these shameless children of mine.'

She used a tone of inflexible authority which was really meant for the little Bakshes. Harbans didn't know this. He ate and drank. The warm liquid stabbed down to his stomach; once there it tore around in circles. Still, from time to time he looked up from the aerated water and rock cake and smiled at Mrs Baksh and Baksh and Foam and the other little Bakshes.

The biscuits were saved.

At last Harbans was finished and he could leave. He was glad. The whole Baksh family frightened him.

Foam walked down the steps with Harbans. They had hardly got outside when they heard someone screaming upstairs.

'Herbert,' Foam said. 'He does always make that particular set of noise when *they* beat him.'

When Foam said *they* Harbans knew he meant Mrs Baksh.

Candidate and campaign manager got into the Dodge and drove on to see Chittaranjan.

II

THE BARGAIN WITH CHITTARANJAN

★

Easily the most important person in Elvira was Chittaranjan, the goldsmith. And there was no mystery why. He looked rich and was rich. He was an expensive goldsmith with a reputation that had spread beyond Elvira. People came to him from as far as Chaguanas and Couva and even San Fernando. Everyone knew his house as the biggest in Elvira. It was solid, two-storeyed, concrete, bright with paint and always well looked after.

Nobody ever saw Chittaranjan working. For as long as Foam could remember Chittaranjan had always employed two men in the shop downstairs. They worked in the open, sitting flat on the concrete terrace under a canvas awning, surrounded by all the gear of their trade: toy pincers, hammers and chisels, a glowing heap of charcoal on a sheet of galvanized iron, pots and basins discoloured with various liquids, some of which smelled, some of which hissed when certain metals were dipped in them. Every afternoon, after the workmen had cleared up and gone home, children combed the terrace for silver shavings and gold dust. Even Foam had done so when he was younger. He hadn't got much; but some children managed, after years of collecting, to get enough to make a ring. Chittaranjan never objected.

No wonder Foam, like nearly everyone else, Hindu, Muslim, negro, thought and spoke of his house as the Big House. As a Hindu Chittaranjan naturally had much influence among the Hindus of Elvira; but he was more than the Hindu leader. He was the only man who carried weight with the Spaniards of Cordoba (it was said he lent them money); many negroes liked him; Muslims didn't trust him, but even they held him in respect.

'You ain't have nothing to worry about, Mr Harbans,' Foam said, speaking as campaign manager, as he and Harbans drove through Elvira. 'Chittaranjan control at least five thousand votes. Add that to the thousand Muslim votes and you win, Mr Harbans. It only have eight thousand voters in all.'

Harbans had been brooding all the way. 'What about that traitor Lorkhoor?'

'Tcha! You worrying with Lorkhoor? Look how the *people* welcoming you, man.'

And really, from the reception the lorry had been getting since it left Baksh's, it didn't look as though Harbans had anything to worry about. The news had gone around that he was in Elvira, campaigning at last. It was just after five o'clock, getting cool, and most people were at home. Children rushed to the roadside and shouted, 'Vote Harbans, man!' Women left their cooking and waved coyly from their front yards, and made the babies at their hips wave too.

Harbans was so morose he left it to Foam to wave and shout back, 'That's right, man! Keep it up!'

Foam's ebullience depressed Harbans more. The bargaining with Baksh had shaken him and he feared that Chittaranjan too might demand stiffer terms. Moreover, he was nervous about the Dodge; and the sweet drink and rock cakes he had had were playing hell with his inside.

'You shy, Mr Harbans,' Foam said. 'I know how it is. But you going to get use to this waving. Ten to one, before this election over, we going to see you waving and shouting to everybody, even to people who ain't going to vote for you.'

Harbans shook his head sadly.

Foam settled into the angle of the seat and the door.

'Way I see it is this. In Trinidad this democracy is a brand-new thing. We is still creeping. We is a creeping nation.' He dropped his voice solemnly: 'I respect people like you, you know, Mr Harbans, doing this thing for the first time.'

Harbans began to dislike Foam less. 'I think you go make a fust-class loudspeaking man, Foam. Where you learn all that?'

'Social and Debating Club. Something Teacher Francis did start up. It mash up now.' He stuck his long head out of the window and shouted encouragement to a group of children at the roadside. 'Soon as I get old enough, going up for County Council myself, you know, Mr Harbans. Sort of campaigning in advance. You want to know how I does do it? Look, I go in a café and I see some poorer people child. Buy the child a sweet drink, man.'

'Sweet drink, eh?'

'Yes, man. Buy him a sweet drink. Cost me six cents. But in five years' time it getting me one vote. Buy one sweet drink for a different child every day for five years. At the end of five years, what you have? Everybody, but everybody, man, saying, "We going to vote for Foam." Is the only way, Mr Harbans.'

'Is a lil too late for me to start buying sweet drink for poorer people children now.'

They were near Chittaranjan's now, and the Dodge slowed down not far from Ramlogan's rumshop.

Ramlogan, a big greasy man in greasy trousers and a greasy vest, was leaning against his shop door, his fat arms crossed, scowling at the world.

'Wave to him,' Foam ordered.

Harbans, his thin hands gripping nervously to the steering wheel, only nodded at Ramlogan.

'You have to do better than that. Particularly that Ramlogan and Chittaranjan don't get on too good.'

'Aah. But why this disunity in our people, Foam? People should be uniting these days, man.'

The Dodge came to a halt. Harbans struggled to put it in neutral.

Foam pointed. 'See that Queen of Flowers tree in Chittaranjan yard, just next door to Ramlogan?'

'Ooh, ooh, is a nice one.' It made him feel Chittaranjan must be a nice man. 'I didn't know that Chittaranjan did like flowers.'

'Chittaranjan *ain't* like flowers.'

Harbans frowned at the Queen of Flowers.

'Chittaranjan say flowers does give cough.'

'Is true.'

'Huh! Don't start talking to Chittaranjan about flowers, eh. Look at the Queen of Flowers again. Flowers in Chittaranjan yard. But look where the root is.'

The root was in Ramlogan's yard. But about eight inches from the ground the Queen of Flowers—just out of perversity, it seemed—had decided to change course. It made almost a right angle, went through the wide-meshed wire fence and then shot up and blossomed in Chittaranjan's yard.

'And look at that Bleeding Heart,' Foam went on. 'Root in Ramlogan yard, but the flowers crawling all up by Chittaranjan bedroom window. And look at the breadfruit tree. Whole thing in Ramlogan yard, but all the breadfruit only falling in Chittaranjan yard. And look at the zaboca tree. Same thing. It look like *obeah* and magic, eh?'

'Ooh, ooh.'

'Now, whenever Ramlogan plant a tree, he planting it right in the middle middle of his yard. But what does happen then? Look at that soursop tree in the middle of Ramlogan yard.'

It was stunted, wilting.

'Ramlogan blight. If you know, Mr Harbans, the amount

of row it does have here on account of those trees. One day Chittaranjan say he want to cut the trees down. Ramlogan chase him with a cutlass, man. Another day Ramlogan say *he* want to go in Chittaranjan yard to collect the breadfruit and the zaboca and flowers from *his* trees. Chittaranjan take up a stick and chase Ramlogan all down Elvira main road.'

Harbans began to get worried about Chittaranjan.

All this while Ramlogan had been eyeing the lorry, heavy brows puckered over deep-set disapproving eyes, fat cheeks sagging sourly, massive arms still crossed. From time to time he hawked leisurely, and hissed out the spittle between the gap in his top teeth.

'Foam,' Harbans said, 'is a good thing I have a campaign manager like you. I only know about Elvira roads. I ain't know about the people.'

'It have nothing like the local expert,' Foam agreed. 'Look out, Mr Harbans, the lorry rolling in the drain!'

The lorry was moving forward, locked towards the gutter at the right. Harbans dived for the hand-brake and pulled it back with a loud ripping sound. 'Oh God, I did *know* I was taking my life in my hands today.' His alarm was double; he knew then that the sign he had had was being confirmed.

Ramlogan gave a short laugh, so sharp and dry it was almost like a word: 'Ha.'

The commotion brought Chittaranjan to his veranda upstairs. The half-wall hid most of his body, but what Foam and Harbans could see looked absurdly small and shrivelled. Spectacles with thin silver rims and thin silver arms emphasized Chittaranjan's diminutiveness.

Foam and Harbans got out of the lorry.

The awning of Chittaranjan's shop had been pulled back; the ground had already been combed that afternoon by children; and only two toy anvils set in the concrete terrace remained of the day's workshop.

'Is you, Mr Harbans?'

'Is me, Goldsmith.'

'Who is the little boy you have with you?'

'Campaign . . .' But Harbans was ashamed to go on. 'Baksh son.'

'And not so little either,' Foam muttered to himself. But he was anxious. He had been talking freely about Chittaranjan in the lorry, dropping the 'Mr', but like nearly everyone else in Elvira he was awed by Chittaranjan, had been ever since he was a boy. He had never set foot in the Big House.

'What Baksh son want with me? He want to see me in any pussonal?'

'Not in any pussonal, Goldsmith. He just come with me.'

'Why he come with you?'

Harbans was beside himself with shyness.

'About the elections,' Foam boomed up.

'Ha,' Ramlogan said from his shop door. 'Ha.'

Chittaranjan turned to talk to someone in his veranda; then he shouted down, 'All right, come up, the both of all-you,' and disappeared immediately.

Foam nudged Harbans and pointed to one side of Chittaranjan's yard. The ground under the breadfruit tree and the zaboca tree was mushy with rotting fruit. 'See what I did tell you,' Foam whispered. 'One frighten to eat it, the other 'fraid to come and get it.'

They went up the polished red steps at the side of the house and came into the large veranda. Chittaranjan was rocking in a morris rocking-chair. He looked even tinier sitting down than he did hunched over the ledge of the veranda wall. He didn't get up, didn't look at them, didn't greet them. He rocked measuredly, serenely, as though rocking gave him an exclusive joy. Every time he rocked, the heels of his sabots clacked on the tiled floor.

'Is a big big house you have here, Goldsmith,' Harbans cooed.

'Tcha!' Chittaranjan sucked his teeth. He had three gold teeth and many gold fillings. 'Biggest house in Elvira, that's all.' His voice was as thin as Harbans's, but there was an edge to it.

Harbans sought another opening. 'I see you is in your home clothes, Goldsmith. Like you ain't going out this evening at all.'

Like Foam, Harbans was struck by the difference between the appearance of the house and the appearance of the owner. Chittaranjan's white shirt was mended and re-mended; the sleeves had been severely abridged and showed nearly all of Chittaranjan's stringy arms. The washed-out khaki trousers were not patched, but there was a tear down one leg from knee to ankle that looked as though it had been there a long time. This shabbiness was almost grand. It awed at once.

Chittaranjan, rocking, smiling, didn't look at his visitors. 'What it have to go out for?' he asked at last.

Harbans didn't know what to say.

Chittaranjan continued to smile. But he wasn't really smiling; his face was fixed that way, the lips always parted, the gold teeth always flashing.

'If you ask me,' Chittaranjan said, having baffled them both into silence, 'I go tell you it have nothing to go out for.'

'Depending,' Foam said.

'Yes,' Harbans agreed quickly. 'Depending, Goldsmith.'

'Depending on what?' Chittaranjan's tone seemed to take its calmness from the evening settling on Elvira.

Harbans was stumped again.

Foam came to the rescue. 'Depending on who you have to meet and what you going to give and what you going to get.'

Chittaranjan relented. 'Sit down. The both of all-you. You want some sweet drink?'

Harbans shook his head vigorously.

Chittaranjan ignored this. 'Let me call the girl.' For the first time he looked at Harbans. 'Nelly! Nalini! Bring some sweet drink.'

'Daughter?' Harbans asked. As though he didn't know about Nalini, little Nelly; as though all Elvira didn't know that Chittaranjan wanted Nelly married to Harbans's son, that this was the bargain to be settled that afternoon.

'Yes,' Chittaranjan said deprecatingly. 'Daughter. One and only.'

'Have a son myself,' Harbans said.

'Look at that, eh.'

'Ambitious boy. Going to take up doctoring. Just going on eighteen.'

Foam sat silent, appreciating the finer points of the bargaining. He knew that in normal circumstances Chittaranjan, as the girl's father, would have pleaded and put himself out to please. But the elections were not normal circumstances and now it was Harbans who had to be careful not to offend.

Nelly Chittaranjan came and placed two wooden negro waiters next to Harbans and Foam. She was small, like her father; and her long-waisted pink frock brought out every pleasing aspect of her slimness. She placed bottles of coloured liquid on the waiters; then went and got some tumblers.

Chittaranjan became a little more animated. He pointed to the bottles. 'Choose. The red one or the orange one?'

'Red for me,' Foam said briskly.

Harbans couldn't refuse. 'Orange,' he said, but with so much gloom, Chittaranjan said, 'You could have the red if you want, you know.'

'Is all right, Goldsmith. Orange go do me.'

Nelly Chittaranjan made a quick face at Foam. She knew him by sight and had had to put up with his daring remarks when she passed him on the road. Foam had often 'troubled' her, that is, whistled at her; he had never 'rushed' her, made a serious pass at her. She looked a little surprised to see him in her father's house. Foam, exaggeratedly relaxed, tried to make out he didn't value the honour at all.

She poured the sweet drinks into the tumblers.

Harbans looked carefully at the wooden waiter next to his chair. But in fact he was looking at Nelly Chittaranjan; doing so discreetly, yet in a way to let Chittaranjan know he was looking at her.

Chittaranjan rocked and clacked his sabots on the floor.

'Anything else, Pa?'

Chittaranjan looked at Harbans. Harbans shook his head.

'Nothing else, Nelly.'

She went inside, past the curtains into the big blue drawing-room where on one wall Harbans saw a large framed picture of the Round Table Conference with King George V and Mahatma Gandhi sitting together, the King formally dressed and smiling, the Mahatma in a loincloth, also smiling. The picture made Harbans easier. He himself had a picture like that in his drawing-room in Port of Spain.

Then Foam had an accident. He knocked the negro waiter down and spilled his red sweet drink on the floor.

Chittaranjan didn't look. 'It could wipe up easy. Tiles, you know.'

Nelly came out, smiled maliciously at Foam and cleaned up the mess.

Chittaranjan stood up. Even in his sabots he looked no more than five feet tall. He went to a corner of the veranda, his sabots clicking and clacking, took up a tall chromium-plated column and set it next to Foam's chair.

'Kick it down,' he said. He looked flushed, as though he was going to break out in sweat.

Harbans said, 'Ooh.'

'Come on, Baksh son, kick this down.'

'Goldsmith!' Harbans cried.

Foam got up.

'Foam! What you doing?'

'No, Mr Harbans. Let him kick it down.'

The column was kicked.

It swayed, then sprang back into an upright position.

'You can't kick this down.' Chittaranjan took the ash-tray with the weighted bottom back to its corner, and returned to his rocking-chair. 'Funny the modern things they making these days, eh? Something my brother in Port of Spain give me.' Chittaranjan looked at Harbans. 'Barrister, you know.'

Foam sat down in some confusion.

Harbans said, 'Your daughter look bright like anything, Goldsmith.'

'Tcha!' Chittaranjan didn't stop rocking. 'When people hear she talk, they don't want to believe that she only have sixteen years. Taking typing-lesson *and* shorthand from Teacher Francis, you know. She could take down prescription *and* type them out. This doctor son you have . . .'

'Oh, he ain't a doctor *yet*.'

'You shoulda bring him with you, you know. I like children with ambition.'

'He was learning today. Scholar and student, you see. But you must come and see him. He *want* to see you.'

'I want to see him too.'

So it was settled.

Harbans was so relieved that Chittaranjan had made no fresh demands, he took a sip of his orange liquid.

Chittaranjan rocked. 'You ain't have to worry about the

election. Once I for you'—he made a small dismissing gesture with his right hand—'you win.'

'The boy father say he for me too.'

Chittaranjan dismissed Baksh with a suck of gold teeth. 'Tcha! What *he* could do?'

Foam's loyalty was quick. 'He control a thousand votes.'

Harbans made peace. 'In these modern days, everybody have to unite. I is a Hindu. You, Goldsmith, is a Hindu. Baksh is Muslim. It matter?'

Chittaranjan only rocked.

Foam said, 'We got to form a committee.'

Chittaranjan widened his smile.

'Committee to organize. Meetings, canvassers, posters.'

Harbans tried to laugh away Foam's speech. 'Things getting modern these days, Goldsmith.'

Chittaranjan said, 'I don't see how committee could bring in more votes than me. If I go to a man in Elvira and I tell him to vote for so-and-so, I want to see him tell me no.'

The cool threatening tone of Chittaranjan's last sentence took Harbans aback. He didn't expect it from such a small man.

'What about that traitor Lorkhoor?' he asked.

But he got no reply because at that moment a loud crash on the galvanized-iron roof startled them all. The negro waiters shuddered. There was a sound of breaking glass.

From inside a woman's voice, weary, placid—Mrs Chittaranjan's—said, 'Breadfruit again. Break a glass pane this time.'

Chittaranjan jumped up, his sabots giving the loudest clack. 'Is that son-of-a-bitch Ramlogan!' He ran to the veranda wall, stood on tiptoe and hunched himself over the ledge. Harbans and Foam looked out with him.

Ramlogan was picking his teeth with unconcern. 'Ha. Ha.'

'Ramlogan!' Chittaranjan shouted, his thin voice edged

and carrying far. 'One of these days I going to mash up your arse.'

'Ha. You go mash up my arse? You ain't even got nothing to sit down on, and *you* go mash up *my* arse?'

'Yes, I go do it. I, Chittaranjan, go do it, so help me God!' He suddenly turned to Foam and Harbans, the fixed smile on his face, and screamed at them: 'Oh, God! Don't let that man provoke me, you hear! Don't let him provoke me!'

Ramlogan left his shop door and walked to the edge of his yard. 'Come down,' he invited, with savage amiability. 'Come down and mash up my arse. Come down and fight. Come down and cut down the breadfruit tree *or* the zaboca tree. Then we go see who is man.'

'Don't worry with the man, Pa.' Nelly Chittaranjan, inside. 'You don't see that the man just want you to low-rate yourself?'

Chittaranjan paid no attention. '*You* is a fighter?' he challenged. '*You?* You ever been to Port of Spain? Go to Port of Spain, ask somebody to show you where St Vincent Street is, walk down St Vincent Street, stop at the Supreme Court and ask them about Chittaranjan. *They* go tell you who is the fighter. Supreme Court know *you* as a fighter?'

Ramlogan hesitated. Chittaranjan had been an expert stick-fighter. He hadn't much of a reach but he made up for that by his nimbleness. And his stick-fighting had often got him into trouble with the police.

Ramlogan couldn't reply. He put his hands on the wire fence.

'Take your fat dirty hand offa my fence,' Chittaranjan snapped. 'A nasty blow-up shopkeeper like you want to put your hand on my fence?'

'All right, all right. One day I going to build my own fence, and then *you* don't touch it, I warning you.'

'But till then, take your fat dirty hand offa my fence.'

Then, unexpectedly, Ramlogan began to cry. He cried in a painful, belly-shaking way, pumping the tears out. 'You don't even want me to touch your fence now.' He wiped his eyes with the back of his big hairy hand. 'But you don't have to be so insultive with it. All right, you ain't want me. Nobody ain't want me. The candidate ain't want me. The three of all-you remain up there complotting against me, and you ain't want me to put my hand on your fence now. *I* don't control no votes, so nobody ain't want me. Just because I don't control no votes.' He stopped for breath, and added with spirit: 'Chittaranjan, the next time one of your wife chickens come in my yard, don't bother to look for it. Because that night I eating good.' He became maudlin again: 'I don't control no votes. Nobody don't want me. But everybody chicken think they could just walk in my yard, as if my yard is a republic.'

Sobbing, he retreated to his shop.

Chittaranjan went back to his rocking-chair. 'Mother arse,' he said, giving a bite to every consonant. 'For three years now, since the man come to live in Elvira, he only giving me provocation.' But Chittaranjan was as poised as before. His face was flushed; but the flush on Chittaranjan's face was, it seemed, as fixed as the smile.

Night fell.

Chittaranjan said, 'You go have to start a rum-account with Ramlogan.' The quarrel might not have been, to judge from Chittaranjan's calm.

Foam nodded. 'Only rumshop in Elvira, Mr Harbans.'

Harbans looked down at his hands. 'I have to buy rum for everybody?'

'Not *every*body,' Chittaranjan said.

Harbans changed the subject. 'What about that traitor Lorkhoor?'

'Lorkhoor ain't got no mind,' Chittaranjan said. 'But he can't worry me. Even supposing Lorkhoor win one thousand Hindu votes for Preacher, that still leave you three thousand Hindu votes. Now, three thousand Hindu votes and one thousand votes—you could depend on *me* for the Spanish votes—that give you four thousand votes.'

'Don't forget the thousand Muslim votes,' Foam boomed.

Chittaranjan acknowledged them distastefully. 'Make five thousand votes. You can't lose.'

'So is only five thousand now, eh?' Harbans said to Foam. 'In the lorry you tell me six thousand. I imagine tomorrow you go tell me four thousand and the day after you go tell me three thousand.'

'Mr Harbans!' Chittaranjan called. 'Mr Harbans, you mustn't talk like that!'

'Nobody can't fool me. I *know* this was going to happen. I had a sign.'

'Five thousand out of eight thousand,' Chittaranjan said. 'You can't lose. Majority of two thousand. Remember, I, Chittaranjan, is for you.'

'This Lorkhoor is a damn traitor!' Harbans exclaimed finally. He became calmer. He looked at Foam and Chittaranjan, smiled and began to coo: 'I sorry, Goldsmith. I sorry, Foam. I was just getting a little down-couraged, that is all.'

'Election fever,' Foam said. 'I know how it is.'

They settled other matters. Chittaranjan accepted the need for a committee, and they decided who were to be members of it. It pleased Harbans to see Chittaranjan growing less frigid towards Foam. At length he broke the news that Foam was the campaign manager. Chittaranjan took it well. It was not a post he coveted, because it was a paid post; everything he did for Harbans, he did only out of the goodness of his heart.

Before they left, Chittaranjan said, 'I coming up to Port of Spain to see that doctor son you have. I *like* ambitious children.'

'He *want* to see you too, Goldsmith.'

Foam and Harbans got into the Dodge.

A small oil lamp burned in Ramlogan's gloomy shop and the man himself was eating his dinner from an enamel plate on the counter.

'Wave to him,' Foam said.

Ramlogan waved back. 'Right, boss!' He was surprisingly cheerful.

'Funny man,' Harbans said, driving off.

'He always ready to play brave brave, but you never know when he going to start crying,' Foam said. 'He lonely really. Wife dead long time. Daughters don't come to see him.'

This time there was no waving and shouting. The youths sitting on the culverts and the half-naked children still straying about were dazzled by the headlights of the Dodge and recognized Harbans only when he had passed. Harbans drove warily. It was Friday evening and the main road was busy. The drinking was to begin soon at Ramlogan's rumshop; the other Friday evening excitement, Mr Cuffy's sermon, had already begun.

Foam pointed out Mr Cuffy's house. A gas lamp in the small rickety veranda lit up Mr Cuffy, an old negro in a tight blue suit, thumping a Bible; and lit up Mr Cuffy's congregation in the yard below, a reverent negro group with many women. The rumble of the Dodge obliterated Mr Cuffy's words, but his gestures were impassioned.

'Mr Cawfee is Preacher right hand man,' Foam said. 'Not one of those negro people there going to vote for you, Mr Harbans.'

'Traitors! Elvira just full of traitors.'

Mr Cuffy and his congregation passed out of sight.

Harbans, thinking of the white women, the black bitch, the loudspeaker van, the seventy-five dollars a month, the rum-account with Ramlogan, the treachery of Lorkhoor, saw defeat and humiliation everywhere.

And then Foam shouted, 'Look, Mr Harbans! Preacher.'

Harbans saw. A tall negro with high frizzy hair, long frizzy beard, long white robe; haloed in the light of the headlamps; walking briskly at the edge of the road, stamping his staff, the hem of his robe dancing above sandalled feet. They saw him leave the road, go across a yard, saw him knock; and as they drove past, saw the door opened for him.

'That is *all* he doing,' Foam said. 'Walking brisk brisk from door to door and knocking and going in and coming out and walking brisk brisk again.'

'What he does talk about when he go in?'

'Nobody ain't know, Mr Harbans. Nobody does tell.'

They stopped at Baksh's house and Foam got off.

'We go have the first committee meeting some time next week, Mr Harbans. It going to give you a encouragement.'

But Foam's hand was still on the door.

'Ooh, I was forgetting.' Harbans dipped into his hip pocket. 'Something. Nothing much, but is a beginning.'

'Is a encouragement,' Foam said, taking the note.

Harbans drove out of Elvira, past the abandoned cocoa-house, past Cordoba, up Elvira Hill, down Elvira Hill. At the bottom of the hill his headlights picked out the two white women on their bicycles.

'It don't mean nothing,' Harbans said to himself. 'I mustn't get down-couraged. It don't mean nothing at all.'

If he only knew, his troubles hadn't started.

III

THE WRITING ON THE WALL

★

In spite of what he had said to Harbans in the lorry about going up for the County Council, Foam hadn't been thinking of going into politics at all. But when Lorkhoor had suddenly begun to campaign for Preacher, Foam announced that he was going to campaign for Harbans. Mrs Baksh objected. But Baksh said, 'It going to be a good experience for the boy.' Baksh had already agreed to support Harbans for two thousand dollars. Foam, however, wanted to do some loudspeaking, like Lorkhoor; and Baksh himself had been talking for some time in Ramlogan's rumshop about the money to be made out of a loudspeaker. So when Harbans came that afternoon, Baksh hadn't said a word about the two thousand dollars but had asked instead for a loudspeaker van and for Foam to be campaign manager.

The rivalry between Foam and Lorkhoor began when Teacher Francis, the new headmaster of the Elvira Government School, formed the Elvira Social and Debating Club. Teacher Francis was a young red-skinned negro who dazzled Elvira with his sharp city dress: sharkskin zoot suit, hot tie knotted below an open collar, two-toned shoes. He was young for a headmaster, but to be a headmaster in Elvira was to be damned by the Trinidad Education Department. (Teacher Francis had been so damned for parading his agnosticism in a Port of Spain school. He had drawn a shapeless outline on the blackboard and asked his class, 'Tell me, eh. That soul you does hear so much about, it look like that, or what?' One boy had been outraged. The boy's father complained to the Director of Education and Teacher Francis was damned to Elvira.) He formed the Elvira Social and Debating Club to encourage things of the mind. The idea was new and the response was big. Lorkhoor quickly became the star of the club. It was Lorkhoor who wrote most of the poems and stories which were read to the club, and one of Lorkhoor's poems had even been printed on the leader page of the *Trinidad Sentinel*, in the special type the *Sentinel* reserves for poetry and the Biblical quotation at the bottom of the leader:

Elvira, awake! Behold the dawn!
It shines for you, it shines for me . . .

In all the discussions, political and religious—Teacher Francis was still hot on religion—Lorkhoor shone and didn't allow Foam or anyone else to shine. Teacher Francis always backed up Lorkhoor; between them they turned the club into a place where they could show off before an audience. They made jokes and puns that went over the heads of nearly everybody else. One day Teacher Francis said, 'People like you and me, Lorkhoor, are two and far between.' Lorkhoor alone roared. At the next meeting Lorkhoor began a review of a film: 'The points in this film are two and far between—the beginning and the end.' People stopped coming to the club; those who came, came to drink—there were always two or three people in Elvira who were having a row with Ramlogan the rumshop owner—and the club broke up.

Teacher Francis and Lorkhoor remained thick. Teacher Francis felt Lorkhoor understood him. He said Lorkhoor was a born writer and he was always sending off letters on Lorkhoor's behalf to the *Sentinel* and the *Guardian* and the *Gazette*. So far nothing had come of that.

And then Foam was really cut up when Lorkhoor got

that job advertising for the cinemas from a loudspeaker van. It was Foam who had heard of the job first, from Harichand the printer, a man of many contacts. Foam applied and had practically got the job when Lorkhoor, supported by Teacher Francis, stepped in. Lorkhoor pointed out that Foam was too young for a driving permit (which was true); that Foam's English wasn't very good (which was true). Lorkhoor pointed out that he, Lorkhoor, had a driving permit (which was true); and his English was faultless (which was an understatement). Lorkhoor got the job and said it was a degradation. But while he drove about Central Trinidad in his loudspeaker van, speaking faultless English to his heart's content, Foam had to remain in Elvira, an apprentice in his father's shop. Foam hated the stuffy dark shop, hated the eternal tacking, which was all he was allowed to do, hated Elvira, at moments almost hated his family.

He never forgave Lorkhoor. The job, which Lorkhoor called a degradation, was his by rights; he would have given anything to get it. And now the election gave him the next best thing. It gave him a loudspeaker of his own and took him out of the shop. He worked not so much for the victory of Harbans and the defeat of Preacher, as for the humiliation of Lorkhoor and Teacher Francis.

★

Even before the committee met, Foam set to work. He got a pot of red paint from Chittaranjan and went around Elvira painting culverts, telegraph poles and tree-trunks with the enthusiastic slogan, VOTE HARBANS OR DIE!

Mrs Baksh didn't like it at all. 'Nobody ain't listening to me,' she said. 'Everybody just washing their foot and jumping in this democracy business. But I promising you, for all the sweet it begin sweet, it going to end damn sour.'

She softened a little when the loudspeaker and the van came, but she still made it clear that she didn't approve. All Elvira knew about the van—it was another example of Baksh's depth—and Mrs Baksh was frightened by the very size of her fortune. She was tempting fate, inviting the evil eye.

Nobody else saw it that way. The little Bakshes clustered around the van while Foam and Baksh made arrangements for lodging it. To get the van into the yard they had to pull down part of the rotting wooden fence and build a bridge over the gutter. Some poorer people and their children came to watch. Baksh and Foam stopped talking; frowned and concentrated and spat, as though the van was just a big bother. And though it wasn't strictly necessary then, they put up the loudspeaker on the van. They spread a gunny sack on the hood, placed the loudspeaker on it and tied it down to the bumper with four lengths of rope.

Baksh spoke only one sentence during the whole of this operation. 'Have to get a proper stand for this damn loud-speaker thing,' he said, resentfully.

After dinner that evening Foam, with his twelve-year old brother Rafiq, went in the van to Cordoba, a good three miles away, to do some more slogans. The Spaniards watched without interest while he daubed VOTE HARBANS OR DIE!

The next evening he went to complete the job.

The first three words of his slogans had been covered over with whitewash and Cordoba was marked everywhere, in dripping red letters, DIE! DIE! DIE!

'That is Lorkhoor work,' Foam said.

Then Rafiq pointed to a wall. The first three words of the slogan were only partially covered over. Three strokes with a dry brush had been used, and between each stroke there was a gap, and the sign read: —TE——N—DIE!

'Ten die,' Rafiq said.

'Come on, man,' Foam said. 'You letting a thing like

that frighten you? You is a man now, Rafiq. And whatever you do,' Foam added, 'don't tell Ma, you hear.'

But that was the first thing Rafiq did.

'*Ten* die!' Mrs Baksh clapped her hand to her big bosom and sat on a bench, still holding the ash-rag with which she had been washing up.

Baksh swilled down some tea from a large enamel cup. 'It don't mean nothing, man. Somebody just trying to be funny, that's all.'

'Oh, God, Baksh, this election sweetness!'

The little Bakshes came into the kitchen.

'Don't mean nothing,' Baksh said. 'It say ten die. It only have nine of we in this house. The seven children and you and me. Was just a accident, man.'

'Was *no* accident,' Rafiq said.

'Oh, God, Baksh, see how the sweetness turning sour!'

'Is only that traitor Lorkhoor playing the fool,' Foam said. 'Let him wait. When *he* start putting up signs for Preacher . . .'

'How it could mean anything?' Baksh laughed. 'It say ten die and it only have nine of we here.'

Mrs Baksh became cooler. A thought seemed to strike her and she looked down at herself and cried, 'Oh, God, Baksh, how we know is only nine?'

★

Though he didn't care for the 'Ten die!' sign and for Mrs Baksh's fears, Foam didn't go out painting any more slogans. Instead he concentrated on the first meeting of the campaign committee.

He decided not to hold the meeting at Chittaranjan's house. The place made him too uncomfortable and he still remembered the malicious smile Nelly Chittaranjan had given him when he knocked his sweet drink over. His own house, the London Tailoring Establishment, was out of the question: Mrs Baksh didn't even want to hear about the election. He decided then to have the meeting in the old wooden bungalow of Dhaniram, the Hindu pundit, who had also been made a member of the committee. At least there would be no complications with Dhaniram's family. Dhaniram's wife had been paralysed for more than twenty years. The only other person in the house was a meek young daughter-in-law who had been deserted by Dhaniram's son only two months after marriage. That was some time ago. Nobody knew where the boy had got to; but Dhaniram always gave out that the boy was in England, studying something.

On the evening of the meeting Foam and Baksh, despite protests from Mrs Baksh, drove over in the loudspeaker van.

From the road Foam could see two men in the veranda. One was Dhaniram, a large man in Hindu priestly dress lying flat on his belly reading a newspaper by an oil lamp. The other man drooped on a bench. This was Mahadeo.

Neither Dhaniram nor Mahadeo was really important. They had been drafted into the committee only to keep them from making mischief. Dhaniram was the best known pundit in Elvira, but he was too fond of gossip and religious disputation, and was looked upon as something of a buffoon. Mahadeo was an out and out fool; everybody in Elvira knew that. But Mahadeo could be useful; he worked on what remained of the Elvira Estate as a sub-overseer, a 'driver' (not of vehicles or slaves, but of free labourers), and as a driver he could always put pressure on his labourers.

When Foam and Baksh came into the veranda Dhaniram jumped up and the whole house shook. It was a shaky house and the veranda was particularly shaky. Dhaniram had kept on extending it at one end, so that the veranda opened out into something like a plain; there were gaps in the floor where the uncured, unplaned cedar planks had shrunk.

'Ah,' Dhaniram said, rubbing his hands. 'Campaign manager. Come to discuss the campaign, eh?'

Everything about the election thrilled Dhaniram. Words like campaign, candidate, committee, constituency, legislative council, thrilled him especially. He was a big exuberant man with a big belly that looked unnecessary and almost detachable.

Mahadeo didn't get up or say anything. He drooped on his bench, a plump little man in tight clothes, his large empty eyes staring at the floor.

There was an explosion of coughing inside the house and a woman's voice, strained and querulous, asked in Hindi, 'Who's there?'

Dhaniram led Foam and Baksh to the small drawing-room and made them look through an open door into a dark bedroom. They saw a woman stretched out on a four-poster. It was Dhaniram's wife. She was lying on her left side and they couldn't see her face.

'Election committee,' Dhaniram said to the room.

'Oh.' She didn't turn.

Dhaniram led Foam and Baksh back to the veranda and seated them on a bench opposite Mahadeo.

Dhaniram sat down beside Mahadeo and began to shake his legs until the veranda shook. 'So the goldsmith fix up, eh? Everything?'

Foam didn't understand.

'I mean, Chittaranjan see the boy? You know, Harbans son.'

'Oh, yes, that fix up,' Baksh said. 'Chittaranjan went to Port of Spain day before yesterday.'

Dhaniram lit a cigarette and pulled at it in the Brahmin way, drawing the smoke through his closed hand. 'Chittaranjan really believe Harbans going to let his son marry Nelly?'

Baksh seized this. 'You hear anything?'

Dhaniram shrugged his shoulders. 'We want some light. *Doolahin*, bring the Petromax,' Dhaniram called.

Baksh noted that though she had been deserted for so long, Dhaniram still called his daughter-in-law *doolahin*, bride.

'How Hari?' Baksh asked. 'He write yet?'

Hari was Dhaniram's son.

'Boy in England, man,' Dhaniram said. 'Studying. Can't study and write letters.'

The *doolahin* brought the Petromax. She looked a good Hindu girl. She had a small soft face with a wide mouth. About eighteen perhaps; barefooted, as was proper; a veil over her forehead, as was also proper. She hung the Petromax on the hook from the ceiling and went back to the kitchen, a smoky room boarded off at one corner of the vast veranda.

Baksh asked, 'How she taking it these days? Still crying?'

Dhaniram wasn't interested. 'She getting over it now. So Chittaranjan really believe that Nelly going to marry Harbans son?'

Mahadeo sat silent, his head bent, his full eyes staring at his unlaced black boots. Foam wasn't interested in the conversation. In the light of the Petromax he studied Dhaniram's veranda walls. There were many Hindu coloured prints; but by far the biggest thing was a large Esso calendar, with Pundit Dhaniram's religious commitments written in pencil above the dates. It looked as though Dhaniram's practice was falling off. It didn't matter; Foam knew that Dhaniram also owned the fifth part of a tractor and Baksh said that was worth at least two hundred dollars a month.

Harbans came, agitated, looking down at the ground, and Foam saw at once that something was wrong.

Dhaniram rose. Mahadeo rose and spoke for the first time: 'Good night, Mr Harbans.'

Dhaniram took Harbans into the drawing-room and Foam heard Harbans saying, 'Ooh, ooh, *how* you is, *maharajin*? We just come to talk over this election nonsense.'

But he looked dejected like anything when he came out and sat on a blanket on the floor.

Dhaniram shouted, '*Doolahin*, candidate here. We want some tea. What sort of tea you want, eh, Mr Harbans? Chocolate, coffee or green tea?'

'Green tea,' Harbans said distractedly.

'What happen, Mr Harbans?' Foam asked.

Harbans locked his fingers. 'Can't understand it, Foam. Can't understand it. I is a old old man. Why everybody down against me?'

Dhaniram was thrilled. He gave a little laugh, realized it was wrong, and tried to look serious. But his eyes still twinkled.

'I drive through Cordoba,' Harbans said, talking down to his hands, his voice thin and almost breaking. 'As soon as the Spanish people see the lorry, they turn their back. They shut their window. And I did think they was going to vote for me. Can't understand it, Foam. I ain't do the Spanish people nothing.'

'Is that traitor Lorkhoor,' Baksh said.

Then Chittaranjan came. He wore his visiting outfit and carried a green book in his hand. He seemed to know the house well because he didn't wait for Dhaniram to introduce him to the invalid inside. As he came up the steps he shouted, 'How you feeling these days, *maharajin*? Is me, Chittaranjan, the goldsmith.'

When he came back out to the veranda, it seemed that Chittaranjan too had bad news. His smile was there, as fixed as his flush; but there was anger and shame in his narrow eyes.

'Dhaniram,' Chittaranjan said, as soon as he sat down and took off his vast grey felt hat, 'we got to make new calculations.'

Dhaniram took Chittaranjan at his word, '*Doolahin!*' he shouted. 'Pencil and paper. New calculations. Committee waiting. Candidate and committee waiting.'

Harbans looked at Chittaranjan. 'What I do the Spanish people for them to turn their back on me?'

Chittaranjan forced the words out: 'Something happen, Mr Harbans. This thing not going to be so easy . . .'

'It don't surprise me, Goldsmith,' Harbans interrupted. 'Loudspeaker van. Campaign manager. Rum-account. Lorkhoor. People turning their back on me. Nothing don't surprise me at all.'

The *doolahin* brought some brown shop-paper. 'It ain't have no pencil. I look everywhere.'

Dhaniram forgot about the election. 'But this is craziness, *doolahin*. I have that pencil six months now.'

'Is only a pencil,' the *doolahin* said.

'Is what *you* think,' Dhaniram said, the smile going out of his eye. 'Is more than just a pencil. Is the principle. Is only since you come here that we start losing things.'

'Your son, fust of all,' Baksh said.

Dhaniram looked at Baksh and the smile came into his eyes again. He spat, aiming successfully at a gap in the floor.

Foam said, 'This is the pencil you was looking for?' From the floor he picked up an indelible pencil of the sort used in government offices. A length of string was attached to a groove at the top.

Dhaniram began to rub himself. 'Ah, yes. Was doing the crossword just before you come in.'

The *doolahin* tossed her head and went back to her kitchen.

Harbans brooded.

All of a sudden he said, 'Chittaranjan, I thought *you* was the big controller of the Spanish vote?'

Everyone noticed that Harbans had called Chittaranjan by his name, and not 'goldsmith'. It was almost an insult.

Yet Chittaranjan didn't seem to feel it. He fidgeted with the book he had brought and said not a word.

Harbans, not getting an answer, addressed his hands. 'In the 1946 elections none of the candidates I know did spend all this money. I have to have loudspeaker van and rum-account with Ramlogan?'

Baksh looked offended. 'I know you mean me, boss. The moment you start talking about loudspeaker van. What you say about 1946 is true. Nobody did spend much money. But that was only the fust election. People did just go and vote for the man they like. Now is different. People learning. You have to spend on them.'

'Yes, you have to spend on them,' Dhaniram said, his legs shaking, his eyes dancing. He relished all the grand vocabulary of the election. 'Otherwise somebody else going to spend on them.'

Mahadeo, the estate driver, raised his right hand, turned his large eyes on Harbans and twitched his thick little moustache and plump little mouth. 'You spending your money in vain, Mr Harbans,' he said gently. 'We win already.'

Harbans snapped, 'Is arse-talk like that does lose election. (Oh God, you see how this election making me dirty up my mouth.) But you, Mahadeo, you go around opening your big mouth and saying Harbans done win already. You think that is the way to get people vote?'

'Exactly,' said Dhaniram. 'People go say, "If he done win, he ain't want my vote."'

'Foam,' Harbans said. 'How much vote you giving me today? Was six thousand when I first see you. Then was five thousand. Is *four* thousand today?'

Foam didn't have a chance to reply because Chittaranjan spoke up at last: 'Yes, Mr Harbans, is four thousand.'

Harbans didn't take it well. 'Look at the mess I getting myself in, in my old old age. Why I couldn't go away and sit down quiet and dead somewhere else, outside Elvira? Foam, take the pencil and paper and write this down. It have eight thousand votes in Naparoni. Four thousand Hindu, two thousand negro, one thousand Spanish, and a thousand Muslim. I ain't getting the negro vote and I ain't getting a thousand Hindu vote. That should leave me with five thousand. But now, Goldsmith, you say is only four thousand. Tell me, I beg you, where we drop this thousand vote between last week Friday and today?'

'In Cordoba,' Chittaranjan said penitently. 'You see for yourself how the Spanish people playing the fool. Just look at this book.'

He showed the green book he had been turning over.

Mahadeo wrinkled his brow and read out the title slowly: '*Let—God—Be—True*.'

As a pundit Dhaniram regarded himself as an expert on God. He looked at the book quizzically and said, 'Hmh.'

'That is all that the Spanish talking about now,' Chittaranjan said, pointing to the book. 'I did know something was wrong the moment I land in Cordoba. Everywhere I look I only seeing red signs saying, "Die! Die!"'

'That is Lorkhoor work,' Foam said.

Chittaranjan shook his head. 'I don't know if any of all-you see two white woman riding about on big red bicycles. If I tell you the havoc they causing!'

'Witnesses!' Harbans exclaimed. 'I know. I had a sign. I shoulda run them over that day.'

No one knew what he was talking about.

'Who they campaigning for?' Baksh asked. 'For Preacher?'

'For Jehovah,' Chittaranjan said. 'They can't touch the Hindus or the Muslims or the negroes, but they wreaking havoc with the Spanish. Everywhere I go in Cordoba, the Spanish people telling me that the world going to end in 1976. I ask them how they know the date so exact and they tell me the Bible say so.'

Dhaniram slapped his thigh. 'Armageddon!' Pundit Dhaniram had been educated at one of the Presbyterian schools of the Canadian Mission where he had been taught hymns and other Christian things. He cherished the training. 'It make me see both sides,' he used to say; and even now, although he was a Hindu priest, he often found himself humming hymns like 'Jesus loves me, yes, I know'. He slapped his thigh and exclaimed, 'Armageddon!'

'Something like that,' Chittaranjan said. 'And these white woman telling the Spanish that they mustn't take no part in politics and the Spanish taking all what these woman say as a gospel.' Chittaranjan sounded hurt. 'I telling you, it come as a big big pussonal blow, especially as I know the Spanish people so long. Look, I go to see old Edaglo, you know, Teresa father. The man is my good good friend. For years he eating my food, drinking my whisky, and borrowing my money. And now he tell me he ain't voting. So I ask him, "Why you ain't voting, Edaglo?" And he answer me back, man. He say, "Politics ain't a divine thing." Then he ask me, "You know who start politics?" You could imagine how that take me back. "Somebody start politics?" I say. He laugh in a mocking sorta way as though he know more than everybody else and say, "You see how you ain't know these little things. Is because you ain't study enough." He, Edaglo, talking like that to me, Chittaranjan! "Go home," he say, "and study the Bible and you go read and see that the man who start politics was Nimrod."'

'Who is Nimrod?' Baksh asked.

Pundit Dhaniram slapped his thigh again. 'Nimrod was a mighty hunter.'

They pondered this.

Harbans was abstracted, disconsolate.

Baksh said, 'What those woman want is just man, you hear. The minute they get one good man, all this talk about mighty hunting gone with the wind.'

Dhaniram was pressing Chittaranjan: 'You didn't tell them about Caesar? The things that are Caesar's. Render unto Caesar. That sort of thing.'

Chittaranjan lifted his thin hands. 'I don't meddle too much in all that Christian bacchanal, you hear. And as I was leaving, he, Edaglo, call me back. Me, Chittaranjan. And he give me this green book. Let God be true. Tcha!'

Mahadeo shook his head and clucked sympathetically. 'Old Edaglo really pee on you, Goldsmith.'

'Not only pee,' Chittaranjan said. 'He shake it.'

And having made his confession, Chittaranjan gathered about him much of his old dignity again.

'Even if the Spanish ain't voting,' Foam said, 'we have four thousand votes. Three thousand Hindu and one thousand Muslim. Preacher only getting three thousand. Two thousand negro and a thousand Hindu. I don't see how we could lose.'

Dhaniram said, 'I don't see how a whole thousand Hindus going to vote for Preacher. Lorkhoor don't control so much votes.'

'Don't fool your head,' Foam said quickly. 'Preacher

help out a lot of Hindu people in this place. And if the Hindus see a Hindu like Lorkhoor supporting Preacher, well, a lot of them go want to vote for Preacher. Lorkhoor going about telling people that they mustn't think about race and religion now. He say it ain't have nothing wrong if Hindu people vote for a negro like Preacher.'

'This Lorkhoor want a good cut-arse,' Baksh said.

Chittaranjan agreed. 'That sort of talk dangerous at election time. Lorkhoor ain't know what he saying.'

Harbans locked and unlocked his fingers. 'Nothing I does touch does turn out nice and easy. Everybody else have life easy. I don't know what sin I commit to have life so hard.'

Everyone fell silent in the veranda, looking at Harbans, waiting for him to cry. Only the Petromax hissed and hummed and the moths dashed against it.

Then the *doolahin* thumped out bringing tea in delightfully ornamented cups so wide at the mouth that the tea slopped over continually.

Dhaniram said, 'Tea, Mr Harbans. Drink it. You go feel better.'

'Don't want *no* tea.'

Dhaniram gave his little laugh.

Two or three tears trickled down Harbans's thin old face. He took the cup, blew on it, and put it to his lips; but before he drank he broke down and sobbed. 'I ain't got no friends or helpers or nothing. Everybody only want money money.'

Mahadeo was wounded. 'You ain't giving *me* nothing, Mr Harbans.' He hadn't thought of asking.

Dhaniram, who had been promised something—contracts for his tractor—pulled at his cigarette. 'Is not as though you giving things to we pussonal, Mr Harbans. You must try and feel that you giving to the people. After all, is the meaning of this democracy.'

'Exactly,' said Baksh. 'Is for the sake of the community we want you to get in the Legislative Council. You got to think about the community, boss. As you yourself tell me the other day, money ain't everything.'

'Is true,' Harbans fluted. 'Is true.' He smiled and dried his eyes. 'You is all faithful. I did just forget myself, that is all.'

They sipped their tea.

To break the mood Dhaniram scolded his daughter-in-law. 'You was a long time making the tea, *doolahin*.'

She said, 'I had to light the fire and then I had to boil the water and then I had to draw the tea and then I had to cool the tea.'

She had cooled the tea so well it was almost cold. It was the way Dhaniram liked it; but the rest of the committee didn't care for cool tea. Only Harbans, taking small, noisy sips, seemed indifferent.

Dhaniram's wife called querulously from her room. The *doolahin* sucked her teeth and went.

Foam said, 'If Lorkhoor getting Hindus to vote for Preacher, I don't see why we can't get negroes to vote for we.'

They sipped their tea and thought.

Dhaniram pulled hard at his cigarette and slapped his dhoti-clad thigh. 'Aha! Idea!'

They looked at him in surprise.

'It go take some money . . .' Dhaniram said apologetically.

Harbans took a long sip of cool tea.

'It go take some money. But not much. Here in Elvira the campaign committee must be a sort of social welfare committee. Supposing one of those negroes fall sick. *We* go go to them. *We* go take them to doctor in *we* taxi. *We* go pay for their medicine.'

Chittaranjan sucked his teeth and became like the formidable Chittaranjan Foam had seen rocking and smiling in his tiled veranda. 'Dhaniram, you talking like if you ain't know how hard these negroes is in Elvira. You ever see any negro fall sick? They just does drop down and dead. And that does only happen when they about eighty or ninety.'

'All right. They don't get sick. But even you say they does dead sometimes. Well, two three bound to dead before elections.'

'You going to kill some of them?' Baksh asked.

'Well, if even *one* dead, *we* go bury him. *We* go hold the wake. *We* go take *we* coffee and *we* biscuits.'

Baksh said, 'And you think that go make the negroes vote for you?'

'It go make them feel shame if they ain't vote for we,' Dhaniram said. 'And if they ain't vote, well, the next time they start bawling for help, they better not come round here.'

Mahadeo lifted his right hand as a warning that he was about to speak again. 'Old Sebastian is one negro who look as though he might dead before elections.'

'Is a good idea,' Foam said. 'And every one of we could buy just one sweet drink for some negro child every day until elections. Different child every day. And the parents. We mustn't only help them if they fall sick or if they dead. If they can't get a work or something. If they going to have a wedding or something. Take the goldsmith here. He could make a little present for negroes getting married.'

Chittaranjan said animatedly, 'Foam, you talking as if I does make jewellery with my own gold. I ain't have no gold of my own. When people want things make, they does bring their own gold.'

And Chittaranjan destroyed an illusion which Foam had

had since he was a boy: he had always believed that the gold dust and silver shavings the children collected from Chittaranjan's workshop belonged to Chittaranjan.

Harbans said, 'Foam, take the pencil and paper and write down all those who sick in Elvira.'

Dhaniram said, 'Mungal sick like anything.'

Mahadeo lifted his hand. 'It have a whole week now that Basdai and Rampiari ain't come out to work. They must be sick too.'

Harbans said, 'Mahadeo, you know you is a damn fool. You think is *Hindu* sick I want Foam to write down?'

Chittaranjan said, 'Like I say, it ain't have no negro sick in Elvira.'

'All right.' Harbans was getting annoyed again. 'Who getting married?'

Chittaranjan said, 'Only Hindu and Muslim getting married. Is the wedding season now. The negro people don't get married so often. Most of them just living with woman. Just like that, you know.'

Harbans said, 'And you can't damn well start taking round wedding-ring to those people as wedding present. So, all we could do is to keep a sharp look-out for any negro who fall sick or who fall dead. That man you talk about, Mahadeo.'

'Sebastian?'

'Keep a eye on him.'

Foam said, 'I believe Mahadeo should handle the whole of that job. He could make a list of all negro who sick or going to dead.'

'Yes.' And Harbans added sarcastically, 'You sure that job ain't too big for you, Mahadeo?'

Mahadeo stared at the floor, his big eyes filling with determination. 'I could manage, Mr Harbans. Old Sebastian is one negro who bound to dead.'

They finished their tea and had some more. Then Harbans sent Foam to get the new posters he had brought in the lorry.

The posters said: HITCH YOUR WAGON TO THE STAR VOTE SURUJPAT ('PAT') HARBANS CHOOSE THE BEST AND LEAVE THE REST. And there was a photograph of Harbans; below that, his name and the star, his symbol.

Mahadeo said, 'It must make a man feel really big sticking his photo all over the place.'

Harbans, unwillingly, smiled.

Chittaranjan asked, 'Where you get those posters print?'

'Port of Spain.'

'Wrong move, Mr Harbans. You shoulda get that boy Harichand to print them.'

'But Harichand ain't got no sorta printery at all,' Harbans said.

'Never mind,' said Chittaranjan. 'People in Elvira wouldn't like that you get your posters print in Port of Spain when it have a Elvira boy who could do them.'

And then Harbans knew. No one in Elvira was fighting *for* him. All Elvira—Preacher, Lorkhoor, Baksh, Chittaranjan, Dhaniram and everybody else—all of them were fighting *him*.

He was nearly seized with another fit of pessimism.

But deep down, despite everything, he knew he was going to win. He cried and raged; but he wanted to fool, not tempt, fate. Then he thought of the sign he had had: the white women and the stalled engine, the black bitch and the stalled engine. He had seen what the first meant. The women had stalled him in Cordoba.

But the dog. What about the dog? Where was that going to stall him?

IV

TIGER

★

Some days passed. The new posters went up. The campaign proceeded. Nothing terrible happened to Mrs Baksh. She became calmer and Foam thought he could start painting slogans again. But now he didn't paint VOTE HARBANS OR DIE! He had had his lesson; it was too easy for the enthusiasm of the slogan to be mistaken for a threat. He painted straight things like WIN WITH HARBANS and WE WANT HARBANS.

One night when Baksh had taken out the loudspeaker van—he said it was to do some campaigning but Mrs Baksh said it was to do some drinking—one night Foam took up his pot of paint and a large brush and went about Elvira, painting new slogans and refurbishing old ones. He didn't take the excitable and untrustworthy Rafiq with him. He took Herbert instead. Herbert was ten and politically and psychically undeveloped. He didn't care for signs or election slogans; and while Foam painted Herbert whistled and wandered about.

Foam did his job with love. He painted even on houses whose owners had gone to bed; and only when he had got as far as the old cocoa-house did he decide it was time to go home.

Herbert hung back a little and Foam noticed that he was walking in a peculiar way, arching his back and keeping his hands on his belly. His belly looked more swollen than usual.

'Your belly hurting, Herbert?'

'Yes, man, Foam. Is this gas breaking me up.'

'Don't worry about it too much. All of we did get gas in we belly when we was small. It does pass.'

'Hope so for truth, man.'

Lights were still on when they got home. They went around to the back of the house. The door was locked from the inside but it wasn't barred; and if you pressed on the middle and pulled and shook at the same time, it fell open. Foam put down the paint-pot and the brush.

'Herbert, when I press down, you pull hard and shake.'

Foam pressed down. Herbert, clutching his belly with one hand, pulled and shook with the other. The door unlocked, and as it did, something fell from Herbert's shirt. In the darkness Foam couldn't see what it was. When he pulled the door open and let out the thin light of the oil lamp inside, he saw.

It was a puppy.

A tiny rickety puppy, mangy, starved; a loose, ribby bundle on the ground. It made no noise. It tried to lift itself up. It only collapsed again, without complaint, without shame.

'Where you pick him up, Herbert?'

'Somewhere.'

'But you can't bring him home. You know how *they* don't like dogs.' *They* was Mrs Baksh.

'Is *my* dog,' Herbert said irrelevantly.

Foam squatted beside the puppy. None of the evening's adventures had disturbed the flies that had settled down for the night around the puppy's eyes. The eyes were rheumy, dead. The puppy itself looked half-dead. When Foam stroked the little muzzle he saw fleas jumping about. He pulled away his finger quickly.

'Take care, Foam. Is them quiet quiet dog does bite, you know.'

Foam stood up. 'You got to feed him good. But how you going to hide him from Ma?'

'*I* go hide him. Got a name for him too. Going to call him Tiger.'

Tiger tried to get up on his haunches. It was as if every tiny rib and every bone were made of lead. But he made it this time, and held the shaky pose.

'See! He recognize the name already,' Herbert said.

Tiger crumpled down again.

'Come on, Tiger,' Herbert said.

Tiger didn't respond.

'What you going to do with him?'

'Take him upstairs. Put him in the bed.'

'And what about Rafiq and Charles and Iqbal?' Foam asked, naming the other Baksh boys. 'Think they go want Tiger to sleep in the same bed with them?'

'We go see.'

The room in which they were was the room behind the tailor shop. It was the only part of the house Baksh had attempted to renovate and smelled of new concrete and new cyp wood. There was a new concrete floor and a new staircase of rough unpainted planks that led to the upper floor. The whole thing was so makeshift because Baksh said he was thinking of pulling down the whole house one day and putting up something better and bigger. The room was called the store-room; but it was used as a dumping-ground for things the Bakshes didn't want but couldn't bring themselves to throw away.

Foam said, 'You can't take up the dog tonight. *They* still waking. What about hiding him under the steps until morning?'

He rummaged among the pile of rubbish under the staircase and brought out a condensed milk case stencilled STOW AWAY FROM BOILERS, two smelly gunny-sacks and many old issues of the *Trinidad Sentinel.* He put the sacks in the case, the newspapers on the sack, and Tiger on the newspapers.

'Under the steps now.'

The door at the top of the stairs opened and some more light flowed down into the store-room.

Mrs Baksh said, 'What the two of all-you complotting and conspiring down there?'

'Nothing,' Foam said. 'We just putting away the paint and thing.'

'And we cleaning up the place,' Herbert added.

Mrs Baksh didn't take them up on that. 'You see your father?'

'Ain't he out with the loudspeaker?' Foam said.

'I know where he is. He just using this election as a big excuse to lift his tail and run about the place. And is what you doing too. Ha! This election starting sweet sweet for some people, but I promising you it going to turn sour before it end.'

She stood at the top of the stairs, broad and dominant.

Herbert, noisily storing away the paint-pot, pushed Tiger's box under the steps as well.

But Tiger had also to be fed.

Foam knew this. He walked up the steps. 'Herbert take in with one belly pain, Ma. All the way home he holding his belly and bawling. I think he hungry.'

'He ain't hungry one little bit. I don't know who ask him to walk about Elvira with all this dew falling.'

Herbert took his cue from Foam. He came out from under the steps, arched his back, and pressed his hands on his belly. 'God, man, how this gas breaking me up!'

Mrs Baksh said, 'But if a stranger hear this little boy talk they go believe I starving him. You ain't eat this evening, Herbert?'

'Yes, Ma.'

'You ain't eat one whole *roti*?'

'Yes, Ma.'

'You ain't eat *bhaji*?'

'Yes, Ma.'

'You ain't drink half a big pot of tea?'

'Yes, Ma.' Herbert drank enormous quantities of tea. He could drink two or three large enamel cups, and when visitors were present, four or five. Mrs Baksh used to boast to her sisters, 'I ain't see nobody to touch Herbert when it come to drinking tea.'

'You eat all that and you drink all that, and you still asking me to believe that you hungry?'

'Yes, Ma.'

'Look, boy! Don't answer me back like that, you hear. You standing up there with your little belly puff out and you looking me in my face and you still bold and brave enough to challenge me? Don't think I forgetting how you shame me in front of that Harbans man, you know.'

Foam said, 'Is not his fault, Ma. Is the gas.'

'Gas! And the other modern thing is appendicitis. Nobody did have gas and appendicitis when I was small. It ain't gas. Is just the sort of gratitude I getting from my own children, after all the pinching and scraping and saving I does do. And tell me, for *who* I pinching and scraping and saving?'

She got no reply.

Her annoyance subsided. 'All right, come up and take out something. If you ain't careful you go get fat and blow-up like me. But I done see that is what you want. Dog eat your shame. Go ahead.'

She stood aside to let them pass and followed them to the grimy little kitchen. From a large blue enamel pot Herbert poured tea, stewed in condensed milk and brown sugar, into an enamel plate. He took half a *roti*, a dry unimaginative sort of pancake, broke it up and dropped the pieces into the tea.

Mrs Baksh stood over him. 'Go ahead. I want to see you eat up all of that.'

Herbert listlessly stirred the tea and *roti*.

'Is so hungry you was? Nobody ain't have to tell me about you, Herbert. Of all the seven children God give me, you have the longest tongue, and your eyes always longer than your tongue.'

Foam couldn't think of anything to get Mrs Baksh out of the kitchen. But distraction came. From one of the inner rooms came a shriek, and a girl's voice shouting, 'I going to tell Ma. Ma, come and see how Zilla pounding me up. She know I can't take blows and still she pounding me up.'

Mrs Baksh moved to the kitchen door. She lowered her voice with sardonic concern: 'Zilla, this evening you was telling me that you had a pain in your foot.' She left the kitchen and went inside. 'I go take away this pain from your foot. I go move it somewhere else.'

Herbert ran down the steps with the tea and *roti*. Upstairs Zilla was being punished. Tiger was unmoved by the screams and slaps and bumping about. When Herbert put the plate of tea and *roti* before him, he didn't know what to make of it. Slowly, instinct overcame inexperience. He sensed it was food. He sought to rise and approach it with dignity, on all four legs; but his legs trembled and folded under him. He let his muzzle lie on the chipped rim of the plate, edged out a tiny languid tongue and dipped it in the tea. Then he dragged the tongue back. He did this a few times; at last, with a show of strength that quite astonished Herbert, he got up on all four legs, trembly and shaky, remained upright, drank and ate.

'Go at it, Tiger boy,' Herbert whispered.

But Tiger ate in his own unemphatic way. Herbert expected him to wag his tail and growl at being handled while he ate; but Tiger ate without overt excitement or relish, philosophically, as though at any moment he expected to see the plate withdrawn as capriciously as it had come.

'Where that boy Herbert gone now?'

Herbert heard Mrs Baksh, and he heard Foam say, 'Went downstairs to bolt and bar the door. I tell him to go down.'

Tiger ate sloppily, squelchily.

Herbert waited, expecting Mrs Baksh to ask for the plate.

'But you and all, Foam, what happening to you? You want to bar the door and your father ain't come home yet?'

'I go call him up.'

The door at the top of the stairs opened, new light ran down the steps and striped Tiger's box, and Herbert heard Foam saying, 'Is all right, Herbert. Don't worry with the door. Come up.'

The room in which the five Baksh boys slept was called the brass-bed room because its only notable feature was a jangly old brass fourposter with a mildewed canopy that sagged dangerously under a mounting load of discarded boxes, clothes and toys. The four younger Baksh boys slept on the brass bed. Foam, as the eldest, slept by himself on an American Army canvas cot.

Herbert squeezed between Rafiq and Charles under the single floursack coverlet. He didn't like sleeping at the edge of the bed because he always rolled off. Iqbal, the youngest, held that position; he never rolled off.

Rafiq was still waking.

Herbert whispered, 'Tell you a secret if you promise not to tell.'

Foam, from the cot, said, 'Herbert, why you don't keep your mouth shut and go to sleep?'

Herbert waited.

He saw Rafiq kiss his crossed index fingers and put them to his eyes, to mean that his eyes would drop out if he told.

'Got a dog,' Herbert whispered. 'Not big, but *bad*.'

'*They* know?'

Herbert shook his head.

'How big?'

'Oh, he have to *grow* a little bit.'

'Call him Rex.'

'Nah. Calling him Tiger. Bad dog. Quiet too. Sort of thing, if *they* allow you, you could write up a signboard and hang it outside: Beware of Bad Dog.'

At that moment they heard the van drive into the yard and after a while they heard Baksh fumbling with the back door. Then there was a rattling and a stumbling, and Baksh began to curse.

Rafiq said, 'The old man drunk again.'

They heard him clattering hastily up the stairs, his curses becoming more distinct.

Then: 'Man!' Baksh cried. 'See a dog. Big dog. Downstairs.'

Herbert nudged Rafiq.

'Is all this campaigning and loudspeaking you doing,' Mrs Baksh said.

'Telling you, man. Big big dog. Downstairs. Walking about. Quiet quiet. Sort of guarding the steps.'

'You go start seeing hell soon, if you ain't careful,' Mrs Baksh said.

Herbert giggled.

'Who bite who?' Mrs Baksh asked. 'You bite the dog, or the dog bite you?'

Rafiq dug Herbert in the ribs.

They listened hopefully; but there was no further excitement. Mumblings from Baksh about the big dog; quiet sarcastic remarks from Mrs Baksh. But no blows; nothing being smashed or thrown through the window.

★

When Herbert got up the next morning, the brass bed was empty. Foam's cot was empty. He jumped out of bed—he slept in his ordinary clothes—and rushed to see what had happened to Tiger.

He had hardly set foot on the steps when Baksh said, 'You sleep well and sound? Come down, mister man. We waiting for you.'

Herbert knew it was all over.

Baksh was saying, 'But I tell you, man, I did see a big big dog here last night. And look how small it come this morning. Is only one thing. Magic. *Obeah*. But who want to put anything on me?'

Mrs Baksh was seated heavily on the cane-bottomed chair from the upstairs veranda. Baksh was standing next to her. In front of them the Baksh children were lined up, including Foam. Tiger's box had been dragged out from under the steps, and Tiger dozed fitfully, curled up on damp *Trinidad Sentinels*.

Mrs Baksh mocked, '"Who want to put anything on me?" Well, ten die. And with the dog it have ten of we in this house now.' Mrs Baksh was calm, ponderously calm. 'Baksh, you going to stand me witness that I tell you that this election beginning sweet sweet, but it going to end sour. You think Preacher is a fool? You think Preacher ain't know that you campaigning against him? You expect him to take that grinning and lying down?'

Baksh said, 'As usual, you didn't listen to *me*. You did think I was drunk. If you did come down last night you woulda see what I was telling you. Telling you, man, was a big big dog last night. Big big dog.'

Tiger half-opened one eye.

'See!' Baksh said. '*He* know. See how sly he looking at me.'

Herbert joined the line, standing beside Rafiq.

Mrs Baksh leaned back in her chair and looked broader than ever. Her bodice tightened and creased right across her bosom; her skirt tightened and creased across her belly. She folded her arms and then put one hand against her jaw. 'Foam, you bring the dog?'

'No, Ma.'

'Zilla, you bring the dog?'

Zilla began to cry.

'But why for you crying? If you ain't bring the dog, you ain't bring the dog, and that is that. You bring the dog?'

Zilla shook her head and sobbed loudly.

Tiger twitched an ear.

'Carol, you bring the dog?'

'Ma, you know I is not that sorta girl.'

And so the questioning went on.

'Herbert, you bring in any dog last night? Herbert, I asking you, you feed any dog outa one of my good good enamel plates that I does only feed humans on?'

'No, Ma.'

'Make sure, you know.'

'I ain't bring no dog, Ma.'

'All right. Foam, go and get the Bible. It in my bureau. Under the parcel with all the photos and the birth certificates.'

Foam went upstairs.

'Baksh, go and bring the shop key.'

Baksh went off with a lot of zest. 'Telling you, man. If only you did listen to me last night!'

'So!' Mrs Baksh sighed. 'So! *No*body ain't bring the dog. It just walk in through a lock door and jump in a condensed milk box.'

Foam and Baksh returned with Bible and key.

Mrs Baksh closed her eyes and opened the Bible at random. 'Ten die,' she sighed. 'Ten die.' She put the key on the open Bible. 'Foam, take one end of the key.'

Foam held one end of the key on the tip of his middle finger and Mrs Baksh held the other end. The Bible hung over the key.

'If nobody ain't going to take back what they say,' Mrs Baksh said, 'this is the only way to find out who bring the dog. All-you know what going to happen. If the Bible turn when I mention anybody name, we go know who bring the dog. Don't say I didn't warn you. Ready, Foam?'

Foam nodded.

Mrs Baksh said, 'By Saint Peter, by Saint Paul, Foam bring the dog.'

Foam replied, 'By Saint Peter, by Saint Paul, Foam *ain't* bring *no* dog.'

The Bible remained steady.

Mrs Baksh began again. 'By Saint Peter, by Saint Paul, Zilla bring the dog.'

Foam replied, 'By Saint Peter, by Saint Paul, Zilla *ain't* bring *no* dog.'

Mrs Baksh, leaning back in her chair, looked solemnly at the Bible, not at the little Bakshes. She fetched a deep sigh and began again, this time on Carol.

Foam's finger started to tremble.

Baksh looked on, pleased. The Biblical trial always appealed to him. Rafiq was excited. Herbert knew he was lost, but he was going to stick it out to the end. Tiger was dozing again, his thin muzzle between his thin front legs; the flies, energetic in the early morning, swarmed about him.

'By Saint Peter, by Saint Paul, Rafiq bring the dog.'

It was going to be Herbert's turn next. He had been through this sort of trial before. He knew he couldn't fool the Bible.

Foam's whole right hand was trembling now, from the strain of having a weight at his finger-tip.

'By Saint Peter, by Saint Paul, Rafiq *ain't* bring *no* dog.'

Another sigh from Mrs Baksh.

Baksh passed a hand over his moustache.

'By Saint Peter, by Saint Paul, Herbert bring the dog.'

'By Saint Peter, by Saint Paul, Herbert *ain't* bring no *dog.*'

The key turned. The Bible turned and fell. The key lay naked, its ends resting on the fingers of Foam and Mrs Baksh.

Rafiq said excitedly, 'I did know it! I did know it!'

Foam said, 'You did know too much.'

'Herbert,' Mrs Baksh said, 'you going to lie against the Bible, boy?'

Rafiq said, 'It must be *obeah* and magic. Last night he tell me it was a big big dog. And he say it was a *bad* dog.' The emphasis sounded sinister.

'Well,' Mrs Baksh said calmly, getting up and smoothing out the creases across her wide belly, 'before I do anything, I have to cut his little lying tail.' She spoke to Baksh, kindly: 'Man, let me see your belt a little bit, please.'

Baksh replied with equal civility: 'Yes, man.'

He undid his leather belt, pulling it carefully through the loops of his khaki trousers as though he wanted to damage neither trousers nor belt. Mrs Baksh took the belt. Herbert began to cry in advance. Mrs Baksh didn't look at him. She held the belt idle for some moments, looking down at it almost reflectively. On a sudden she turned; and lunged at Herbert, striking out with the belt, hitting him everywhere. Herbert ran about the small room, but he couldn't get out. The back door was still barred; the door that led to the tailor shop was still padlocked. Unhurried, Mrs Baksh stalked him. The belt gave her ample reach. Once she struck Baksh. She stopped and said, 'Och. Sorry, man.'

'Is all right, man. Mistake.'

Herbert bawled and screeched, making the siren-like noise that had so disturbed Harbans that Friday afternoon some weeks before. The other little Bakshes looked on with fascination. Even Foam was affected. Rafiq's excitement turned to horror. Zilla wept.

Then Foam called in his stern booming voice, 'All *right*, Ma.'

Mrs Baksh stopped and looked at him.

Baksh looked at him.

Mechanically Mrs Baksh passed the belt back to Baksh.

Herbert sat on the steps, his eyes and nose streaming. His sobs, half snuffle and half snort, came at regular intervals.

Tiger dozed on, his ears twitching.

Mrs Baksh sat down on the chair, exhausted, and began to cry. 'My own son, my biggest son, talking to me so!'

Baksh tried to soothe her.

'Go away. Is your fault, Baksh. Is this election sweetness that sweeten you up so. And now you seeing how sour it turning. You having people throwing all sorta magic and *obeah* in my house, you having all my sons lying to my face, and you having my biggest son talk to me like if I is his daughter. Is your fault, Baksh. This election sweetness done turning sour, I tell you.'

'You see, Foam?' Baksh said. 'It make you happy? Seeing your mother cry?'

'I ain't tell she nothing. She was going to bless the boy, that is all.'

'Take that dog outa my house!' Mrs Baksh screamed, her face twisted and inflamed. 'If that dog don't go, I go go.' She cried a lot more. 'Oh God, Baksh! Now I have to waste a whole day. Now I have to go and take Herbert and get the spirit off him.'

From the steps Herbert said, 'I ain't got *no* spirit on me.'

Baksh said, 'You keep your little tail quiet, mister man. Like you ain't had enough.' He said to Mrs Baksh, 'I can't think of nobody who could drive away a spirit as good as Ganesh Pundit. He was the man for that sort of thing. But he take up politics now.'

That reminded Mrs Baksh. 'This election sweetness! Man, I telling you, it turning sour.'

'Where you want me take the dog?' Foam asked.

'Just take him outa the house,' Mrs Baksh said, wiping her eyes. 'That is all I want. But don't take him away in broad daylight. Is bad enough already having *obeah* coming inside here. Don't take it out for everybody to see. Ten die. What more Preacher have in mind than to make all of we come thin thin like that dog? And then for all ten of we to dead. What more?'

Baksh was struck by his wife's interpretation. 'Take that dog outa my house!' he ordered. 'And don't give that dog any of my food, you hear. That dog going to suck the blood outa all of we if you don't get him outa here quick sharp.'

Tiger woke up and looked dreamily at the scene.

★

Mrs Baksh took Herbert for a spiritual fumigation to a gentleman in Tamana who, following the celebrated mystic masseur Ganesh at a distance, dabbled in the mystic.

And when Baksh saw Preacher on the road that morning, walking as briskly as ever, he crossed himself.

V

ENCOUNTERS

★

Things were crazily mixed up in Elvira. Everybody, Hindus, Muslims and Christians, owned a Bible; the Hindus and Muslims looking on it, if anything, with greater awe. Hindus and Muslims celebrated Christmas and Easter. The Spaniards and some of the negroes celebrated the Hindu festival of lights. Someone had told them that Lakshmi, the goddess of prosperity, was being honoured; they placed small earthen lamps on their money-boxes and waited, as they said, for the money to breed. Everybody celebrated the Muslim festival of Hosein. In fact, when Elvira was done with religious festivals, there were few straight days left.

That was what Lorkhoor, Foam's rival, went around preaching from his loudspeaker van that morning: the unity of races and religions. Between speeches he played records of Hindi songs and American songs.

'People of Elvira, the fair constituency of Elvira,' Lorkhoor said. 'Unite! You have nothing to lose but your chains. Unite and cohere. Vote for the man who has lived among you, toiled among you, prayed among you, worked among you. This is the voice of the renowned and ever popular Lorkhoor begging you and urging you and imploring you and entreating you and beseeching you to vote for Preacher, the renowned and ever popular Preacher. Use your democratic rights on election day and vote one, vote all. This, good people of Elvira, is the voice of Lorkhoor.'

Lorkhoor took a good deal of pleasure in his unpopularity. He offended most Indians, Hindus and Muslims; and Preacher's negro supporters looked on him with suspicion. Mr Cuffy didn't like Lorkhoor. Mr Cuffy was Preacher's most faithful supporter. Preacher was the visionary, Mr Cuffy the practical disciple. He was a grey-headed negro who ran a shoe-repair shop which he called The United African Pioneer Self-Help Society. Every Friday evening Mr Cuffy held a prayer-meeting from his veranda. He wore his tight blue serge suit and preached with the Bible in one hand. On a small centre table he had a gas lamp and a framed picture of a stabbed and bleeding heart. On the last few Fridays, to ward off the evil he feared from Lorkhoor, Mr Cuffy had been giving resounding sermons on treachery.

So, when Lorkhoor's van came near, Mr Cuffy, some tacks between his purple lips, looked up briefly and muttered a prayer.

Lorkhoor stopped the van outside Mr Cuffy's shop and, to Mr Cuffy's disgust, made a long speech over the loud-speaker before jumping out. He was slim and tall, though not so tall or slim as Foam. He had a broad bony face with a thriving moustache that followed the cynical curve of his top lip and drooped down a bit further. He had grown the moustache after seeing a film with the Mexican actor, Pedro Armendariz. In the film Armendariz spoke American with an occasional savage outburst in Spanish; it was the Spanish outbursts that thrilled Lorkhoor. Teacher Francis loyally if sorrowfully agreed that the moustache made Lorkhoor look like the Mexican; but Lorkhoor's enemies thought other-wise. Foam called Lorkhoor Fu-Manchu; that was how Mr Cuffy thought of him too.

'Heard the latest, Mr Coffee?'

Here was another reason for Lorkhoor's unpopularity: his stringent determination to speak correct English at all times. He spoke it in a deliberate way, as though he had to weigh and check the grammar beforehand. When Lorkhoor spoke like that outside Elvira, people tried to overcharge him. They thought him a tourist; because he spoke correct English they thought he came from Bombay.

'Good *morning*,' Mr Cuffy said.

Lorkhoor recognized his social blunder. 'Morning, Mr Coffee.'

Mr Cuffy frowned, the wrinkles on his black face growing blacker. 'I is not something you does drink, sir.'

The people of Elvira called Mr Cuffy 'Cawfee'. Lorkhoor, a stickler for correctness, called him 'Coffee'. Mr Cuffy preferred 'Cawfee'.

'Heard the latest?'

'Ain't hear nothing,' Mr Cuffy said, looking down at the ruined black boot in his hand.

'Propaganda, Mr Cawfee. Blackmail and blackball.'

Mr Cuffy regarded Lorkhoor suspiciously; he thought his colour was being mocked.

'*Obeah*, Mr Cawfee.'

Mr Cuffy tacked a nail. 'God hath made man upright.'

'Yes, Mr Cawfee. However, this propaganda is pernicious.'

Mr Cuffy tacked another nail. 'But they have found out many inventions.'

'Something about a dog.'

'Ain't know nothing about no dog.'

'Could destroy the whole campaign, you know.'

'That go satisfy you, eh, Mr Lorkhoor? That go satisfy your heart?'

'Mr Cawfee, I'm only informing you that the opposition are spreading the pernicious propaganda that Preacher is working *obeah*.'

'Who give you the right to call the gentleman Preacher?'

'Mr Preacher, then.'

'Mr Preacher go look after everything. Don't worry your head too much, you.'

'Still, Mr Cawfee, keep your eyes open. Nip the rumour in the bud. And see if they try to work any *obeah* against us. Could frighten off many votes, you know, if they try to work any *obeah* and magic against Mr Preacher.'

Bicycle bells trilled from the road and Lorkhoor and Mr Cuffy saw two white women with sunglasses standing beside red pudgy-tyred American bicycles. Pennants from both cycles said AWAKE!

Mr Cuffy grumbled a greeting.

The shorter woman took a magazine from her tray and held it before her like a shield.

The taller woman said, 'Can we interest you in some good books?'

'I've read too many lately,' Lorkhoor said.

He was ignored.

Mr Cuffy looked down. 'Ain't want no magazine.' But his manner was respectful.

Miss Short said happily, 'Oh, we know you don't *like* us.'

Mr Cuffy looked up. 'You know?'

'Course we do. We're Witnesses.'

'This election business,' Mr Cuffy said. 'You in this election business, like everybody else?'

Miss Short curled her thin lips. 'We have nothing to do with politics.'

'It's not a divine institution,' said Miss Tall, 'but a man-made evil. After all, who started the politics you have in Elvira today?'

'British Government,' Mr Cuffy said. He looked puzzled.

The Witnesses rested their case.

'We had to fight for it,' Lorkhoor said.

Miss Short looked at him sympathetically. 'Why, I don't believe you're even a Christian.'

'Of course not,' Lorkhoor snapped. 'Look at Jacob. Defend Jacob. Defend Abraham.' It was something he had got from Teacher Francis.

'We *must* study the Bible together,' Miss Short said. 'What do you do Sunday afternoons?'

Mr Cuffy's puzzlement was turning to exasperation. 'Look, who you come to see? Me? Or he?'

Miss Tall said, 'The magazine my friend is holding shows how the prophecies in the Bible are coming true. Even the troubles of Elvira are in the Bible. Elections and all.'

'Who won?' Lorkhoor asked.

'Who *are* you?' Miss Short asked.

'I'm the village intellectual.' It was a tried sentence; it had the approval of Teacher Francis.

'We must study the Bible together.'

'Leave my election campaign alone first.'

Mr Cuffy's disapproval of Lorkhoor was melting into admiration.

'About this magazine,' Miss Tall persisted. 'You have no interest at all in seeing how the Bible's prophecies are coming true?'

'I'm not ambitious,' Lorkhoor said.

The women left.

'The devil ain't no fool,' Mr Cuffy said. 'He does send pretty woman to tempt us. But were I tempted?' He used the tone and grammar of his Friday evening sermons. 'No, sir, I were not.'

'You were not,' Lorkhoor said. 'But about this *obeah* affair, Mr Cawfee. If they try any fast ones, let me know. We have to plan move for move. And now we have those Witnesses encouraging people not to vote. We have to think of something to counter that as well.'

'You is really a atheist?'

'Freethinker really. Agnostic.'

'Oh.' Mr Cuffy looked reassured.

★

This Mahadeo, the estate-driver, was a real fool. He just had to make a list of sick and dying negroes in Elvira—it was the only thing he could be trusted with—and he had to make a lot of noise about it.

That midday, shortly after Lorkhoor had left Mr Cuffy, Mahadeo, plump and sweating in his tight khaki driver's uniform, came up to Mr Cuffy's shop and tried to open a conversation with him. Mr Cuffy had relapsed into a mood of gloomy suspicion; opening a conversation with him was like opening a bottle of beer with your teeth. Mr Cuffy wasn't liking anything at all at that moment; he wasn't liking the Witnesses, wasn't liking this talk of *obeah*, wasn't liking Lorkhoor.

Mahadeo took off his topee. 'Working hard, Mr Cawfee?'

Silence. Mr Cuffy wasn't liking Mahadeo either.

Mahadeo scratched the mauve sweat-stains under his arms. 'Elections, Mr Cawfee.'

No reply.

'Progress, Mr Cawfee. Democracy. Elvira going ahead.'

'Why you don't go ahead yourself and haul your arse outa my yard?'

Mahadeo's eyes began to bulge, hurt but determined. 'One of the candidates want my help in the election, Mr Cawfee.'

Mr Cuffy grunted.

Mahadeo brought out his red pocket-notebook and a small pencil. 'I have to ask you a few questions, Mr Cawfee.' He tried some elementary flattery: 'After all, you is a very important man in Elvira.'

Mr Cuffy liked elementary flattery. 'True,' he admitted. 'It's God's will.'

'Is what I think too. Mr Cawfee, how your negro people getting on in Elvira?'

'All right, I believe, praise be to God.'

'You sure, Mr Cawfee?'

Mr Cuffy squinted. 'How you mean?'

'*Every*body all right? Nobody sick or anything like that?'

'What the hell you up to, Mahadeo?'

Mahadeo laughed like a clerk in a government office. 'Just doing a job, Mr Cawfee. Just a job. If any negro fall sick in Elvira, you is the fust man they come to, not true?'

Mr Cuffy softened. 'True.'

'And *no*body sick?'

'*No*body.' Mr Cuffy didn't care for the hopeful note in Mahadeo's voice.

Mahadeo's pencil hesitated, disappointed. 'Nobody deading or dead?'

Mr Cuffy jumped up and dropped the black boot. '*Obeah!*' he cried, and took up an awl. '*Obeah!* Lorkhoor was right. You people trying to work some *obeah*. Haul your tail outa my yard! Go on, quick sharp.'

'How you mean, *obeah*?'

Mr Cuffy advanced with the awl.

'Mr Cawfee!'

Mahadeo retreated, notebook open, pencil pointing forward, as protection. 'Just wanted to help, that is all. And this is the thanks I getting. Just wanted to help, doing a job, that is all.'

'Nobody ask for your help,' Mr Cuffy shouted, for Mahadeo was now well away. 'And listen, Mahadeo, one thing I promising you. If anybody dead, anybody at all, you going to be in trouble. So watch out. Don't try no magic.

If anybody dead, anybody. *Obeah!*' Mr Cuffy bawled. '*Obeah!*'

Mr Cuffy sounded serious.

And now Mahadeo was really worried.

★

Mahadeo wouldn't have got into that mess if Baksh had kept his mouth shut. Mrs Baksh had warned him not to say anything about Tiger. But nothing like it had ever happened to him and he wanted people to know. Nearly everybody else in Elvira had some experience of the supernatural; when the conversation turned to such matters in Ramlogan's rumshop, Baksh had had to improvise.

As soon as Mrs Baksh and Herbert left for Tamana, Baksh went to see Harichand the printer and caught him before he started for his printery in Couva.

Harichand, the best-dressed man in Elvira, was knotting his tie in the Windsor style before a small looking-glass nailed to one of the posts in his back veranda. He listened carefully, but without excitement.

'Nothing surprising in what you say,' he said at the end.

'How you mean, man, Harichand? Was a big big dog...'

'If you think *that* surprising, what you going to think about the sign I had just before my father dead?'

'Sign, eh?' It was a concession, because Baksh had heard Harichand's story many times before.

'Two weeks before my father dead,' Harichand began, blocking his moustache with a naked razor-blade. 'Was a night-time. Did sleeping sound. Sound sound. Like a top. Eh, I hear this squeaky noise. Squeaky squeaky. Like little mices. Get up. Still hearing this squeaky noise. Was a moonlight night. Three o'clock in the morning. Moonlight making everything look like a belling-ground. Dead and funny. Squeak. Squeak. Open the window. No wind at all.

All the trees black and quiet. Squeak. Squeak. Road looking white in the moonlight. White and long. Squeak. Squeak. Lean out. No wind. Nothing. Only squeak, squeak. Look down. Something in the road. Black, crawling. Look down again. Four tiny tiny horses harness together. Big as little puppies. Black little horses. And they was pulling a funeral huss. Squeak. Squeak. Huss big as a shoebox.'

Harichand put away the razor-blade.

'Two weeks later, my father dead. Three o'clock in the morning.'

'But talking about puppies,' Baksh said. 'This thing was a big big dog last night. I just open the back door and I see it. Walking about in a funny limping way. You know how Haq does walk? Limping, as though he walking on glass? This dog was walking about like Haq. It ain't say nothing. It just look at me. *Sly*. I get one frighten and I run upstairs. In the morning is a tiny tiny puppy, thin, all the ribs showing. But the same coloration.'

Harichand bent down to shine his shoe. 'Somebody trying to put something on you.' His tone was matter-of-fact.

'Was a big dog, man.'

'Just don't feed it,' Harichand said.

'Feed it! Preacher ain't catching me so easy.'

'Ah, is Preacher, eh?' Harichand gave a knowing chuckle. 'Election thing starting already?'

'We helping out Harbans.'

'Harbans ain't getting *my* vote. Eh, the man ain't bring nothing yet for me to print.'

'How you could say that, man? We fixing up something for you.'

'Mark you, I ain't begging nobody. But if you want my vote, you want my printery. It have a lot of people who wouldn't like it if they know you wasn't treating me nice.'

'We fixing you up, man. So just don't feed it, eh?'

'Well, I waiting to see what all-you bringing. Just don't feed it. And try to get it outa the house.'

And then Baksh ran around telling his story to nearly everyone who wasn't too busy to listen. He had to listen to many stories in return. Etwariah, Rampiari's mother, told (in Hindi) how two days after her husband died she saw him standing at the foot of her bed. He looked at her and then at the baby—he had died the day Rampiari was born—and he cried a little before disappearing. Etwariah cried a lot when she told the story and Baksh had to cry too; but he couldn't keep on crying with Etwariah and in the end he had to leave, very rudely.

So it went on all morning. The story of Tiger got round nearly everywhere. Lorkhoor heard and told Mr Cuffy.

★

Before Rafiq went to school Foam called him to the little ajoupa at the back of the house and said, 'Rafiq, you is a nasty little good-for-nothing bitch.'

Rafiq began to sniffle.

'You pretending you ain't know why I calling you a bitch?'

'I ain't tell no lie.'

Foam slapped him. 'No, you ain't tell no lie,' he mimicked. 'But you tell.'

'The Bible turn for itself. I didn't have nothing to do with it.'

Foam slapped him again. 'How else Ma know, unless you did tell she about the dog?'

Rafiq began to cry. 'I didn't know she was going to bless Herbert.'

'When Herbert come back this evening from Tamana, I want you to beg his pardon. And I want you to give him that red-and-blue top you hiding on top the brass bed.'

'Is my top. I thief it from a boy at school. Big Lambie.'

'I want you to give Herbert the top.'

'Not going to give it. You could do what you like. Touch me again and I going to tell Ma.'

'Rafiq! What sorta obscene language you using? Where you pick up those words? Ma ever hear you using those sorta words?'

'What sorta words?'

'Again, Rafiq? I just have to tell Ma now.'

Rafiq understood blackmail. 'All right, I going to give the top to Herbert.'

★

One of the first things Foam bought with his campaign manager's salary was an expensive pair of dark glasses. He wore them whenever he took out the loudspeaker van.

He was cruising down Ravine Road—if you could cruise down any road in Elvira—when he saw Nelly Chittaranjan coming back from school. She was walking briskly, head a little high.

Foam slowed up and gave a little election speech. Nelly Chittaranjan turned and saw and turned away again, head a little higher.

Foam followed her with the van.

'Want a lift home, girl?'

She didn't reply. He followed.

'Foreman, I will kindly ask you to stop following me about.'

'Why you so formal? Is because you getting married to Harbans son? Call me Foam, man, like everybody else.'

'Some people in Elvira don't know their elders and betters.'

He gave a dry laugh. 'Ah, is because of the dark glasses that you can't recognize me!'

'Foreman, please drive off. Otherwise I will just have to tell my father.'

Foam sang:

> *'Tell, tell,*
> *Till your belly full of rotten egg.'*

'Simple things amuse small minds, I see.'

'Look, girl, you want this lift or you ain't want it? Don't waste my time. Is work I have to work these days.'

'Huh! I don't see what sort of work you could ever do.'

'I is your father boss in this election, you know.'

'Huh!' But she stopped.

The van stopped too. Foam rested an elbow on the door. 'Just managing Harbans campaign for him. That is all. Seventy-five dollars a month. See these glasses? Guess how much.'

'Sixty cents.'

'Garn. Twelve dollars, if you please.'

'Huh!'

'You like the old loudspeaking voice?' He gave a loud and vigorous demonstration.

'You mean to say you learn off all that by heart?'

'Nah! Just make it up as I go along. Want to hear some more?'

She shook her head. 'It *is* hot. You can give me a lift to the end of Ravine Road.'

'Only up to there, eh? Ah, you shame to let the old man see you with me.' He opened the door for her. 'Now that you is practically a married woman.'

He drove off with much noise, and settled down with one hand on the steering wheel, his back in the angle of the seat and door. He looked reposed and casual.

'So little Nelly getting married off, eh?'

He was embarrassing her.

'I don't see why you shame about it. You marrying a doctor, man. You could take down prescriptions *and* type them out. Especially with doctors' handwriting so hard to read.'

He had gone too far. It looked as though she might cry. 'I don't want to get married, Foreman.'

He hadn't thought of that. 'What you want to do then?'

'I want to go to the Poly.'

He couldn't make anything of that. 'Well, things could always mash up. From what I hear, Harbans ain't too anxious to see you as a daughter-in-law either.'

She wept. 'I want to go to the Poly.'

'Poly, eh?'

'In London. Regent Street.'

'Oh.' He spoke as though he knew it well. 'Teacher Francis been putting ideas in your head. Well, you never know what could happen between now and election day.' He paused. 'Look, you like dogs?'

Weeping, Nelly Chittaranjan remembered refinement. 'I adore dogs.'

Foam stamped on the brakes and brought the van to a noisy halt. 'Look, I ain't want that sort of talk. I ask you if you like dogs. You answer me yes or you answer me no. None of this educative nonsense, you hear. You ain't gone to the Poly yet.'

She stopped crying.

She said, 'I like dogs.'

'You is a nice girl. I have a dog—well, small dog, puppy really. Can't keep it home. You want to look after it?'

She nodded.

He was surprised. 'Giving it to you. Wedding present from Foam. What time you does stop taking lessons from Teacher Francis in the evening?'

'Half-past eight.'

'See you at quarter to nine. Where we meet today.'

She got off at the end of Ravine Road.

★

In the afternoon Chittaranjan put on his visiting outfit, left Mrs Chittaranjan to look after the two workmen downstairs, and went out to campaign for Harbans. Chittaranjan's visiting outfit was as special as his home clothes. Item number one was an untorn white shirt, size thirteen, with the sleeves carefully rolled up—not rolled, folded rather—and when it wasn't in use it hung on its own hanger in Chittaranjan's expensive, spacious and practically empty wardrobe. Chittaranjan was extra careful with this shirt. He didn't like to have it washed too often because that weakened the material; but he never liked keeping a shirt in use for more than two months at a time. He wore it as little as possible, and only on special occasions; Chittaranjan liked a shirt to grow dirty gradually and gracefully. Item number two was a pair of brown gaberdine trousers which he kept flat between *Trinidad Sentinels* under his mattress. Item number three was a pair of brown shoes, old, cracked, but glittering; this replaced the sabots he wore at home. The fourth and last item of Chittaranjan's visiting outfit was a vast grey felt hat, smooth, ribbonless, with only one stain, large, ancient and of oil, on the wide brim.

When Elvira saw Chittaranjan in this outfit, it knew he meant business.

Chittaranjan campaigned.

At first things went well. But then Chittaranjan found people a little less ready to commit themselves. They talked about *obeah* and magic and dogs. But they always yielded in the end. Only Rampiari's husband, who had cut his foot with a hoe, played the fool. At the best of times Rampiari's husband was a truculent lout; now he was in pain and ten times worse. He had been there in the morning when Baksh had come to Etwariah with the story of Tiger; and he made a big thing of it. He said he wasn't going to vote for anybody because he didn't want anybody to put any *obeah* on him, he didn't believe in this new politics business, politicians were all crooks, and nobody was going to do anything for him anyway.

Chittaranjan listened patiently, his hat on his knees.

When Rampiari's husband was finished, Chittaranjan asked: 'When you does want money borrow, Rampiari husband, who you does come to?'

'I does come to you, Goldsmith.'

'When you does want somebody to help you get a work, who you does come to?'

'I does come to you, Goldsmith.'

'When you want letter write to the Government, who you does come to?'

'I does come to you, Goldsmith.'

'When you want cup borrow, plate borrow, chair borrow, who you does come to?'

'I does come to you, Goldsmith.'

'When you want *any* sort of help, Rampiari husband, who you does come to?'

'I does come to you, Goldsmith.'

'So when *I* want help, who I must come to?'

'You must come to me, Goldsmith.'

'And when I want this help to put a man in the Legislative Council, who I must come to?'

'You must come to me, Goldsmith.'

'You see, Rampiari husband, the more bigger people *I* know, the more I could help *you* out. Now tell me, is beg I have to beg you for *your* sake?'

'You ain't have to beg, Goldsmith.'

Chittaranjan stood up and put his hat on. 'I hope your foot get better quick.'

'When you see Mr Harbans, Goldsmith, you go tell him, eh, how bad my foot sick.'

Chittaranjan hesitated, remembering Harbans's refusal to have anything to do with the Hindu sick or the Hindu dead.

Rampiari's husband said, 'Preacher coming to see me tomorrow.'

'What *Preacher* could do for you? A man like you ain't want only sympathy. You want a lot more.'

The sick man's eyes brightened. 'You never say a truer word, Goldsmith. *Whenever* I want help, I does come to you.'

Chittaranjan smiled; the sick man smiled back; but when he was outside Chittaranjan muttered, 'Blasted son of a bitch.'

Still, it was a successful afternoon, despite Rampiari's husband and all that talk about *obeah*.

But the *obeah* talk worried him. It could lose votes.

VI

ENCOUNTERS BY NIGHT

★

Mrs Baksh came back to Elvira, her mission accomplished. Herbert had received his spiritual fumigation; and she brought back mysterious things—in a small brown parcel—which would purify the house as well.

'Ganesh Pundit was really the man for this sort of mystic thing,' Baksh said. 'Pity he had to take up politics. Still, that show how good he was. The moment he feel he was losing his hand for that sort of thing, he give up the business.'

'The fellow we went to was all right,' Mrs Baksh said. 'He *jharay* the boy well enough.'

Herbert looked chastened indeed. His thin face was stained with tears, his eyes were still red, the edges of his nostrils still quivering and wet. He kept his mouth twisted, to indicate his continuing disgust with the world in general.

Mrs Baksh had been feeling guilty about Herbert. She said to Baksh, for Herbert to hear, 'Herbert didn't give the fellow much trouble, you know. He behave like a nice nice boy. The fellow say that the fust thing to do when a spirit come on anybody is to beat it out. It ain't the person you beating pussonal, but the spirit.'

Herbert sniffed.

Baksh said, 'People ain't want to believe, you know, man, that the big big dog I see last night turn so small this morning. Nobody ain't want to believe at all at all. Everybody was surprise like anything.'

Mrs Baksh sank aghast into her cane-bottomed chair. 'But you know you is a damn fool, Baksh. You mean you went around *telling* people?'

'Didn't tell them *every*thing. Didn't mention nothing about Preacher or about *obeah*. Just say something about the dog. It ain't have nothing wrong if I tell about the dog. Look, Harichand tell me about the time he did see some tiny tiny horses dragging a tiny tiny funeral huss. Was a moonlight night. Three o'clock . . .'

'Everybody know about Harichand huss. But that was only a *sign*.'

'Sign, eh? And this thing—this dog business—that—that is *obeah* and magic, eh? Something bigger?'

'Yes, you damn fool, yes.'

'Nobody did believe anyway. Everybody thought I was lying.'

'You *was* lying, Pa,' Herbert said. 'Was a puppy last night and is a puppy today.'

Baksh was grateful for the diversion. 'Oh God! Oh God! I go show that boy!'

He tried to grab Herbert; but Herbert ducked behind Mrs Baksh's chair. He knew that his mother was in a sympathetic mood. And Baksh knew that in the circumstances Herbert was inviolate. Still, he made a show. He danced around the chair. Mrs Baksh put out a large arm as a barrier. Baksh respected it.

'Oh God!' he cried. 'To hear a little piss-in-tail boy talking to me like that! When I was a boy, if I did talk to my father like that, I woulda get my whole backside peel with blows.'

'Herbert,' Mrs Baksh said. 'You mustn't tell your father he lie. What you must say?'

'I must say he tell stories,' Herbert said submissively. But he perked up, and a faint mocking smile—which made him look a bit like Foam—came to his lips.

'No, Herbert, you mustn't even say that your father does tell stories.'

'You mean I mustn't say *any*thing, Ma?'

'No, son, you mustn't say anything.'

Baksh stuck his hands into his tight pockets. 'Next time you say anything, see what happen to you, mister man. I beat you till you pee, you hear.'

Herbert had a horror of threats of that sort; they seemed much worse than any flogging.

'I talking to you, mister man,' Baksh insisted. 'Answer me.'

Herbert looked at his mother.

She said, 'Answer him.'

He said, 'Yes, Pa.'

Baksh took his hands out of his pockets. He was mollified but continued to look offended. He couldn't fool Herbert though. Herbert knew that Baksh was only trying to prevent Mrs Baksh attacking *him*.

Baksh got in his blows first. 'You call yourself a mother, and this is the way you bringing up your children. To insult their father and call him liar to his face. This is what you *encouraging* the children to do, after they eating my food since they born.'

Mrs Baksh, tired and very placid now, said, '*You* carry them nine months in your belly? You nurse them? You clean them?'

Baksh's moustache twitched as he looked for an answer.

Before he found one Mrs Baksh returned to the counter-attack. 'Who fault it is that this whole thing happen?' Her brow darkened and her manner changed. 'Is this election sweetness that sweeten you up, Baksh. But see how this sweetness going to turn sour sour. See.'

She was righter than she knew.

★

All that day Tiger remained in his box under the steps, dozing or lying awake and futile. Foam fed him surreptitiously; but Tiger was unused to food and in the afternoon he had an attack of hiccoughs. He lay flat on his side, his tiny ribs unable to contain the convulsions of his tiny belly. The hiccoughs shook him with more energy than he had ever shown; they lifted him up and dropped him down again on the sodden newspapers; they caused curious swallowing noises in his throat. His box became wetter and filthier. Foam, for all his toughness, was squeamish about certain things, and Tiger's box was never cleaned. But Foam fed Tiger, often and unwisely; and it gave him much pleasure when once, stretching out his hand and passing a finger down Tiger's muzzle, he saw Tiger raise his eyes and raise his tail.

And now he had to get rid of Tiger.

'Put him in a bag and take him away in the van,' Mrs Baksh said after dinner.

'Take him far,' Baksh added. 'Far far.'

'All *right,*' Foam said, with sudden irritation. 'All right, don't rush me. I going to take him so far, he not going to offend your sight *or* your heart.'

Mrs Baksh almost cried. 'Is only since the elections that this boy talking to me like that, you know.'

Baksh saw a chance to redeem himself. 'Boy, you know you talking to your mother? Who carry you for nine months in their belly? Who nurse you?'

Mrs Baksh said, 'Why you don't shut your tail, Baksh?'

'The two of all-you quarrel,' Foam said, and went downstairs.

He took a clean gunny sack, held it open and rolled it down to make a nest of sorts; lifted Tiger from his box, using newspaper to keep his hands clean, and put him in the nest.

Herbert tiptoed down the steps.

'Ey, Herbert. Come down and throw away this dirty box somewhere in the backyard. It making the whole house stink.'

'Foam, what you going to do with him?'

Foam didn't reply. His irritation lingered.

Tiger sprawled in the nest of sacking, heaving with hiccoughs.

'Foam, Tiger going to dead?'

Foam looked at Herbert. 'No. He not going to dead.'

'Foam! You not going to kill him?'

He didn't know what he was going to do. When he had spoken to Nelly Chittaranjan about Tiger, it was only to make conversation, to stop her from crying.

Tiger made choking noises.

Foam stood up.

'Foam! You not going to *kill* Tiger?'

Foam shook his head.

'Promise, Foam. Kiss your fingers and promise.'

'You know I don't believe in that sort of thing.'

'Don't kill him, Foam. *You* don't believe in this *obeah* business, eh, Foam?'

Foam sucked his teeth. 'That boy give you the top?'

'Rafiq?' Herbert brightened. 'Yes, he give me the top.'

'Good, throw away that old box. It stinking.'

Herbert touched Tiger's nose with the tip of his index finger. Tiger's eyes didn't change; but his tail lifted and dropped.

★

Nelly Chittaranjan hadn't been thinking when she agreed to meet Foam that evening and take the dog. Now, sitting in Teacher Francis's drab drawing-room and only half listening while he talked, she wasn't so sure about the dog or about Foam. She didn't believe the dog existed at all. But the thought of meeting a boy at night in a lonely lane had kept her excited all afternoon. She had never walked out with any boy: it was wrong; now that she was practically engaged, it was more than wrong. Mr Chittaranjan was modern enough in many ways—the way he had given her an education and the way he furnished his house and kept it shining with new paint—but he wasn't advanced enough to allow his only daughter to walk out with a boy before she was married. Nelly didn't blame him. She knew she was being married off so quickly only because she hadn't been bright enough to get into one of the girls' high schools like La Pique. Thinking of La Pique, she thought of the Poly, and then she thought of Harbans's son, the boy she was going to marry. She had seen him once or twice in Port of Spain when she had gone to stay with her aunt (the wife of the barrister, the donor of the chromium-plated ashtray in Chittaranjan's veranda). He was a fat yellow boy with big yellow teeth, a giggling gum-chewer, always taking out his wallet to show you his latest autographed picture of some American actress, and you were also meant to see the crisp quarter-inch wad of new dollar notes. Still, if she had to marry him, she had to; it was her own fault. She would have preferred the Poly though. Teacher Francis had met someone who had actually been. There were *dances* at the Poly! Foam didn't even know what the Poly was. But he was no fool. He couldn't talk as well as that Lorkhoor; but Lorkhoor was a big show-off; she preferred Foam. Foam was crazy. Those sunglasses. And those long speeches he shot right off the reel, just like that. She had wanted to laugh all the time. Not that the speeches were funny; it was the over-serious way Foam spoke them. And yet he could never make her feel that the whole thing was more than a piece of skylarking. A boy trying to be mannish!

And making up that story about a dog, just to meet her!

Teacher Francis had to pull her up. 'But what making you laugh all the time so for, Miss Chittaranjan?' Teacher Francis reserved standard English only for prepared statements. 'I was saying, the thing about shorthand is practice. When *I* was studying it, I use to even find myself writing shorthand on my pillow.' That was how he always rounded off the lesson.

Nelly looked at the dusty clock on the ochre and chocolate wall. It was twenty past eight; she was meeting Foam at a quarter to nine.

But this was the time when Teacher Francis, the lesson over, his coat off, his tie slackened a little lower than usual, liked to talk about life. He was talking about the election. A bitter subject for him ever since Lorkhoor had, without warning or explanation, deserted him to campaign for Preacher.

'This new constitution is a trick, Miss Chittaranjan. Just another British trick to demoralize the people.'

Nelly, her pen playing on her pad, asked absently, 'Who you voting for, Teach?'

'Not voting for nobody at all.'

'You talking like the Witnesses now, man, Teach.'

He gave a sour laugh. 'No point in voting. People in Elvira don't know the *value* of their vote.'

Nelly looked up from her pad. 'It look to me that a lot of them know it very well, Teach.'

'Miss Chittaranjan, I don't mean nothing against your father, Miss Chittaranjan. But look at Lorkhoor. Before this election, I did always think he was going to go far. But now . . .' Teacher Francis waved a hand and didn't finish the sentence. 'Elvira was a good friendly place before this universal suffrage nonsense.'

'Teach! You mean to say you against democracy?'

He saw he had shocked her. He smiled. 'Is a thing I frown on, Miss Chittaranjan.'

'Teach!'

'I am a man of radical views, Miss Chittaranjan.'

Nelly put down her pen on her notebook. 'My father would be *very* interested, Teacher Francis.'

He saw the notebook. 'Miss Chittaranjan! You been taking down what I was saying, Miss Chittaranjan!'

She hadn't. But she snapped the book shut and rose.

'I was just throwing off ideas, Miss Chittaranjan. You mustn't think I is a fascist.'

She prepared to leave. '*I* don't think anything, Teacher Francis. But if my father hear that you don't approve of democracy or the elections, he wouldn't approve of me coming to you for lessons, I could tell you.'

It was what Teach feared.

'I was just talking, Miss Chittaranjan. Idea-mongering. Fact is, as a teacher, I have to be impartial.'

'I know what you mean. You want to play both sides.'

'No, Miss Chittaranjan, no.'

She didn't wait to hear any more.

He wandered about his bare, cheerless government house, feeling once again that, since the defection of Lorkhoor, Elvira had become a wilderness.

Ravine Road was pitch dark. There was no moon, no wind. The tall featureless bush hunched over the road on one side; on the other side the dry ravine was black, blank. When Foam turned off the headlamps, all the night noises seemed to leap out at the van from the bush, all the croakings and stridulations of creatures he couldn't see, drowning the heaving of Tiger on the seat next to him.

Then the noises receded. Foam heard the beat of a motor engine not far away. Soon he saw headlights about two hundred yards down the slope where the road turned. The vehicle had taken the corner too quickly: the headlights made a Z. Then Foam was dazzled.

The driver shouted, 'Yaah!'

It was Lorkhoor.

'Yaah! We will bury Harbans! Yaah!'

Quick as anything, Foam put his head out of the window and shouted back, 'Put money where your mouth is! You traitor!'

'Yaah!'

And Lorkhoor was gone.

But Lorkhoor wasn't alone in his van. Foam was sure he had seen a woman with him; she had ducked when the van passed. He was really a shameless liar, that boy. He said it was a degradation to get mixed up with Elvira politics, yet he was campaigning for Preacher. He said he didn't care for women, that marriage was unnatural, and here he was driving out of Elvira at night with a woman who wasn't anxious to be seen.

'I too glad we not fighting on the same side this election,' Foam said aloud.

★

Nelly Chittaranjan came, coy but uneasy. 'Well, Foreman,' she said ironically. 'You bring this famous dog?'

He switched on the top light of the van.

'Oh God, Foreman! A dog!'

He didn't understand why she was annoyed.

'Is a mangy little mongrel puppy dog, Foreman. It sick and it stink.'

'For a little dog you calling him a lot of big names, you know.'

She was in a temper. 'Look at the belly, Foreman. Colic.'

'Is why I ask *you*. It ain't have nobody else in Elvira who would look after a sick dog.'

She couldn't go back on her word. But she was angry with Foam; she felt he had made a fool of her. What was she going to do with the dog anyway?

Foam said, 'Your father send a message. Committee meeting at your house. I could give you and your dog a lift.'

She got in without a word.

'For a educated girl, Miss Chittaranjan, you know you ain't got no manners? They not going to like that at the Poly. Nobody ever teach you to say thanks?'

She tossed her head, smoothed out her frock, edged away from Tiger and sniffed loudly.

Foam said, 'You go get used to it.'

Then the trouble started.

They heard a curious noise at the side of the road. It was part gurgle, part splutter, part like a thirsty dog lapping up water.

Then a squeaky breathless voice exclaimed, 'This is the thing that does start the thing!'

Foam had some trouble in making out Haq, the Muslim fanatic.

He got out of the van.

'Haq, you is a old *maquereau*. God give you the proper *maquereau* colour. Black. You so damn black nobody could see you in the night-time.'

Haq was trembling with excitement. His stick rapped the ground, he looked more bent than usual. 'You, Foreman Baksh, call me what you like. But I going to tell your father. For a Muslim you ain't got no shame. Going out with a kaffir woman.'

Nelly looked down at Tiger beside her; she was too stupefied to say or do anything.

Foam defended her. '*You* calling she kaffir? You make yourself out to be all this religious and all this Muslim and all this godly, and still you ain't got no shame. Dog eat your shame. You is a dirty old *maquereau*, old man.'

'This is the thing that does start the thing,' Haq repeated, his squeaky voice twittering out of control. For a precarious moment he lifted his weight off his stick and used the stick to point at Nelly. 'This is the thing.' He made a noise that could have been a titter or a sob, and leaned on his stick again. In the darkness all that Foam could see clearly of Haq were the whites of his eyes behind his glasses and his white prickly beard.

'What *thing* you see, *maquereau*?'

'I see everything.' Haq tittered, sobbed again. 'This is the thing that does start the thing.'

'Tell me what thing you see, *maquereau*.'

'All right, all right, you calling me rude words.' He whined one word and spat out another. 'You don't understand the hardship I does have to put up with.'

'You not getting one black cent from me, you nasty old *maquereau*.'

'I not young and strong like you. I is a old man. You calling me rude words and you want to see me cry. Well, all right. I go cry for you.'

And Haq began to cry. It sounded like chuckling.

'Cry, *maquereau*.'

Nelly spoke at last: 'Leave him, Foreman.'

'No, I want to see the old *maquereau* cry.'

Haq sobbed, 'I is a old man. All you people making Ravine Road a Lovers' Lane. First Lorkhoor and now you. All-you don't understand the hardship a old man does have.' He wiped his cheeks on his sleeve. Then he cried again. 'I is a widow.'

Foam got into the van.

'You tell anybody about this *thing* you see, Haq, and I promising you that you going to spend the rest of your days in a nice hospital. You go start using rubber for bones.'

Haq sobbed and gurgled. 'Kill me now self. You is young and strong. Come on and kill me one time, and bury me right here in Ravine Road, all your Lovers' Lane.'

To start the engine Foam turned off the headlights. Again the noises sprang out from the bush and Haq cried out in the dark, 'Kill me, Foreman. Kill me.'

'*Maquereau*,' Foam shouted, and drove off.

He had enjoyed the encounter with Haq, a man he had never liked; because of Haq's tales he had often been flogged when he was younger.

But Nelly was feeling flat and frightened.

'Don't worry,' Foam said. 'He wouldn't say anything. Not after that tongue-lashing I give him.'

She was silent.

Between them Tiger heaved and croaked.

He dropped them both off at a trace not far from Chittaranjan's.

★

He found Mahadeo and Chittaranjan waiting for him. Chittaranjan had changed into his home clothes and, rocking in his own tiled veranda, was as dry and formidable as ever. Mahadeo was still in his khaki uniform.

There was no light in the veranda. Chittaranjan said they didn't need one, they didn't want to write anything, they only wanted to talk.

Presently Foam heard Nelly arrive. He heard her open the gate at the side of the shop downstairs and heard her come up the wooden steps at the back.

Chittaranjan called out, 'Is you, daughter?'

'Yes, Pa, is me.'

'Go and put on your home clothes,' Chittaranjan ordered. 'And do whatever homework Teacher Francis give you. No more running about for you tonight.'

Foam looked at Chittaranjan. He was smiling his fixed smile.

For some moments no one in the veranda said anything. Foam was thinking about Tiger; Mahadeo was thinking about Mr Cuffy; Chittaranjan rocked and clacked his sabots on the floor.

At last Chittaranjan said to Foam, 'This Mahadeo is a real real jackass.'

Mahadeo remained unmoved, his large eyes unblinking. He had just told Chittaranjan of his unhappy interview with Mr Cuffy that morning.

'I is a frank man,' Chittaranjan said, spreading out his palms on the arms of his rocking-chair. 'I does say my mind, and who want to vex, let them vex.'

Mahadeo wasn't going to be annoyed. He continued to look down at his unlaced boots, stroked his nose, cracked his fingers, passed his thick little hands through his thick oily hair and mumbled, 'I was a fool, I was a fool.'

Chittaranjan wasn't going to let him off so easily.

'Course you was a fool. And you was a double fool. And this boy father was a triple fool.'

'How you mean?' Foam asked.

Chittaranjan smiled more broadly. 'So your father was having trouble with a dog, eh?'

Foam looked down.

'And so your father think that the best way to get people votes is to run about saying that Preacher putting *obeah* and magic on him?' Chittaranjan was caustic, but bland. 'Tell me, that go make a *lot* of people want to vote against Preacher, eh?'

Mahadeo was still preoccupied with his morning adventure. 'It look, Goldsmith, like we have to give up that plan now for burying dead negroes and looking after sick ones.'

For the first time in his life Foam heard Chittaranjan laugh, a short, corrosive titter. 'Eh, but Mahadeo, you smart, man. You work out that one all by yourself?'

Mahadeo smiled. 'Yes, Goldsmith.'

Foam was attending with only half a mind. He was straining to catch all the noises inside the house. The coolness he had shown in Ravine Road was beginning to leave him in Chittaranjan's veranda; the thought of Haq unsettled him now. He heard sounds of washing-up; he heard Mrs Chittaranjan singing the theme song from the Indian film *Jhoola*.

Mahadeo was saying, 'Was a good plan though, Goldsmith. Goldsmith, ain't it did look to you that Sebastian was one negro who was bound to dead before elections?'

Chittaranjan smiled and rocked and didn't reply.

Mahadeo suffered. He passed his hands through his hair and said, 'I sorry, Goldsmith. I was a fool, I was a fool.'

Inside Nelly was moving about. Foam heard the thump and slap of her slippers. Everything seemed all right so far.

Mahadeo scratched the back of his neck to indicate perplexity and contrition. Chittaranjan remained impassive. Mahadeo tried to crack his fingers again; but nothing came: they had been cracked too recently. 'Goldsmith, this new talk about *obeah* could frighten off a lot of votes.'

Chittaranjan spoke up. 'On one side we have the Witnesses telling people not to vote. And now this boy father decide to tell people that if they vote for Harbans, Preacher going to work magic and *obeah* on them. All-you go ahead. See if that is the way to win election.'

Mahadeo forgot his own error. 'In truth, Goldsmith, this boy father does talk too much.'

Foam was about to retort, but Chittaranjan challenged

him: 'You got any sorta plan, Foam? To make the Spanish people vote, and to get other people to vote without getting frighten of Preacher *obeah*?'

Foam shook his head.

Chittaranjan rocked. 'I have a plan.'

They attended.

'It ain't Preacher who working *obeah*,' Chittaranjan said. 'Is the Witnesses. That is the propaganda we have to spread.'

'Is a master-idea,' Mahadeo said.

Foam was cautious. 'Just a minute, Goldsmith. All right, we go about saying that the Witnesses working *obeah*. But what Preacher going to say?'

Chittaranjan's gold teeth flashed in the pale light that came through the thickly curtained drawing-room doorway. 'You is a smart boy, Foam. You does ask the correct question. He'—Chittaranjan jerked his chin towards Mahadeo who stared stolidly at his boots—'he ain't have the brains to think of things like that.'

Mahadeo looked up and asked, 'What Preacher going to say, Goldsmith?'

Chittaranjan stopped rocking. 'Is like this. Preacher hoping to get some Spanish votes too. He wrong, but it good to let people hope sometimes. If the Spanish ain't voting, Preacher suffering. So, already Preacher hisself start saying that the Witnesses working *obeah*. If we say the same thing, the Witnesses ain't got a chance. People go start getting frighten of the Witnesses and we go get back all the votes of the Spanish people in Cordoba who saying they ain't voting because politics ain't a divine thing. Tcha!' Chittaranjan sucked his teeth; the ingratitude and stupidity of the Spaniards still rankled.

Mahadeo scratched the back of his head and passed a finger down his nose. 'You know what you have that we ain't have, Goldsmith? Is brains you have, Goldsmith.'

Chittaranjan snubbed Mahadeo. 'Wasn't my idea. Today I hear people talking about *obeah* and today I hear Lorkhoor going around saying that it wasn't Preacher working *obeah*, but the Witnesses. And I sit down and I hold my head in my two hands and I puzzle it out and I see that even out of this boy father stupidness, starting all this talk about dog and *obeah*, we could make some profit.'

Foam gave his approval. But he was a little bitter that it was Lorkhoor who had thought of a way to counter the Witnesses. After all, the Witnesses were to be defeated by talk of *obeah* and magic; and this *obeah* and magic was nothing other than Tiger, Herbert's Tiger.

Inside, footsteps were measured, ordinary. Mrs Chittaranjan was singing.

Tiger was going to be all right. At least for the night.

VII

DEAD CHICKEN

★

And the next day, in spite of Chittaranjan's plan, Harbans was in trouble, big trouble.

The day began badly, you might almost say with an omen. Foam had an accident outside Chittaranjan's shop. Only a chicken was involved, but the repercussions of the accident were to shake Elvira before dusk.

It was just about midday when the accident happened. Ramlogan had closed his rumshop for the regulation hours from twelve to four. Chittaranjan's two workmen had disappeared somewhere into the back of the shop to eat—Mrs Chittaranjan gave them food and they ate squatting on the floor downstairs. Just then the two rival loudspeaker vans approached one another.

Foam gave his speech everything. 'People of Elvira, vote for the only honourable man fit to become an Honourable Member of the Legislative Council of Trinidad and Tobago. Vote for Mr Surujpat Harbans, popularly known to all and sundry as Pat Harbans. Mr Harbans is your popular candidate. Mr Harbans will leave no stones unturned to work on your behalf. People of Elvira, this is the voice of Foreman Baksh, popularly known to all and sundry as Foam, this is the voice of Foam Baksh asking you—not begging you or imploring you or beseeching you or entreating you—but asking you and telling you to vote for the honourable and popular candidate, Mr Pat Harbans. Mr Harbans will leave no stones unturned to help you.' There was a pause. 'But you must put him in fust.'

Then Lorkhoor spoke and Foam, honourably, remained silent. Lorkhoor said, in his irritating educated voice, 'Ladies and gentlemen of the fair constituency of Elvira, renowned in song and story, this is the voice of the renowned and ever popular Lorkhoor. Lorkhoor humbly urges every man, woman and child to vote for Mr Thomas, well known to you all as Preacher. Preacher will leave no stone unturned to help you. I repeat, ladies and gentlemen, no *stone* unturned.'

The vans were about to cross. Foam, remembering Lorkhoor's taunt the evening before, leaned out and shouted, 'Yaah! We going to bury Preacher! And he won't have nobody to preach at his funeral.'

Lorkhoor shouted back, 'When you bury him, make sure to leave no stone unturned.'

The vans crossed. Lorkhoor shouted, 'Foreman Baksh, why not speak English for a change?'

'Put money where your mouth is,' Foam retorted, although he knew that the words had no relevance to their present exchange. And as he spoke those words he pulled a little to the right to avoid Lorkhoor's van, felt a bump on his radiator, heard a short, fading cackle, and knew that he had damaged some lesser creature. He waited for the shouts and abuse from the owner. But there was nothing. He looked back quickly. It was a chicken, one of Chittaranjan's, or rather, Mrs Chittaranjan's. He drove on.

★

That happened just after noon. Less than three hours later a breadfruit from Ramlogan's tree dropped so hard on Chittaranjan's roof that the framed picture of King George V and Mahatma Gandhi in the drawing-room fell.

Chittaranjan rushed to the kitchen window, pushed aside his wife from the enamel sink where she was scouring pots and pans with blue soap and ashes, and shot some elaborate Hindi curses at Ramlogan's backyard.

Ramlogan didn't retaliate, didn't even put his head out of his window.

Mrs Chittaranjan sighed.

Chittaranjan turned to her. 'You see how that man Ramlogan provoking me? You see?'

Mrs Chittaranjan, ash-smeared pot and ashy rag in hand, sighed again.

'You see or you ain't see?'

'I see.'

Chittaranjan was moved to further anger by his wife's calm. He put his head out of the Demerara window and cursed long and loud, still in Hindi.

Ramlogan didn't reply.

Chittaranjan was at a loss. He spoke to Mrs Chittaranjan. 'A good good picture. You can't just walk in a shop and get a picture like that every day, you know. Remember how much time I spend passe-partouting it?'

'Well, man, it have one consolation. The picture ain't break.'

'How you mean? It *coulda* break. Nothing in this house ain't safe with that man breadfruit dropping all over the place.'

'No, man. Why you don't go and hang back the picture up?'

'Hang it back up? Me, hang it back up? Look, *you* don't start provoking me now, you hear. I ain't know what I do so, for everybody to give me all this provocation all the time.'

'But, man, Ramlogan *ain't* provoking you today. The breadfruit fall, is true. But breadfruit ain't have a mind.

Breadfruit don't stop and study and say, "I think I go fall today and knock down the picture of Mahatma Gandhi."'

'Stop giving me provocation!'

'And Ramlogan, for all the bad cuss you cuss him, he ain't even come out to answer you back.'

'Ain't come out! You know why he ain't come out? You know?' And running to the window, he shouted his own answer: 'Is because he ain't no fighter. You know who is the fighter? I, Chittaranjan, is the fighter.' He shook his short scrawny arms and beat on the enamel sink. Then he pulled in his head and faced Mrs Chittaranjan. 'My name in the Supreme Court for fighting. Not any stupid old Naparoni Petty Civil—ha!—but *Supreme* Court.' He sat on the paint-spotted kitchen stool and said ruminatively, 'I is like that. Supreme Court or nothing.' He chuckled. 'Well, if Ramlogan go on like this, Supreme Court going to hear from me again, that is all.' He spoke with rueful pride.

'Man, you know you only talking.' Mrs Chittaranjan was being provocative again.

Chittaranjan pursed and unpursed his lips. 'Only talking, eh?'

But he was quite subdued. Ramlogan's perverse silence had put him out. He sat smiling, frowning, his sabots on the cross-bar of the stool, his small sharp shoulders hunched up, the palms of his small bony hands pressing hard on the edges of the seat.

Mrs. Chittaranjan returned to her pans. She scoured; the ash grated; she sang the song from *Jhoola*.

Chittaranjan said, slowly, 'Going to fix him up. Fix him good and proper. Going to put something on him. Something good.'

The singing stopped. 'No, man. You mustn't talk so. *Obeah* and magic is not a nice thing to put on anybody.'

'Nah, don't stop me, I begging you. Don't stop me. I can't bear *any* more provocation again.'

'Man, why you don't go and hang back the picture up?'

'Put something on him before *he* put something on we.'

Mrs Chittaranjan looked perturbed.

Chittaranjan saw. He drove home his point. 'Somebody try to put something on Baksh day before yesterday. Dog. Was big big in the night and next morning was tiny tiny. So high.'

'*You* see the dog?'

'You laughing. But I telling you, man, we got to put something on him before he put something on we. And it ain't we alone we got to think about. What about little Nalini?'

'Nelly, man? Little Nelly?'

His wife's anxiety calmed Chittaranjan. He got up from the stool. 'Going to hang back the picture up,' he announced.

He clattered down the wooden back steps in his sabots and went to the little dark cupboard behind the shop. In this cupboard he kept all sorts of things: pails and basins for his jewellery work, ladders and shears and carpenter's tools, paint-tins and brushes, tins full of bent nails he had collected from the concrete casings when his house was being built. There was no light in the cupboard—that was part of his economy. But he knew where everything was. He knew where the hammer was and where the nail-tin was.

When he opened the door a strong smell met his nostrils. 'That white lime growing rotten like hell,' he said. He felt for the hammer, found it. He felt for the nail-tin. His fingers touched something hard and fur-lined. Then something slimy passed over his hand. Then something took up the loose flesh at the bottom of his little finger and gave it a sharp little nip.

Chittaranjan bolted.

One sabot was missing when he stood breathless against the kitchen door.

'Man,' he said at last. 'Man, dog.'

'Dog?'

'Yes, man.'

'Downstairs?'

'Yes, man. Store-room. Lock up in the store-room.'

Mrs Chittaranjan nearly screamed.

'Just like the one Baksh say he see, man. They send it away but it come back. To we, man, to we.'

★

Ramlogan had heard the breadfruit fall and heard all the subsequent curses from Chittaranjan. But he didn't reply because a visitor had just brought him important news.

The visitor was Haq.

Haq had come at about half-past two, gone around to that side of Ramlogan's yard which was hidden from Chittaranjan's, and beaten on the gate. The gate answered well: it was entirely made up of tin advertisements for Dr Kellogg's Asthma Remedy, enamelled in yellow and black.

Ramlogan shouted: 'Go away. I know who you is. And I know who send you. You is a police and your wife sick and you want some brandy really bad for she sake, and you go beg and I go sell and you go lock me up. And I know is Chittaranjan who send you. Go away.'

Chittaranjan had indeed caught Ramlogan like that once.

Haq drummed again. 'I is not a police. I is Haq. Haq.'

'Haq,' came the reply, 'haul your black arse away from my shop. You not getting nothing on trust. And too besides, is closing time.'

Haq didn't go away.

At length Ramlogan came out, smelling of Canadian Healing Oil, and unchained the gate. He had been having his siesta. He was wearing a pair of dirty white pants that showed how his fat legs shook when he walked, and a dirty white vest with many holes. And he was in his slippers: dirty canvas shoes open at the little toes, with the heels crushed flat.

'What the hell you want, black Haq?'

Haq put his face close up to Ramlogan's unshaved chin. 'When you hear me! When you hear me!'

Ramlogan pushed him away. 'You ain't bound and 'bliged to spit on me when you talk.'

Haq didn't seem to mind. 'When you hear,' he twittered, his lower lip wet and shining. 'Just wait until you hear. It not going to be black Haq then.'

Ramlogan was striding ahead, flinging out his legs, shaking and jellying from his shoulders to his knees.

They went to the room behind the shop. Here Ramlogan cooked, ate and slept. It was a long narrow room, just the size of the rumshop. *Trinidad Sentinels* covered the walls and sheltered many cockroaches. The one window was closed; the air was hot, and heavy with the sweet smell of Canadian Healing Oil.

Ramlogan said grumpily, 'You wake up a man when a man was catching a little sleep, man,' and he lay down on his rumpled bed—a mattress thrown over some new planks—scratching easily and indiscriminately. He yawned.

Haq leaned his stick against the rum crates in a corner and eased himself into the sugar-sack hammock hanging diagonally across the room.

Ramlogan yawned and scratched. 'Before you start, Haq, remember one thing. No trust. Remember, no trust.'

He pointed to the only picture on his walls, a coloured diptych. In one panel Haq saw the wise man who had never given credit, plump—though not so plump as Ramlogan—and laughing and counting what looked like a fortune. In the other panel the incorrigible creditor, wizened, haggard, was biting his nails in front of an empty money chest. Ramlogan had a copy of this picture in his shop as well.

'In God we trust, as the saying goes,' Ramlogan glozed. 'In man we bust. *As* the saying goes.'

'I ain't come to beg,' Haq said. 'If you ain't want to hear what I have to say, I could just get up and walk out, you know.'

But he made no move to go.

He talked.

Ramlogan listened. And as he listened, his peevishness turned into delight. He rolled on his dirty bed and kicked up his fat legs. 'Oh, God, You is good. You is really good. Was this self I been waiting and praying for, for a long long time. Ha! So Chittaranjan is the fighter, eh? He in the Supreme Court for fighting, eh? Now we go show this Supreme Court fighter!'

Then the breadfruit fell. Then Chittaranjan cursed.

Haq waited. Ramlogan did nothing.

'Go on and tell him now,' Haq urged. 'Answer him back.'

'It could wait.' And Ramlogan began to sing: 'It could wait-ait, it could-ould wait-ait.'

He stopped singing and they both listened to Chittaranjan cursing. Ramlogan slapped his belly. Haq giggled.

'Let we just remain quiet like a chu'ch and listen to *all* that he have to say,' Ramlogan said. He clasped his hands over his belly, looked up at the sooty corrugated-iron ceiling, smiled and shut his eyes.

Chittaranjan paused. All that could be heard in Ramlogan's room was the whisking of cockroaches behind the *Trinidad Sentinels* on the wall.

Chittaranjan began again.

'He talking brave, eh, Haq? Let him wait. Haq, you black, but you is a good good friend.'

Haq was about to speak, but Ramlogan stopped him: 'Let we *well* listen.'

They listened until there was nothing more to listen to.

Haq said, 'Ramlogan, you is my good good friend too. You is the only Hindu I could call that.'

Ramlogan sat up and his feet fumbled for the degraded canvas shoes.

'I is a old man, Ramlogan. My shop don't pay, like yours. People ain't buying sweet drink as how they use to. I is a widow too. Just like you. But I ain't have your strength.'

'All of we have to get old, Haq.'

'That boy Foam say he going to send me to hospital.'

'Foam only full of mouth, like his father.'

'He did beg and beg me not to tell nobody. Wasn't for *my* sake I break my word.'

Ramlogan stood up, stretched, and passed his big hairy hands over his big hairy belly. He walked over to the rum crates and took out a quarter bottle.

'A good Muslim like you shouldn't drink, you know, Haq.'

Haq looked angrily from the quarter bottle to Ramlogan. 'I is a *very* old man.'

'And because you is very old, you want to take over my shop?' Ramlogan put back the bottle of rum. 'You done owing me more than thirty dollars which I know these eyes of mine never even going to smell again.'

It was true. Haq had caught Ramlogan when Ramlogan was new in Elvira.

Haq said, 'Is so it does happen when you get old. Give me.'

He took the rum, dolefully, and hid it in an inside pocket of his loose serge jacket. 'Sometimes, eh, Ramlogan, I could drop in by you for a little chat, like in the days when you did fust come to Elvira?'

Ramlogan nodded. 'You is a bad Muslim, Haq, and you is a bad drinker.'

Haq struggled to rise from his hammock. 'I is a old man.'

Ramlogan hurried him outside and chained the gate after him.

Haq came out well pleased, but trying hard to look dejected, to fool the two workmen in Chittaranjan's yard. They weren't looking at him; they were staring in astonishment at something he hadn't seen. He kept his eyes on the ground and fumbled with his jacket to make sure that his rum was safe. He limped a few paces; then, knowing that people would suspect equally if he appeared too dejected, he looked up.

And halted.

There, limping out of Chittaranjan's yard into the hot afternoon sun, was the animal all Elvira had heard about. Tiny, rickety. Dangerous. Tiger.

'Where that dog going?' Haq cried. And he hoped it wasn't to his place.

★

Tiger came out into the road and turned left.

It was nearly half-past three. Children were coming back from school, labourers from the estate. Only people in government service were still at work; they would knock off at four.

The news ran through Elvira. Baksh's puppy, the *obeah*-dog, the one that had been sent away, was back.

Tiger limped on. Schoolchildren and labourers stood silently at the verge to let him pass. Faces appeared behind raised curtains. People ran up from the traces to watch. No one interfered with Tiger and he looked at no one. His hiccoughs had gone. He tottered, wobbled, and went on, as though some force outside him were pushing him on to a specific destination.

Mr Cuffy saw and was afraid.

Rampiari's husband was afraid. 'You is my witness, Ma,' he said to his mother-in-law, 'that when the goldsmith come yesterday to ask for my vote, I tell him I didn't want to meddle in this politics business. You is my witness that he beg and beg me to vote.'

Mahadeo, his thoughts on the sick and dying negroes of Elvira, saw. When he passed Mr Cuffy he didn't look up.

Mr Cuffy shouted, 'Remember, Mahadeo, if anybody dead before this elections . . .'

Mahadeo walked on.

Tiger walked on.

Baksh, Mrs Baksh, Foam and all the six young Bakshes knew.

'Shut up the shop!' Baksh ordered. 'And shut up the gate. Nobody dog ain't walking into my yard as they well please.'

Mrs Baksh was pale. 'This sweetness, man, this election sweetness.'

Baksh said, 'Foam, I ain't want to get Bible and key again. You did or you didn't take away that dog last night?'

'I tell you, man.'

'Oh God, Foam! Things serious. Don't lie to me at this hour, you know.'

Foam sucked his teeth.

Herbert said, 'But we ain't even know is the same dog.'

'Yes,' Baksh said eagerly. 'Exactly. How we know is the same dog?'

Mrs Baksh beat her bosom. 'I *know*, Baksh.'

Tiger came on, indifferent as sea or sky. He didn't walk in the centre of the road, as people wished he would; he walked at the edge, as if he wished to hide in the grass.

Christians, Hindus and Muslims crossed themselves. To make sure, some Hindus muttered *Rama, Rama* as well.

Tiger came around the bend of the road.

'Is Tiger!' Herbert said.

'Sweetness! Sourness!'

Rafiq said, 'Ten die.'

'But look how small the mister man dog is, eh?' Baksh said. 'You know, he get even smaller now. Small as a rabbit and thin as a matchstick.'

Herbert said, 'Still, small as he is, he coming.'

'Herbert,' Mrs Baksh pleaded, 'you ain't cause enough trouble and misery?'

Baksh said, 'Not to worry, man. For all we know, the dog just going to walk straight past the house. After all, that fellow in Tamana did well *jharay* Herbert.'

'I *know*, Baksh. And everybody in Elvira know too. Look how they looking. They looking at the dog and then they looking at we. And they laughing in their belly, for all the serious face they putting on. Oh God, Baksh, this sweetness!'

Foam said, 'I don't see why all-you making this big set of fuss for. All I could see is a thin thin dog, break-up like hell, that look as though he ain't eat nothing since he born.'

Tiger staggered on.

Baksh said, 'Look, man. What you worried for? He ain't even trying to cross the road yet.'

'Baksh, I know. He go cross when he want to cross. That dog know his business, I telling you. Oh, Baksh, the mess you get me in!'

Herbert said, 'Oh. He ain't even stopping.'

Mrs Baksh, crying, asked, 'You want it to stop, Herbert? Just answer me that. My own child want the dog to stop?'

Herbert said, 'Well, it ain't stopping.'

'What I did tell you?' Baksh said. He laughed. 'Wonder *who* house little mister man dog going to. Come to think of it, you know, man, it ain't even the same dog. The one we did have had a white spot on the right foot in front. This one ain't have no white spot. Not the same dog really.' He turned his back to the veranda wall and faced his family. 'Don't know why everybody was getting so excited. All right, all right, the show over.' He clapped his hands and snapped his fingers at the young Bakshes. 'Show over. Back to your reading and your studies. Homework. Educate yourself. Jawgraphy and jawmetry. Nobody did give *me* a opportunity to educate myself. . . .'

'Dog coming back,' Foam said. 'He stop and turning.'

They all scrambled to look.

Tiger was limping brokenly across the road.

'Somebody feed that dog here!' Baksh shouted. 'Nobody not going to tell me that somebody ain't feed that dog here.'

Tiger dragged himself across the plank over the gutter. Then the strength that had driven him so far was extinguished; he collapsed on his side, his eyes vacant, his chest and belly heaving.

'He behaving as if he come home,' Herbert said.

'Herbert, my son, my own son,' Mrs Baksh said. 'What come over you, son? Tell me what they do to you, to make you *want* that dirty dog. Tell me, my son.'

Herbert didn't reply.

Mrs Baksh broke down completely. She cried and her breasts and belly shook. 'Something going to happen, Baksh. In this house.'

'Ten die,' Rafiq said.

Baksh slapped him.

'Suppose that dog just lay down there and dead,' Baksh said. 'Oh God, Foam, you want me to believe that you ain't feed that dog here? That dog behave too much as if he know where his bread butter, you hear.'

Foam shrugged his shoulders.

Baksh said, 'Man, what going to be the best thing? For the dog to live or dead?'

Mrs Baksh pressed her hands against her eyes and shook her head. 'I don't know, Baksh. I just don't know what is the best thing.'

But Herbert knew what he wanted. 'Oh, God,' he prayed, 'don't let Tiger dead.'

★

Ramlogan didn't know about Tiger's passage through Elvira. After Haq left he remained in his narrow dark room, savouring the news Haq had brought. He couldn't go back to sleep. He remained on his bed, completely happy, looking up at the corrugated-iron roof until the alarm clock went off on the empty rum crate at his bedside. It was an alarm clock he had got many years before for collecting empty Anchor Cigarette packets; the dial had letters in the place of eleven numerals and read SMOKE ANCHOR 6. The dial was yellow and the glass, surprisingly uncracked, was scratched and blurred. Every midday when he shut his shop Ramlogan set the alarm for a quarter to four. That gave him time to anoint himself with Canadian Healing Oil, dress and make some tea before he opened the shop again at four.

That afternoon, routine became delicious ritual. He was lavish with the Canadian Healing Oil. He rubbed it over his face and worked it into his scalp; he poured some into his palm and held it to his nostrils to inhale the therapeutic vapours; the only thing Ramlogan didn't do with Canadian Healing Oil was drink it. He dressed leisurely, humming the song from *Jhoola*. He made his tea, drank it; and having some moments to spare, went out into his yard. The stunted and dead plants in the centre didn't offend him that afternoon, and he looked almost with love on the breadfruit tree and the zaboca tree at the edge of the yard. He was particularly fond of the zaboca tree. He had stolen it not long after he had come to Elvira, from a lorry that was carrying a whole load of small zaboca trees in bamboo pods. The lorry had had a puncture just outside his shop; he had gone out to look; and when the driver went off to look for a pump, Ramlogan had taken a bamboo pod and walked off with it into his own yard. The tree had grown well. Its fruit was high-grade. You could tell that by just looking at it. It was none of your common zaboca, all stringy and waterlogged. That afternoon it didn't grieve Ramlogan at all that he hadn't tasted one of the fruit.

It was time to open the shop. He climbed over the greasy counter, thinking, as he did so, that after the election, when Harbans had settled his account, he would get a nice zinc counter. And perhaps even a refrigerator. For lager. People were drinking more lager and it didn't do for him to keep ice wrapped up in a dirty sugar-sack. And sometimes the ice-lorry didn't even come.

He lifted the solid bar that kept the shaky front doors secure, humming the song from *Jhoola*. He remembered he had picked up the song from Mrs Chittaranjan next door, and stopped humming. He opened the doors, squinting against the sudden dazzle of the afternoon sun. He looked down.

Before him, laid squarely in the middle of his doorway, was a dead chicken.

VIII

DEAD DOG

★

He recognized the chicken at once.

It was one of Mrs Chittaranjan's clean-necked chickens, white and grey, an insistent, impertinent thing that, despite repeated shooings and occasional lucky hits with stones and bits of wood and empty Canadian Healing Oil bottles, continued to come into his yard, eat his grass, dig up his languishing plants and leave its droppings everywhere, sometimes even in the back room and in the shop.

It was the chicken Foam had hit earlier that day.

Ramlogan had known the chicken since it was hatched. He had known its mother and managed to maim her in the leg when she came into his yard one day with all her brood. The rest of that particular brood had disappeared. They had been stolen, they had grown up and been eaten or they had just died. Only the hardy clean-necked chicken had survived.

For a moment Ramlogan was sad to see it lying dead at his feet.

He looked up at Chittaranjan's veranda.

Chittaranjan was waiting for him. 'Look at it good, Ramlogan. It not going to worry you again. That fowl on *your* nasty conscience.'

Ramlogan was taken by surprise.

'You is a fat blow-up beast. You can't touch no human, so you take it outa a poor chicken. You is a bad wicked beast. Look at it good. Take it up. Cook it. Eat it. Eat it and get more fat. Ain't is that you say you want to do for a long long time? Now is your chance. Cook it and eat it and I hope it poison you. You kill it, you wicked beast, you Nazi spy.'

Ramlogan hadn't recovered. 'Who you calling a Nazi spy?'

'You. You is a Nazi spy. You is wuss than Hitler.'

'And because I is wuss than Hitler, you come and put this dead fowl on my doorstep?'

'But ain't it make your heart satisfy, you wuthless beast? Ain't it bring peace and satisfaction inside your fat dirty heart to see the poor little chicken dead?'

'Eh! But who tell you I kill your fowl? I ain't kill nobody fowl, you hearing me?'

'You is a wuthless liar.'

Ramlogan lifted his leg to kick the chicken from his doorstep. But something Chittaranjan said arrested him.

'Kick it,' Chittaranjan said. 'And I bet your whole fat foot drop off and rotten. Go ahead and kick it.'

Ramlogan was getting angry. 'You just want to put something on me, eh? You is a big big fighter, and all you could do is put magic and *obeah* on me, eh? You is a Supreme Court fighter?'

'What you asking me for? *You* ever see the inside of any court?'

Ramlogan strode over the dead chicken and walked slowly to the edge of his yard. He said, genially, 'Chittaranjan, come down a little bit. Come down and tell me I is a Nazi spy.'

And Ramlogan put his hand on the wire fence.

'Take your fat dirty hand offa my fence!'

Ramlogan smiled. 'Come down and take my hand off. Come down, take my hand offa your fence and tell me I is a Nazi spy.'

Chittaranjan was puzzled. Ramlogan had never before

refused to take his hands off the fence. He had contented himself either with crying and promising to build his own fence, or with saying, 'All right, I taking my hand offa your fence, and I going inside to wash it with carbolic soap.'

'Come down,' Ramlogan invited.

'I not going to dirty my hands on you.' Chittaranjan paused. 'But is my fence still.'

Inspiration came to Ramlogan. 'Why you don't put a fence around your daughter too?'

He scored.

'Nalini?' Chittaranjan asked, and his tone was almost conversational.

'Yes, Nalini self. Little Nelly. Ha.' Ramlogan gave his dryest laugh.

'Ramlogan! What you want with my daughter?'

Ramlogan shook the wire fence. 'Ha. *I* don't want nothing with your daughter. But I know who want though.'

'Ramlogan! Who you is to take my daughter name in your mouth in vain? You, a man like you, who should be running about kissing the ground in case she walk on it.'

'*Walk*? Ha. Little Nelly tired with walking, man. She lying down now.'

'Ramlogan! You mean you sell everything from that rumshop of yours? You ain't even keep back a penny shame? Is the sort of language to hear from a old, hard-back, resign man like you?'

Ramlogan addressed Chittaranjan's workmen under the awning. They had been studiously inattentive throughout. 'Tell me, is something *I* make up?'

The workmen didn't look at him.

Ramlogan said, 'When girl children small, they does crawl, as the saying goes. Then they does start walking. Then they does lie down. *As* the saying goes. Ain't something I sit down and invent.'

'Who invent it?' Chittaranjan screamed. 'Your mother?'

Ramlogan said solemnly, 'Chittaranjan, I beg you, don't cuss my mother. Cuss me upside down as much as you want, but leave my mother alone.' He paused, and laughed. 'But if you want to learn more about Nelly, why you don't ask Foam?'

'Foam? Foreman? Baksh son?'

'Campaign manager. Ha. *Nice* boy. Nice *Muslim* boy.'

Chittaranjan lost his taste for battle. 'Is true? Is true, Ramlogan? You ain't making this up?'

'Why you asking me for? Ha. Ask little Nelly. Look, little Nelly coming back from school. Ask she.' Ramlogan pointed.

From his veranda Chittaranjan saw Nelly coming up the road.

'Proper student and scholar, man,' Ramlogan said. 'The girl going to school in the day-time and taking private lessons in the night-time. I know I is a Nazi spy, and I know I is a shameless hard-back resign man, but I is not the man to stand up between father and daughter.'

He gave the fence a final shake, went and picked up the chicken and flung it into Chittaranjan's yard. 'It get fat enough eating my food,' he said. 'Cook it and eat it yourself. Supreme Court fighter like you have to eat good.'

He went back to his counter.

Nelly had stayed behind at school, as she always did, to help correct the exercises of the lower classes and rearrange the desks after the day's upheaval. She was head pupil, a position more like that of unpaid monitor. On the way home she had heard about Tiger and seen him lying in the Bakshes' yard. She knew then that her parents must have found him and turned him out.

She overdid the cheerfulness when she saw Chittaranjan. 'Hi, Pops!'

Chittaranjan didn't like the greeting. 'Nalini,' he said sadly, 'don't bother to go round by the back. Come up here. I have something to ask you.'

She didn't like his tone.

'Oh dog, dog,' she muttered, going up the red steps to the veranda, 'how much more trouble you going to cause?'

★

The Bakshes in their dilemma—whether they wanted Tiger dead or alive—were fortunate to get the advice of Harichand the printer.

Harichand was coming home after his work in Couva. No taxi-driver cared to come right up to Elvira, and Harichand was dropped outside Cordoba. He had to walk the three miles to Elvira. He enjoyed it. It kept his figure trim; and when it rained he liked sporting the American raincoat he had acquired—at enormous cost, he said—on one of his trips to Port of Spain. He was the only man in Elvira who possessed a raincoat; everybody else just waited until the rain stopped.

Baksh was sitting in his veranda, looking out as if to find a solution, when he saw Harichand and pointed to Tiger prostrate in the yard.

'Ah, little puppy dog,' Harichand said cheerfully. 'Thought you did get rid of him.'

'It come back, Harichand.'

'Come back, eh?' Harichand stooped and looked at Tiger critically. 'Thin thing.' He stood up and gently lifted Tiger's belly with the tip of a shining shoe. 'Ah. Preacher put something strong on you if dog come back.'

'Come up, Harichand,' Baksh said. 'It have something we want to ask you.'

Harichand had an entirely spurious reputation as an amateur of the mystic and the psychic; but the thing that encouraged Baksh to call him up was the limitless confidence he always gave off. Nothing surprised or upset Harichand, and he was always ready with a remedy.

'I have a pussonal feeling,' Baksh began, seating Harichand on a bench in the veranda, 'I have a pussonal feeling that somebody feed that dog here.'

'Feed, eh?' Harichand got up again and took off his coat. His white shirt was spotless. One of Harichand's idiosyncrasies was to wear a clean shirt every day. He folded his coat carefully and rested it on the ledge of the veranda wall. Then he sat down and hitched up his sharply creased blue serge trousers above his knees. 'Somebody feed it, eh? But did tell you not to feed it. Wust thing in the world, feeding dog like that.'

Mrs Baksh came up. 'What go happen if the dog dead, Harichand?'

Harichand hadn't thought of that. 'What go happen, eh?' He passed the edge of his thumb-nail along his sharp little moustache. 'If it dead.' He paused. 'Could be dangerous. You never know. You went to see somebody about it?'

She mentioned the name of the mystic in Tamana.

Harichand made a face. 'He all right. But he don't really *know*. Not like Ganesh Pundit. Ganesh was the man.'

'Is that I does always say,' Baksh said. He turned to Mrs Baksh. 'Ain't I did tell you, man, that Ganesh Pundit was the man?'

'Still,' Harichand said consolingly, 'you went to see somebody. He give you something for the house and he *jharay* the boy?'

'He well *jharay* him,' Mrs Baksh said. 'Baksh tell you about the sign, Harichand?'

'Sign? Funeral huss?'

'Not *that*,' Baksh said quickly. '*We* had a sign. Tell him, man.'

Mrs Baksh told about the 'Ten Die!' sign.

'Did see it,' said Harichand. 'Didn't know was *your* sign.'

Baksh smiled. 'Well, was *we* sign.'

Harichand said firmly, 'Mustn't let the dog dead.'

'But you did tell me not to feed him,' Baksh said.

'Didn't tell me about your sign,' said Harichand. 'And too besides, didn't exactly say that. Did just say not to feed it *inside* the house. Wust thing in the world, feeding dog like that inside.'

'Feed him outside?' Baksh asked.

'That's right. Outside. Feed him outside.'

Harichand stood up and looked down at Tiger.

'Think he go dead, Harichand?' Mrs Baksh asked.

'Hm.' Harichand frowned and bit his thin lower lip with sharp white teeth. 'Mustn't *let* him dead.'

Baksh said, 'He look strong to you, Harichand?'

'Wouldn't exactly *call* him a strong dog,' Harichand said.

Baksh coaxed: 'But is thin thin dogs like that does live and live and make a lot a lot of mischief, eh, Harichand?'

Harichand said, 'Trinidad full of thin dogs.'

'Still,' Baksh said, 'they *living*.'

Harichand whispered to Baksh, 'Is thin dogs like that does breed a lot, you know. And breed fast to boot.'

Baksh made a big show of astonishment, to please Harichand.

'Yes, man. Dogs like that. Telling you, man. See it with my own eyes.' Harichand caught Mrs Baksh's eye. He said, loudly, 'Just feed it outside. Outside all the time. Everything going to be all right. If anything happen, just let me know.'

He hung his coat lovingly over his left arm and straightened his tie. As he was leaving he said, 'Still waiting for those election printing jobs, Baksh. If Harbans want my vote, he want my printery. Otherwise . . .' And Harichand shook his head and laughed.

*

Soon Tiger was passing through Elvira again, this time in the loudspeaker van. Foam and Herbert were taking him, on instructions, to the old cocoa-house.

*

Chittaranjan called.

Baksh said, 'Going out campaigning, Goldsmith?'

For Chittaranjan was in his visiting outfit.

Chittaranjan didn't reply.

'Something private, eh, Goldsmith?'

And Baksh led Chittaranjan upstairs. But Chittaranjan didn't take off his hat and didn't sit down in the cane-bottomed chair.

'Something serious, Goldsmith?'

'Baksh, I want you to stop interfering with my daughter.'

Baksh knit his brows.

Chittaranjan's flush became deeper. His smile widened. His calm voice iced over: 'It have some people who can't bear to see other people prosper. I don't want nobody to pass over their *obeah* to me and I ain't give my daughter all that education for she to run about with boys in the night-time.'

'You talking about Foam, eh?'

'I ain't talking about Foam. I talking about the man who instigating Foam. And that man is you, Baksh. I is like that, as you know. I does say my mind, and who want to vex, let them vex.'

'Look out, you know, Goldsmith! You calling me a instigator.'

'I ain't want your *obeah* in my house. We is Hindus. You is Muslim. And too besides, my daughter practically engage already.'

'Engage!' Baksh laughed. 'Engage to Harbans son? You have all Elvira laughing at you. You believe Harbans going to let his son marry your daughter? Harbans foolish, but he ain't that foolish, you hear.'

For a moment Chittaranjan was at a loss.

'And look, eh, Goldsmith, Foam better than ten of Harbans sons, you hear. And too besides, you think *I* go instigate Foam to go around with *your* daughter? Don't make me laugh, man. Your daughter? When it have five thousand Muslim girl prettier than she.'

'I glad it have five thousand Muslim girl prettier than she. But that ain't the point.'

'How it ain't the point? Everybody know that Muslim girl prettier than Hindu girl. And Foam chasing *your* daughter? Ten to one, your daughter ain't giving the poor boy a chance. Let me tell you, eh, every Hindu girl think they in paradise if they get a Muslim boy.'

'What is Muslim?' Chittaranjan asked, his smile frozen, his eyes unshining, his voice low and cutting. 'Muslim is everything and Muslim is nothing.' He paused. 'Even negro is Muslim.'

That hurt Baksh. He stopped pacing about and looked at Chittaranjan. He looked at him hard and long. Then he shouted, 'Good! Good! I glad! I glad! Harbans ain't want no Muslim vote. Harbans ain't going to *get* no Muslim vote. You say it yourself. Negro and Muslim is one. All right. Preacher getting every Muslim vote in Elvira.'

Baksh's rage relaxed Chittaranjan. He took off his hat and flicked a finger over the wide brim. 'We could do without the Muslim vote.' He put on his hat again, lifted his left arm and pinched the loose skin just below the wrist. 'This is pure blood. Every Hindu blood is pure blood. Nothing mix up with it. Is pure Aryan blood.'

Baksh snorted. 'All-you is just a pack of kaffir, if you ask me.'

'*Madinga!*' Chittaranjan snapped back.

They traded racial insults in rising voices.

Mrs Baksh came out and said, 'Goldsmith, I is not going to have you come to my house and talk like that.'

Chittaranjan pressed his hat more firmly on his head. 'I is not *staying* in your house.' He went through the brass-bed room to the stairs, saying, 'Smell. Smell the beef and all the other nastiness they does cook in this house.' He matched the rhythm of his speech to his progress down the steps: 'A animal spend nine months in his mother belly. It born. The mother feed it. People feed it. It feed itself. It grow up. It come big. It come strong. Then they kill it. Why?' He was on the last step. 'To feed Baksh.'

Baksh shouted after him, 'And tell Harbans he have to win this election without the Muslim vote.'

'We go still win.'

And Chittaranjan was in the road.

'What I tell you, Baksh?' Mrs Baksh exclaimed. 'See how sour the sweetness turning?'

'Look, you and all,' Baksh said, 'don't start digging in my tail, you hear.'

Mrs Baksh smoothed her dress over her belly. 'Why you didn't talk to the goldsmith like that? No, you is man only in front of woman. But Baksh, you just put one finger on me, and Elvira going to see the biggest bacchanal it ever see.'

Baksh sucked his teeth. 'You talking like your mother. Both of all-you just have a lot of mouth.'

'Go ahead, Baksh. You finish already? Go ahead and insult the dead. This election make you so shameless. If it was to me that the goldsmith was talking, I woulda turn my hand and give him a good clout behind his head. *I* know that. But you, you make me shame that you is the father of my seven children.'

Baksh said irritably, trying to turn the conversation, 'You go ahead and talk. And let the goldsmith talk and let Harbans talk. But no Muslim ain't going to vote for Harbans. Just watch and see.'

★

It was growing dark when Foam and Herbert brought Tiger to the cocoa-house. Years before, labourers were paid to keep the very floor of the cocoa-woods clean; now the woods were strangled in bush that had spread out to choke the cocoa-house itself. When Foam was a child he had played in the cocoa-house, but it was too dangerous now and no one went near it.

Foam and Herbert broke a path through from the road to the house. They had brought a box, gunny sacks and food for Tiger. While Foam hunted about for a place safe enough to put Tiger, Herbert explored.

Herbert knew all about the ghost of the cocoa-house, but ghosts, like the dark, didn't frighten him. The ghost of the cocoa-house was a baby, a baby Miss Elvira herself had had by a negro servant at the time the cocoa-house was being built. The story was that she had buried it in the foundations, under the concrete steps at the back. Many people, many Spaniards in particular, had often heard the baby crying; some had even seen it crawling about in the road near the cocoa-house.

Herbert climbed to the ceiling and tried to push back the sliding roof: the roof was sliding so that the beans could dry in the sun and be covered up as soon as it began to rain. He pushed hard, but the wheels of the roof had rusted and stuck to the rails. He pushed again and again. The wheels grated on the rails, the whole house shook with a jangle of corrugated-iron sheets and a flapping of loose boards, and wood-lice and wood-dust fell down.

Herbert called out, 'Foam, the roof still working.'

'Herbert, why you so bent on playing the ass? Look how you make Tiger frighten.'

Tiger was indeed behaving oddly. He had staggered to his feet, for the first time since his marathon afternoon walk; and for the first time since he had been discovered, was making some sound. A ghost of a whine, a faint mew.

Herbert came down to see.

Tiger mewed and tottered around in his box, as though he were trying to catch his tail.

Herbert was thrilled. 'You see? He getting better.' He remembered Miss Elvira's baby. 'Dog could smell spirits, you know, Foam.'

The tropical twilight came and went. Night fell. Tiger's mews became more distinct. Whenever Foam stepped on the rotting floor the cocoa-house creaked. Outside in the bush croak was answering screech: the night noises were beginning. Tiger mewed, whined, and swung shakily about in his box.

Foam tried to force Tiger to lie down; the position seemed normal for Tiger; but Tiger wasn't going to sit down or lie down and he wasn't going to try to get out of his box either. The darkness thickened. The bush outside began to sing. Foam could just see the white spots on Tiger's muzzle. A bat swooped low through the room, open at both ends.

'Can't leave him here,' Foam said aloud. 'Herbert!'

But Herbert wasn't there.

'Herbert!'

He lit a match. For a moment the spurt of flame blinded

him. Then the rotting damp walls, stained with the ancient stain of millions of cocoa-beans, defined themselves around him. He looked up at the roof.

'Herbert!'

He walked back to the box. Shadows flurried on the walls.

'Take it easy, Tiger.'

The match went out. He dropped it but didn't hear it fall. It must have gone through one of the holes in the floor.

'Herbert! You up on the roof? Boy, take care you don't fall and break your tail, you hear.'

He felt his way to the broken entrance. The house creaked, the galvanized-iron roof shivered.

'Herbert!'

In the night his voice sounded thinner. He couldn't see anything, only the blackness of bush all around. The road and the van were a hundred yards away.

Then: 'Foam! Foam!' he heard Herbert screaming, and ran back inside. The sudden rumbling of the house made him stop and walk. Tiger he couldn't see at all now, only heard him whining and striking against the sides of his box.

'Foam! Foam!'

He walked to the other end of the room, lighting matches to see his way across the holes in the floor.

'Look, Foam!'

He went down the solid concrete steps at the back. They were the only solid thing left in the cocoa-house. The ground sloped down from the road and the steps at the back were about eight feet high, nearly twice as high as those in front. A solid concrete wall supported the solid concrete steps. Foam lit a match. The surface of the steps was still smooth and new, as though it had been finished only the week before. Tall weeds switched against Foam's legs. The weeds were already damp with dew. The match flickered in his cupped hands.

'Look, Foam, under the steps here.'

Herbert was almost hysterical. Foam did what he had been told to do in such circumstances. He slapped Herbert, with great dexterity, back-hand and forward-hand. Herbert pulled in his breath hard and kept back his sobs.

Foam lit another match.

Under the steps he saw a dead dog and five dead puppies. The mother had its mouth open, its teeth bared. She was the dog Harbans had hit that afternoon weeks before.

Her eyes were horribly inanimate. Her chest and belly were shrunken. Her ribs stood out, hard. Damp black earth stuck to her pink blotched dugs, thin and slack like a punctured balloon. The puppies were all like Tiger. They had died all over their mother, anyhow.

The match went out.

'She didn't have no milk or nothing to feed them,' Herbert said.

Foam squatted in the darkness beside the dead dog. 'You talking like a woman, Herbert. You never see nothing dead before?'

'Everybody only know how to say, "Mash, dog!"' The words came between sobs. 'Nobody know how to feed it.'

'That is all you could think about, Herbert? Food? It look as if *they* right, you know.'

'What we going to do with them, Foam?'

Foam laughed. 'I got a master-idea, Herbert.' He got up and lit a match, away from the dead puppies. 'I going to get the cutlass.'

'What for, Foam?'

'Dig a hole and bury the mother. You coming with me or you staying here to cry over the dogs?'

'I coming with you, Foam. Don't go.'

They dug a shallow hole and buried the mother. Herbert trimmed a switch, broke it in two, peeled off the bark and tied the pieces into a cross. He stuck it on the grave.

Foam pulled it out. 'Where you learn that from?'

'Is how they does do it in the belling-ground, Foam.'

'Eh, but you turning Christian or something?'

Herbert saw his error.

'Come on now,' Foam said cheerfully. 'Help me take these dead puppies in the van.'

Foam's business-like attitude calmed Herbert. 'What we going to do with *five* dead puppies, Foam?'

Foam laughed. 'Ah, boy, you go see.'

Herbert trusted Foam. He knew that whatever it was, it was going to be fun.

'But what about Tiger, Foam? We could leave him here? He wouldn't grieve too much?'

Foam said confidently, 'Only place for Tiger now is right here. Don't worry about Tiger. He going to be all right.'

★

They got home late and found Baksh, Mrs Baksh and Zilla in the store-room. Teacher Francis was there too. Foam was surprised. Teacher Francis had come to the Baksh house only once before, to say that if Rafiq didn't buck up at school he was going to turn out just like Foam.

'Ah,' Baksh said heavily to Foam and Herbert. 'Campaign manager and little mister man. Where you was out so late? I did tell you to put away the dog or I did tell you to build a mansion for it?'

Herbert smiled. 'We was out campaigning.' He winked at Foam.

'That prove what I was saying about the elections, ma'am,' Teacher Francis said to Mrs Baksh. 'A little boy like Herbert ain't have no right to go out campaigning.'

Mrs Baksh was on her best behaviour for the teacher. 'Is what I does forever always keep on telling the father, Teach. Beg pardon, Teach.' She turned to the boys. 'All your food take out and waiting for all-you in the kitchen. It must be cold as dog nose now.'

Herbert went noisily up the stairs. Foam sucked his teeth and followed.

'I don't mean anything against you, Mr Baksh,' Teacher Francis went on, 'but the fact is, the *ordinary* people of Elvira don't really appreciate that voting is a duty and privilege.' That was part of the speech he had prepared for the Bakshes. 'Duty and privilege, ma'am.'

'Is what I does forever always keep on telling the father, Teach. Hear what the teacher say, Baksh? I been telling him, Teach, a hundred times if I tell him one time, that this election begin sweet sweet for everybody, but the same sweetness going to turn sour sour in the end. Zilla, you ain't hear me use those self-same words to your father?'

'Yes, Ma.'

'Yes, ma'am. Election bringing out all sort of prejudice to the surface. To the surface, ma'am.'

Mrs Baksh crossed her powerful arms and nodded solemnly. 'You never say a truer word, Teach. In all my born days nobody ever come to my own house—my own house, mark you—and talk to me like how the goldsmith come and talk to me this afternoon.'

Teacher Francis delivered the rest of his statement: 'I have been turning over this and similar ideas in my mind from time to time. From time to time. Yesterday evening I stated them in general terms—in general terms—to Miss Chittaranjan. Mrs Baksh, Miss Chittaranjan took down every word I said. *In shorthand*.'

Mrs Baksh opened her eyes wide, swung her head slowly,

very slowly, from side to side and gave a cluck of horror. 'Look at that, eh, Teach. In shorthand.'

'You could trust somebody as stuck-up as Nelly Chittaranjan to do a low thing like that,' Zilla said.

'And Mrs Baksh, Miss Chittaranjan thinks I am a fascist.' He paused; he had come to the end of his statement. 'Mrs Baksh, I look like a fascist to you?'

'No, Teach. You ain't look like a fascist. Not to me anyway.'

Zilla said, 'Don't worry your head with Nelly Chittaranjan, Teach. She just a little too hot for man sheself. These small thin girls like Nelly Chittaranjan like man.'

'Beg pardon, Teach,' Mrs Baksh said. 'I have to talk to my sister here.' She turned to Zilla. 'Yes, *ma commère*? Small thin girls like man? How you know? You does like man yourself?' She turned to Teacher Francis again. 'Beg pardon, Teach. But these children these days is like if dog eat their mind and their shame.'

Zilla hung her head.

Teacher Francis came to the point. 'And then this evening, Mrs Baksh, Mr Chittaranjan come to see me. He come in cool cool and he tell me dry dry that Nelly not coming for no more lessons from me. It ain't the money I worried about, Mrs Baksh. Is the fact that I don't like people misunderstanding my views. I have to think of my job.'

It certainly wasn't the ten dollars a month alone that worried Teacher Francis. He knew that what Chittaranjan did today the rest of Elvira did tomorrow. If all the parents stopped sending their children to him for private lessons, he would be in a spot.

Foam, an enamel cup in his hands, came down the steps.

Teacher Francis was saying, 'That is why I come to see you, Mrs Baksh. I know how your husband and Mr Chittaranjan working on the same side in the elections, and I would be glad like anything if you could tell Mr Chittaranjan that I is not really a fascist. Fact is, I ain't taking no sides in this election at all.'

'Is the best best thing, God knows, Teach,' Mrs Baksh said.

Foam gave a loud dry laugh. 'Eh, Teacher Francis, why you want *we* to tell the goldsmith for? Why you don't ask Lorkhoor? He could run about telling it with his loud-speaking van.'

And Foam had his first triumph.

He had been waiting a long time to spurn a suppliant Teacher Francis. He had had extravagant visions of the moment. The reality seemed made to order, and was sweet.

Teacher Francis accepted the rebuke sadly. 'Lorkhoor let me down, man. Prove my point again, ma'am. Is the election that spoil Lorkhoor.'

But it had given Foam his first triumph.

'Lorkhoor is a damn traitor if you ask me,' Foam said.

'*Nobody* ain't ask you,' Baksh said. 'And look, eh, I ain't want to hear nobody bad-talking Lorkhoor in this house.'

Foam was baffled.

Baksh said, '*You*, you was out campaigning, eh? Campaigning for that dirty Hindu Harbans. Dog eat your shame? It look like dog eat *all* my children shame.'

Foam said, 'But look, look. What happening? Ain't you done take Harbans money and everything?'

If Teacher Francis hadn't been there Baksh would have spat. 'Money, eh? The money doing me a lot of good? A lot of good! Ten die. Big dog in the night turning tiny tiny in the morning. Send him away and he come back. A lot of good!'

Teacher Francis realized he had been talking in vain. Baksh was no good to him as an intermediary with Chittaranjan.

Foam said, 'Well, I take Harbans money and I give him my word. I going to still help Harbans.'

'I *want* you to help Harbans,' Baksh said. 'I going to help Preacher. I ain't stopping you doing nothing. You is a big man. Your pee making froth. How *much* votes you control, Foam?'

Teacher Francis, unhappy, bemused, got up and left.

Then Baksh told about Chittaranjan's visit.

'All right, you supporting Preacher,' Foam said, and Mrs Baksh noted that for the first time Foam was talking to his father man-to-man. 'Preacher could give you anything?'

Baksh smiled. 'It ain't *Preacher* who going to give me anything. Don't worry, you. I calculate everything already. Everything.'

IX

THE RETREAT OF THE WITNESSES

★

Mahadeo was a worried man. He haunted Elvira, checking up on negroes, anxious lest any of them fell ill or, worse, died.

Hindus misunderstood his purpose and resented his partiality. Rampiari's husband said, 'What the hell? Hindus does fall sick too.' And so, despite his strict instructions not to meddle with them, Mahadeo found himself making out a long list of sick Hindus to present to Harbans. That was one worry.

His big worry was Old Sebastian.

That evening in Dhaniram's veranda he had been pretty confident that Sebastian would die before polling day; and in the happy days before his interview with Mr Cuffy he had kept a hopeful eye on him. Every morning he passed Sebastian's hut and saw him sitting on a backless kitchen chair before his front door, a stunted unlit pipe in his mouth, making fish-pots from strips of bamboo, an inexplicable and futile occupation because Sebastian had no connection whatever with the sea and the fish-pots only remained and rotted in his yard. Mahadeo would ask, 'How you feeling this morning, Sebastian?' And Sebastian would smile—he hardly spoke—showing his remaining teeth, isolated and askew as if some oral explosion had destroyed the others. In the afternoon Mahadeo would pass again, after the day's work on the estate, and repeat his question; and Sebastian would smile again.

Some days Mahadeo felt Sebastian wasn't going to die at all. That was before Mr Cuffy.

Mahadeo distrusted and feared Mr Cuffy. He was old, he was black, he lived alone, he preached, and he read the Bible. And Mahadeo could never forget a disquieting encounter he had had with him as a boy. One Saturday morning he had gone into Mr Cuffy's yard to watch Mr Cuffy whitewashing the walls of his house. Mr Cuffy frowned and muttered, but Mahadeo paid no attention. On a sudden Mr Cuffy had turned and vigorously worked the whitewash brush over Mahadeo's face.

And now Mr Cuffy was Sebastian's guardian.

Sebastian began to look very old and fragile. Mahadeo asked after his health with genuine concern and Sebastian suddenly revealed himself as a very sick man. He had aches and pains all over; stiff joints; and a dangerous stiffness in the neck. Everything that surrounded Sebastian seemed dangerous—the chair he sat on, the old thatched roof over his head. Mahadeo begged him to be careful with the penknife he used on his fish-pots, begged him not to lift heavy weights, begged him not to go for walks in the night dew, and not to get wet. Mahadeo backed up his advice with a shilling or so which Sebastian took easily, without acknowledgment, as though it was money from the government.

On the morning after Foam knocked down Mrs Chittaranjan's clean-necked chicken, Mahadeo, sweating in his tight khaki uniform, walked past Sebastian's hut.

And there was no Sebastian.

★

He forgot about the labourers on the estate waiting for him to measure out their tasks for the day. He hurried across the shaky bridge into Sebastian's yard. He had to warn Sebastian about that bridge: it was dangerous, made only of lengths of bamboo piled up with dirt. He knocked on Sebastian's door and there was no reply. He tried the door. It was locked. He walked around the hut, but every cranny in the walls was blocked up. That was what he himself had advised, to protect Sebastian from draughts.

'Sebastian!' Mahadeo called. 'You all right?'

There was a gap about three inches high running all around the hut between the walls and the eaves of the thatched roof. Mahadeo decided to climb. He would get up on the narrow window-ledge and hope it didn't come down with him. He tried to climb in full uniform. The dirt wall was too smooth to give him a grip and the tight khaki jacket hindered his arms. He took off the jacket, then took off his boots. Still, the wall was too smooth and the window-ledge too high to help him. He pressed the big toe of his right foot against the wall and tried again. He felt the wall give under his toe. He looked down. He had made a hole in Sebastian's wall, about eight inches from the ground. He went down on all fours and lowered his head. Some strands of tapia grass in the wall barred his view. He poked a finger in. Before he could pull away the grass he heard a shout from the road.

'Mahadeo! What the hell you think you doing?'

Still on all fours, he looked up. It was Mr Cuffy.

'Not doing nothing,' he said.

'Mahadeo, what get into you to make you play the ass so?'

Mahadeo rose and put his bare feet into his laceless boots.

'You see Old Sebastian this morning, Mr Cawfee?'

'Ain't see nobody,' Mr Cuffy said sullenly. '*What* you was looking for so?'

'Was Old Sebastian I was looking for, Mr Cawfee.'

'And is so you does always look for Sebastian? Look, Mahadeo, if anything happen to Sebastian, you go be surprise . . .'

At this moment Baksh shouted from a little way down the road, 'Hear about this thing at Cordoba, Mr Cawfee?'

'Going up there right now,' Mr Cuffy said.

'When I did tell people,' Baksh said, 'nobody did want to believe. Everybody did just run about saying Baksh is a big mouther, eh?'

'What happen at Cordoba?' Mahadeo asked.

Mr Cuffy looked at Mahadeo. It was the look he had given him when he pasted his face with the whitewash brush. 'Something *funny* happen up there last night, Mahadeo. I hear something about a dead.'

Mahadeo stared.

'Let him go and see for hisself,' Baksh said.

Mahadeo didn't wait. He ran as much as he could of the way to Cordoba. Even before he got there he saw the crowd blocking up the road. It was mostly a Spanish crowd—he could tell that by the dress—but there were people from Elvira as well.

The crowd made a wide circle around something in the road. The Spaniards were silent but uneasy; they actually seemed happy to have the outsiders from Elvira among them.

Mahadeo was stared at. A path was opened for him.

'Look,' he heard someone say in the acrid Spanish accent. 'Let him look good.'

★

Five dead puppies were symmetrically laid out on a large cross scratched right across the dirt road. One dead puppy was at the centre of the cross and there was a dead puppy at each of the four ends. Below was written, in huge letters:

AWAKE!

And all around, on palings and culverts, Cordoba was still red with Foam's old, partly obliterated slogans: DIE! DIE!

Mahadeo, sweating, panting, gave a chuckle of relief. The Spaniards looked at him suspiciously.

'I did think it was Sebastian,' Mahadeo said.

There were murmurs.

Mahadeo felt someone pull the sleeve of his uniform. He turned to see Sebastian, smiling, the empty pipe in his mouth. He almost embraced him. 'Sebastian! You here! You ain't there!'

The murmurs swelled.

Fortunately for Mahadeo, Baksh and Mr Cuffy came up just then, and almost immediately Foam arrived in the van and began to campaign.

Foam said, 'Is those Witnesses. They can't touch nobody else, so they come to meddle with the poor Spanish people in Cordoba. Telling them not to vote, to go against the government. Who ever see white woman riding around on red red bicycle before, giving out green books?'

Baksh wasn't thinking about politics. 'Aha!' he cried. 'Aha! Just look at those dogs. Said same coloration, said same shape, said same everything, as in *my* dog. But nobody did want to believe. Well, look now.'

Mr Cuffy crossed himself. 'Mahadeo, this is your work?'

'Ain't my work, Mr Cawfee. I just come and see it.'

'Want to know something?' Baksh said. 'For all the tiny those dogs look tiny this morning, they was big big dogs last night. I telling all-you, man. Come in that night. Eleven o'clock. Open the door. See this mister man dog, big big, walking about quiet quiet and *sly*. . . .'

'Is those damn Witnesses,' Foam said.

'. . . next morning, is a tiny tiny puppy.'

'Jesus say,' Foam said, 'we have to give Caesar's things back to Caesar. Witnesses tell you different.'

'I always say this,' Mr Cuffy said. 'God hath made man upright, but they have found out many inventions.'

A Spaniard asked, 'But *what* they trying to do to we?'

'Do to you!' Foam said. 'Do to you! They ain't begin yet. Ain't they was talking about the world blowing up in 1976? And ain't you was listening? They was talking and you was listening. Well, look.' And he pointed to the puppies.

Baksh said, 'Nobody can't try nothing on me. I know how to handle them. *My* dog *didn't* dead.'

Harichand the printer came up, dressed for work.

'Ah,' he said. 'More puppy dogs.' He squatted and examined the ground like a detective. 'Dead, eh? Awake, eh?' He stood up. 'Witnesses. Serious. Very serious. Ganesh was the man to handle a thing like this.'

'But what we going to do, Mr Harichand?'

'Do, eh? What you going to do.' Harichand thought. 'Just don't feed no Witnesses,' he said decisively. 'Don't feed no Witnesses. Funny, five little puppy dogs like that. Like your dog, eh, Baksh?'

Baksh smiled. 'Tell them about it, Harichand. And tell them about the sign too.'

Harichand said, 'Yes, things really waking up in Elvira. But don't feed no Witnesses.'

Baksh said, 'But you did tell me it was Preacher who set the fust dog on me, Harichand.'

Mr Cuffy frowned at Harichand.

Harichand said quickly, 'Didn't exactly say it *that* way. Said *a* preacher was putting something on you. Didn't say what *sort* of preacher. What about those printing jobs, Baksh? If Harbans want my vote, he want my printery, I telling you.'

Baksh said, 'Harbans could haul his arse.'

Harichand laughed. 'Election thing, eh? You changing sides? Who you for now?'

Baksh said, 'Preacher. Eh, you ain't hear the bacchanal?'

Mr Cuffy spat loudly. '*Obeah! Obeah!*'

The Spaniards looked on in dismay.

'*Obeah!*' Mr Cuffy cried. 'That is what all-you trying to work. Lorkhoor, and now you, Baksh. Tomorrow I go hear that Harbans come over to Mr Preacher side too. All-you only making a puppet-show of Mr Preacher. Mahadeo!' Mr Cuffy called. 'You trying something, eh?'

'I ain't trying nothing, Mr Cawfee.' Mahadeo turned to Sebastian. 'Come on, Sebastian, let we go home.'

Sebastian, smiling, stepped away from Mahadeo's hand.

Mahadeo followed. 'Come, Sebastian, you only tireding out yourself. You should go home and rest, man.' He pressed a shilling into Sebastian's palm. Sebastian smiled and allowed himself to be led away.

Mr Cuffy shouted, 'Look after him good, you hear, Mahadeo.'

And then Chittaranjan was seen coming up to Cordoba. He was in his visiting outfit.

Harbans—the candidate—heard about the row between Baksh and Chittaranjan and hurried down that noon to Elvira. He didn't want to inflame either of the disputants, so he went straight to Pundit Dhaniram to find out what was what.

That day Dhaniram was not being a pundit. He was in his other, more substantial role as the owner of one-fifth of a tractor. No dhoti and sacred thread; but khaki trousers, yellow sports shirt, brown felt hat and brown patent leather shoes. When Harbans drove up, Dhaniram was standing on his sunny front steps, humming one of his favourite hymns:

What though the spicy breezes
Blow soft o'er Ceylon's isle;
Though every prospect pleases,
And only man is vile;
In vain with lavish kindness
The gifts of God are strown;
The heathen, in his blindness,
Bows down to wood and stone.

He was about to leave, but he stayed to tell Harbans all about Foam and Nelly, and Baksh and Chittaranjan.

Harbans seemed more concerned about the loss of Baksh and the thousand Muslim votes than about the loss of honour of his prospective daughter-in-law. Dhaniram wasn't surprised.

'In the old days,' Dhaniram said, talking about Nelly, and sounding Harbans further, 'you coulda trust a Hindu girl. Now everything getting modern and mix up. Look, Harichand tell me just the other day that he went to San Fernando and went to a club place up there and he see Indian girls'—Dhaniram had begun to whisper—'he see Indian girls openly soli-citing.' He made the word rhyme with reciting. 'Openly soli-citing, man.'

'Openly soli-citing, eh,' Harbans said absently. 'Ooh, ooh. Send for some pencil and paper.'

'*Doolahin!*' Dhaniram called, loosening his black leather belt and sitting on the bench. 'Pencil and paper. And make it quick sharp.'

The *doolahin* brought out some brown paper and the old pencil with the string attached to the groove at the top. She said irritably, 'Why you don't keep the pencil tie round your waist?' And before Dhaniram could say anything she ran back to the kitchen.

'See?' Dhaniram said. 'Only two years she husband leave

she to go to England to study, and you see how she getting on. In the old days you think a daughter-in-law coulda talk like that to a father-in-law? In fact'—Dhaniram was whispering again—'it wouldn't surprise me if *she* ain't got somebody sheself.'

'Ooh, ooh, Dhaniram, you mustn't talk like that.' Harbans was sitting cross-legged on the floor, making calculations on the brown paper. 'We lose the Muslim vote. That is one thousand. We can't get the negro vote. Two thousand and one thousand make three thousand. About a thousand Hindus going to vote for Preacher because of that traitor Lorkhoor. So, Preacher have four thousand votes. I have three thousand Hindus and the Spanish ain't voting.' He flung down the pencil. Dhaniram picked it up. Harbans said calmly, 'I lose the election, Pundit.'

Dhaniram laughed and loosened his belt a bit more. 'Lemmesee that paper,' he said, and lay down flat on his belly and worked it out. He looked perplexed. 'Yes, you lose. It *look* like if you lose.' He passed his hand over his face. 'Can't make it out, man. It did look like a sure thing to me. Sure sure thing.'

Harbans cracked his fingers, turned his palms downwards and studied the grey hairs and wrinkles on the back. 'I is a old man,' he said. 'And I lose a election. That is all. Nothing to cry about.' He looked up and smiled with his false teeth at Dhaniram.

Dhaniram smiled back.

Harbans broke down. 'How much money Preacher spend? Tell me, Pundit, how much money Preacher spend for him to beat me in a election?'

Dhaniram said, 'This democracy is a damn funny thing.'

At that moment Lorkhoor came up in his loudspeaker van. 'Preacher is gaining new support. Ladies and gentlemen, this is the voice of Lorkhoor. The enemy's ranks are thinning and Preacher will win. . . .'

From her room Dhaniram's wife asked in Hindi, 'What is he saying?'

Dhaniram translated for her.

The *doolahin*, adjusting her veil, rushed out on bare feet.

'Back inside, *doolahin*,' Dhaniram said. 'Is not the sort of thing a married woman should listen to.'

She didn't obey right away.

'Here,' Dhaniram said. 'Take back this paper. *And* the pencil.'

She practically snatched them.

'See?' Dhaniram said. 'See what I was telling you? It only want for she to hear a man voice and she excited long time.'

Lorkhoor drove off noisily, shouting, 'Yaah! We will bury Harbans!'

Harbans all the while kept looking down at his hands.

Dhaniram sat on the bench again, lit a cigarette and began shaking his legs. The gravity of the situation thrilled him; he couldn't dim the twinkle in his eyes; he smiled continually.

A visitor came.

Harbans said, 'Go away, if is me you want to see. I ain't got no more money to give.'

The visitor was Mahadeo, still in his uniform, holding a sweated khaki topee in his hands. His big eyes shone mournfully at the floor; his cheeks looked swollen; his thick moustache gave an occasional twitch over his small full mouth.

'Sit down,' Dhaniram said, as though he was inviting Mahadeo to a wake.

Mahadeo said, 'I have a message from the goldsmith.'

Harbans shook away his tears. 'You is faithful, Mahadeo.'

Mahadeo's sad eyes looked sadder; his full mouth became fuller; his eyebrows contracted. 'Is about Rampiari husband,' he said hesitantly. 'He sick. Sick like anything.'

'Rampiari husband is a Hindu, as you damn well know,' Dhaniram said.

'Aah, Mahadeo,' Harbans said, smiling through his tears. 'You is unfaithful, too?'

'Yes, Mr Harbans. No, Mr Harbans. But the goldsmith, Mr Chittaranjan, did promise Rampiari husband that you was going to see him. He sick bad bad. He cut his foot with a hoe.'

Harbans looked down at his hands. 'I ain't got no more money for nobody. All it have for me to do is to settle Ramlogan rum-account and leave Elvira for good. Why *I* fighting election for?'

Dhaniram said, 'Is God work.'

'How the hell is God work? Is God work for Preacher to beat me in a election? How much money Preacher spend? You call that God work?'

Mahadeo said, 'Preacher gone to see Rampiari husband.'

Harbans jumped up. 'Preacher ain't got no *right* to meddle with the Hindu sick.' He paced so thunderously about the veranda that Dhaniram's wife, inside, complained. 'All right,' he said. 'What about that list of negro sick you was going to make?'

Mahadeo hesitated.

Dhaniram, who had suggested the care of sick negroes, stopped shaking his legs.

Mahadeo explained about Mr Cuffy.

Harbans was silent for a while. Then he exploded: 'Traitors! Spies! Haw-Haw! I ask you, Mahadeo, to keep a eye on negro sick and I come today and find that you is *feeding* them.' He wagged a long thin finger. 'But don't worry your head. I not going to cry. I going to fight all of all-you. I not going to let any of all-you make me lose my election, after all the hard work I put in for Elvira.'

Dhaniram's legs began to shake again; he pulled at his cigarette; his eyes twinkled.

Then Harbans's fight seemed to die. 'All right,' he said resignedly. 'All right, suppose I go to see Rampiari husband'—he gave a short grim laugh—'and I pay the entrance fee, what guarantee I have that Rampiari husband going to vote for me?'

Dhaniram stood up and crushed his cigarette under his shoe. 'Ah, the main thing is to *pay* the entrance fee.'

Harbans went absent-minded.

'The people of Elvira,' Dhaniram said, tightening his belt, 'have their little funny ways, but I could say one thing for them: you don't have to bribe them twice.'

'But what about Baksh?'

'Baksh,' Dhaniram said, 'is a damn disgrace to Elvira.'

They went to see Chittaranjan.

★

They found Chittaranjan unruffled, bland, in his home clothes, rocking in his veranda. Obviously he was in the highest spirits.

'Who say the Spanish ain't voting?' Chittaranjan said. And he told them about the five dead puppies in Cordoba. 'Bright and early those two white woman Witnesses come up on their fancy bike. The Spanish ain't talk to them, ain't look at them. The five dead puppies alone remain in the road and the Spanish go inside their house and lock up the door. The white woman had to go away. Who say the Spanish ain't voting?'

Harbans hid his joy. He didn't want to tempt fate again.

Dhaniram calculated. 'We draw up even with Preacher now. Four thousand apiece.'

Chittaranjan rocked. 'Wait. Watch and see if Preacher don't lose his deposit.'

Harbans said, 'Goldsmith, I shoulda tell you this a long time now.' And he disclosed the sign he had had weeks before: the Witnesses, the black bitch, the engine stalling.

Chittaranjan gave his corrosive titter. 'You *shoulda* tell me, Mr Harbans. You woulda save both of we a lot of worry. One sign is bad. But when you get *two* signs in one day, is different. They does cancel out one another. Just as how the dog cancel out the Witnesses.'

Dhaniram wanted Chittaranjan to talk about the row with Baksh. He said, 'I did always say we could give Preacher the Muslim vote. We could do without Baksh and Baksh son.'

'Dhaniram,' Chittaranjan said, 'you know me. I does say my mind, and who want to vex, let them vex. But you talking like a fool. Those dead puppies in Cordoba, who you think put them there?'

'Foam?' Harbans said. 'Ooh. You mean Foam is still faithful?'

'But I thought you did have a row with the father, man,' Dhaniram said.

'With the father, yes. But not with the son.' Chittaranjan glanced at Harbans. 'Is the father who put him up to *try*.'

Dhaniram frowned and began to shake his legs, slowly. 'Don't like it. Baksh want something more. He got something at the back of his mind.'

Chittaranjan clacked his sabots. 'Course he got! Baksh ain't no fool. Baksh have everything calculate already.'

Dhaniram tried once more. He cocked his head to one side and said, 'I feel I hearing little Nelly walking inside. She ain't gone to school today?'

Chittaranjan didn't look at Dhaniram but at Harbans who, his head bent, had gone absent-minded. Chittaranjan said, 'No school for she today. After all, she practically engage already.'

Harbans didn't look up.

'I say,' Chittaranjan said, slowly, incisively, 'how you want me to still send Nelly to school, when she practically *engage*?'

Harbans woke up. 'Wouldn't be right,' he said hurriedly, 'especially when the girl practically engage already.'

Chittaranjan looked triumphantly at Dhaniram.

★

The Witnesses stayed away from Cordoba and Elvira.

X

THE NEW CANDIDATE

★

The campaigns began to swing.

Preacher made his house-to-house visits. Mr Cuffy preached political sermons on Friday evenings. Lorkhoor blazed through the district.

Chittaranjan revisited Cordoba and won back the votes the Witnesses had seduced. Foam, loyal to Harbans, toured with his loudspeaker van, and neither Baksh nor Mrs Baksh objected. Harichand got orders for posters. Whenever Pundit Dhaniram officiated at a Hindu ceremony he urged his listeners to vote for Harbans.

Mahadeo kept a sharp, panicky eye on Old Sebastian. The man seemed to wilt more and more every day, and Mahadeo was giving him five shillings, sometimes two dollars a week to buy medicines.

Harbans resigned himself to visiting the Hindu sick. Whenever he came to Elvira and saw Mahadeo, he asked first, 'Well, how much Hindu sick today? And what-and-what is the various entrance fee?' Mahadeo would take out his little red notebook and say, 'Mungal not so good today. Two dollars go settle him. Lutchman complaining about a pain in his belly. He got a big family and the whole house have six votes. I think you better give him ten dollars. Five dollars for the least. Ramoutar playing the fool too. But he so ignorant, he can't even make a X and he bound to spoil his vote. Still, give him a dollar. It go make people feel that you interested.'

Harbans's rum-account with Ramlogan rose steeply. But Ramlogan maintained to all the drinkers that he was impartial. 'Once this election bacchanal over,' he said, 'I have to live with everybody, no matter who they vote for.' Chittaranjan never went inside the shop. He and Foam devised rum-vouchers that could be exchanged only at Ramlogan's. Harichand printed the vouchers.

And, secure in the cocoa-house, Tiger began to flourish.

★

But Baksh was doing nothing at all about the election. The thousand Muslim voters of Elvira looked to him in vain for a lead. He wasn't campaigning for Preacher and he wasn't campaigning against Harbans. He remained in his shop and sewed dozens of khaki shirts, working with a new, sullen concentration. He refused to talk about the election, refused almost to talk at all. This sudden reticence won him a lot of attention and respect in Ramlogan's rumshop. But if he didn't talk much, his actions were larger. He brought down his thick glass heavily on the counter; he smacked his lips and twisted his face as though the puncheon rum tasted like castor oil; he spat copiously and belched often, bending forward, blowing out his cheeks and rubbing his belly, like one who suffers. When people asked him about the election he only gave an odd, ironic little smile. Altogether he behaved like a deep man with a deep secret.

This finally annoyed Mrs Baksh. 'You have everybody laughing at you. When this election nonsense did first begin, you ain't ask nobody, you ain't look right, you ain't look left, you jump in. Now, when everybody washing their foot and jumping in, you remaining quiet, sitting on your fat tail like a hatching fowl.'

'Well, all right. I ain't doing nothing. What you want me to do? You think I would let two shot of cheap grog fool me? Look, is not for my sake I worrying, you know. If I trying to make anything outa this election, is for you and the children, you hear, not for me.'

Mrs Baksh would say with scorn, 'Even little Foam bringing home seventy-five dollars when the month end.'

Baksh's silent inactivity worried Harbans and his committee as much as Preacher's silent campaigning.

Messages from Baksh were always reaching the committee.

Some were boastful. 'Baksh say he just got to walk around Elvira *one* time, saying all that he know, and everybody going to forget Harbans.'

Some were cryptic. 'Baksh say *he* ain't got to do nothing to make Harbans lose. Harbans doing that hisself.'

Some were threatening. 'Baksh say Harbans could do what he want before the elections, but Harbans going to lose the election on election day itself.'

But Baksh himself did nothing.

Chittaranjan alone refused to be alarmed. He said, 'Baksh ain't no fool. Baksh know what he want. And the sad thing is that he going to get what he want. But *we* mustn't make the fust move. We would be low-rating weself if we do that.'

★

Foam wasn't happy about two things.

He would have liked to confess to Chittaranjan that it was he who had run over the clean-necked chicken; but he just didn't have the courage. Then there was Nelly. He felt especially guilty about her. Chittaranjan had taken her out of school and stopped her going anywhere; she remained in the house all day.

Perhaps Foam would have confessed about the chicken if Chittaranjan had been at all cool towards him; but Chittaranjan showed himself surprisingly, increasingly amiable.

He encouraged Foam to visit the Big House and gave him many sweet drinks. Only, Mrs Chittaranjan did the honours now, not Nelly. Foam responded by making it clear that he wasn't interested in Nelly. He said, often and irrelevantly, that he couldn't understand why people got married, that he wasn't interested in marriage at all, hardly interested in girls even. Chittaranjan seemed to approve. 'Well, what happen between your father and me ain't have nothing to do with you.'

Then, when Chittaranjan thought he had proved to everyone in Elvira that Nelly's honour was safe; that Foam was a good boy whom he trusted absolutely; that Baksh was the envious troublemaker; then he sent Nelly off to Port of Spain, to stay with his brother, the barrister.

He was a lonely man after that. Outside, canvassing in his visiting outfit, he was the powerful goldsmith, the great controller of votes. But at home, in his torn khaki trousers, patched shirt and sabots, Foam knew him as a sad humiliated man. He never rushed to the veranda wall to shout at Ramlogan. He heard his chickens being shooed and struck and made to squeal in Ramlogan's yard, and he did nothing.

When Foam was in the Big House one day, a breadfruit and three over-ripe zabocas fell on the roof. Foam waited. Chittaranjan kept on rocking and pretended he hadn't heard.

Foam decided to confess.

He said, 'Goldsmith, that clean-neck fowl . . .'

'Oh, that.' Chittaranjan waved a hand, anxious to dismiss the subject. 'That cook and eat long time now. Didn't have no disease, you know.'

'Shoulda say this before, but was me who kill it. Knock it down with the loudspeaking van.'

Chittaranjan paused, just perceptibly, in his rocking; a

look of surprise, relief passed over his face; then he rocked again. When he spoke he didn't look at Foam. 'All right, you kill it right enough. But who did want to see it dead?'

Foam didn't answer.

Chittaranjan waved a tired hand towards Ramlogan's yard. 'He. He wanted to see it dead. If the chicken dead now and eat, that not on your conscience.'

Foam didn't follow the reasoning; but it pleased him to see Chittaranjan look a little less oppressed. A little less grieved.

Foam said, 'It did grieve Ramlogan like anything to see it dead. He tell Pa so the day after. Is what he tell Pa and is what Pa tell me. Ramlogan say he did know the chicken from the time it hatch, and he did watch it grow up. He say it was like a child to him, and when it dead it was a pussonal loss.'

Chittaranjan looked even less grieved.

★

The big quarrel, coming after three years of intermittently explosive hostility, had in fact purged Chittaranjan of much of his animosity towards Ramlogan. He had never been sure that it was Ramlogan who had killed the chicken; but coming upon it so soon after discovering Tiger in the cupboard, he had felt that he had to do something right away. Now he realized the enormity of his accusation. Ramlogan had, justly, got the better of him in that quarrel; and would always get the better of him in any future quarrel: Nelly's dishonour was a more devastating argument than his ownership of the fence or his appearance in the Supreme Court.

He had had his fill of enmity. He wanted to change his relationship with the man. He called Mrs Chittaranjan and said, 'That breadfruit that fall, and those three zaboca, pick them up and put them in the basket I bring back from San Fernando and take them over to Ramlogan.'

Mrs Chittaranjan didn't show surprise. She was beyond it. She packed the fruit in the basket and took it across. Ramlogan's shop was open. It was early morning and there were no customers.

Ramlogan was reading the *Sentinel*, his large hairy head down, his large hairy hands pressing on the chipped and greasy counter. When he saw Mrs Chittaranjan he went on reading with an air of absorption, reading and saying, 'Hm!' and scratching his head, aromatic with Canadian Healing Oil. In truth, he was deeply moved and trying to hide it. He too was ripe for reconciliation. He had always wanted to wound Chittaranjan; but now that he had, he regretted it. He knew he had gone too far when he attacked the honour of the man's daughter; he felt ashamed.

'Ah, *maharajin*,' he said at last, looking up and smoothing out the *Sentinel* on the counter.

Mrs Chittaranjan placed the basket of fruit on the counter and pulled her veil decorously over her forehead.

'Breadfruit,' Ramlogan said, as though he had never seen the fruit before. 'Breadfruit, man. And zaboca, eh? Zaboca. One, two, three zaboca.' He pressed a zaboca with a thick forefinger. 'Ripe too.'

Mrs Chittaranjan said, 'He send it.'

'It have nothing I like better than a good zaboca and bread. Nothing better.

'Yes, it nice,' Mrs Chittaranjan said.

'Nice like anything.'

'He send it. He tell me to take up the breadfruit and the three zaboca and bring it for you in this basket.'

Ramlogan passed a hand over the basket. 'Nice basket.'

'He bring it from San Fernando.'

Ramlogan turned the basket around on the greasy

counter. 'Very nice basket,' he said. 'It make by the blind?'

'He say I have to bring back the basket.'

Ramlogan emptied the basket, hugging the fruit to his breast. Mrs Chittaranjan saw the basket empty, saw the fruit in a cluster against Ramlogan's dirty shirt. Then she saw the cluster jog and heave and heave and jog.

Ramlogan was crying.

Mrs Chittaranjan began to cry in sympathy.

'We is bad people, *maharajin*,' Ramlogan sobbed.

Mrs Chittaranjan pressed a corner of her veil over her eyes. 'It have some good in everybody.'

Ramlogan clutched the fruit to his breast and shook his head so violently that tears fell on the breadfruit. 'No, no, *maharajin*, we is more bad than good.' He shook down some more tears and lifted his head to the sooty galvanized-iron roof. 'God, I is asking You. Tell me why we is bad.'

Mrs. Chittaranjan stopped crying and took the basket off the counter. 'He waiting for me.'

Ramlogan brought his head down. 'He waiting?'

She nodded.

Ramlogan ran with the fruit to the back room and then followed Mrs Chittaranjan out of the shop.

Chittaranjan was leaning on the wall of his veranda.

Ramlogan shouted, 'Hello, brothers!'

Chittaranjan waved and widened his smile. 'You all right, brothers?'

'Yes, brothers. She bring the breadfruit and the zaboca for me. Ripe zaboca too, brothers.'

'They did look ripe to me too.'

Ramlogan was near the wire fence. He hesitated.

'Is all right, brothers,' Chittaranjan said. 'Is much your fence as mine.'

'Nice fence, brothers.'

Chittaranjan's two workmen were so astonished they stopped working and looked on, sitting flat on the concrete terrace under the awning, the bracelets which they were fashioning held between their toes.

Ramlogan spoke sharply to them: 'What the hell happen to all-you? The goldsmith paying all-you just to meddle in other people business?'

They hurriedly began tapping away at their bracelets.

From the veranda Chittaranjan said, 'Let them wait until I come down.' He clattered down the front steps. 'Is this modern age. Everybody want something for nothing. I work for every penny I have, and now you have these people complaining that they is poor and behaving as though other people depriving them.'

Ramlogan, grasping the fence firmly, agreed. 'The march of time, brothers. As the saying goes. Everybody equal. People who ain't got brain to work and those who use their brain to work. Everybody equal.'

Ramlogan invited Chittaranjan over to the shop and seated him on an empty rum crate in front of the counter. He gave him a glass of grapefruit juice because he knew Chittaranjan didn't drink hard liquor.

They talked of the degeneracy of the modern age; they agreed that democracy was a stupid thing; then they came to the elections and to Baksh.

Chittaranjan, sipping his grapefruit juice without great relish—he still had a low opinion of Ramlogan's cleanliness—said: 'This democracy just make for people like Baksh. Fact, I say it just make for negro and Muslim. They is two people who never like to make anything for theyself, and the moment *you* make something, they start begging. And if you ain't give them, they vex.'

Ramlogan, thinking of Haq, assented with conviction.

'And if you give them,' Chittaranjan went on, 'they is ungrateful.'

'As the saying goes, however much you wash a pig, you can't make it a cow. *As* the saying goes.'

'Look at Baksh. Everybody else in Elvira just asking for one little piece of help before they vote for any particular body. Baksh is the only man who want three.'

Ramlogan scratched his head. 'Three bribe, brothers?'

'Three. Baksh done calculate everything ready.'

'The old people was old-fashion, but they was right about a lot of things. My father, when he was deading, tell me never to trust a Muslim.'

'Muslim, negro. You can't trust none of them.'

They told tales of the ingratitude and treachery of these races. When Chittaranjan left, he and Ramlogan were good friends.

After that, every morning when Ramlogan got up he went out into his yard and called, 'How you is, brothers?' And Chittaranjan came to his veranda and said, 'All right, brothers. And how *you* is?'

Soon they started calling each other 'bruds'.

★

Then Ramlogan had an unfortunate idea. He wanted among other things to make some gesture that would seal his friendship with Chittaranjan. One day he announced that he was going to give a case of whisky to the committee of the winning candidate. He didn't make it more specific than that because he wished to preserve his impartiality, but he had no doubt that Harbans would win. Chittaranjan understood and was grateful. And the rest of Elvira was astonished by this act of the laxest generosity from someone who was not even a candidate. Which was one of Ramlogan's subsidiary intentions.

He talked a lot about his offer. This was to have disastrous consequences.

★

It was not until the week before nomination day that Baksh showed his hand. Two indirect messages came from him.

First, Foam announced: 'Pa say he thinking of going up for the elections hisself.'

'Damn traitor!' Harbans said, and added calmly, 'But he ain't got a chance. He only control the thousand Muslim votes.'

'Is that he say hisself,' Foam said. 'He say is the only thing that keeping him back.'

And then Ramlogan hurried across to Chittaranjan one lunch-time and said in a whisper, although there was no need to whisper: 'Bruds, Baksh was in the shop today. He ask me whether I would vote for him if he went up for the elections.'

Chittaranjan said, 'He ask you to tell me?'

Ramlogan said in a softer whisper, 'He particularly ask me *not* to tell you, bruds.'

'But he ask you about three four times not to tell me?'

Ramlogan looked surprised at Chittaranjan's sagacity. 'He did *keep* on asking me not to tell you. Is the reason *why* I come over to tell you.'

Chittaranjan said simply, 'Well, Baksh just got to get bribe number two now, that is all.'

And when Harbans came to Elvira Chittaranjan told him, 'Mr Harbans, you could take it from Chittaranjan that you win the elections.'

Harbans preferred not to show any excitement.

Chittaranjan said, 'Baksh send a message.'

'Another message again?'

'He want to go up.'

'Ooh.'

'You have to go and see him and make it appear that you begging him to go up for the elections hisself. Once the Muslims don't vote for Preacher, we all right.'

Harbans smiled and wagged a finger at Chittaranjan. 'Ooh, but you is a smart man, Goldsmith. Ooh, ooh. Split the opposition vote, eh?'

Chittaranjan nodded. 'But when you go to see him, don't just dip your hand in your pocket. Don't do nothing until you see everything in black and white.'

Harbans went to see Baksh.

He was sitting at his sewing-machine near the door, to get the light, and working with honest concentration.

Harbans cooed. 'Aah, Baksh. How you is? I hear that you thinking of going up for this election stupidness yourself.'

Baksh bit off a piece of loose thread from the shirt he was making. Thread between his teeth, he gave a dry laugh. 'Ho! Me? Me go up for election, a poor poor man like me? Whoever give you that message give it to you wrong. I ain't got no money to go up for no election. Election ain't make for poor people like me.'

Harbans cooed again. 'Still, the fact that you was even thinking of going up show, Baksh, that you is a ambitious man. I like people with ambition.'

'Is very nice of you to say those few kind words, Mr Harbans. But the fact is, and as the saying goes, I just ain't got the money. Two hundred and fifty dollars deposit alone. Posters. Canvassers. Agents. Is a lot of money, Mr Harbans.'

'Ooh, not more than five hundred dollars.' Harbans paused. 'For a fust try.'

'Don't forget the two hundred and fifty dollars deposit.'

'No, man. Two hundred and fifty and five hundred. All right?'

The machine hummed again. Baksh sewed thoughtfully, shaking his head. 'Elections is a lot more expensive than that, Mr Harbans. You know that yourself.' He took up the shirt and bit off another piece of thread. 'I would say three thousand dollars, plus the deposit money.'

Harbans laughed nervously and almost put his hand on Baksh's bowed shoulder. 'Ooh, ooh, Baksh. You making joke, man. Three thousand for your fust little try? A thousand.'

'Two thousand five hundred, plus the deposit money.'

'Two five. Ooh, Baksh. Come, man. One five.'

Baksh was sewing again. 'In the old days, as you know, Mr Harbans, before the war, you coulda take up six cents and go in a shop and buy a bread and some butter and a tin of sardine and even a pack of cigarettes into the bargain. Today all you could buy with six cents is a Coca-Cola. I is a man with a big family. I can't fight elections with one thousand five hundred dollars.'

'You don't *want* more than two thousand dollars, Baksh,' Harbans said, the coo gone from his voice. 'And if you ain't careful you damn well have to find the deposit money out of that same two thousand.' He cooed again: 'Two thousand, eh, Baksh?'

'*Plus* the deposit money.'

'Plus the deposit money.'

'It not going to be much of a fight for two thousand dollars, Mr Harbans. I warning you. I is a man with a big big family.'

'Is a fust try,' Harbans said. 'You could always try again. This democracy not going to get up and run away.'

Baksh sewed and bit thread, sewed and bit thread. 'It would be nice if I could start off my campaign right away.'

Harbans remembered Chittaranjan's warning. 'Ooh, but you is impatient, man. Right away? Give it a little time, man, Baksh. We never know what could happen between now and nomination day, eh?'

Baksh was surprisingly complaisant. 'Fair is fair. Nothing until after nomination day. Two thousand, plus the deposit money.'

'Plus the deposit money.'

Mrs Baksh came into the shop, combing out her long hair with a large gap-toothed comb.

Harbans went absent-minded.

Mrs Baksh held her hair in front of her bodice and combed. Particles of water sped about the room. She cleared the comb of loose hair, rolled the hair into a ball, spat on it a few times and flung it among the dusty scraps in a corner.

The sewing-machine hummed.

Mrs Baksh said, 'I was wondering who was doing all the talking.'

Harbans looked up. 'Ah. Ooh. How you is, Mrs Baksh?'

'Half and half. How the campaign?'

'Ooh, so-so. We trying to get your husband to go up hisself.'

Mrs Baksh stopped combing and tossed her hair over her shoulders.

Baksh sewed, not stopping to bite thread.

'Baksh, what the hell I hearing?'

'Hearing, man? Mr Harbans here come and beg me to go up for the elections, that is all.'

'Mr Harbans beg you? Baksh, you know you talking arseness?'

'It go be a good experience for him.' Harbans smiled at Mrs Baksh. He got no response. 'Ooh. Two thousand dollars.'

'Plus the deposit money,' Baksh said to Mrs Baksh.

'It look as if your brains drop to your bottom, Baksh. This election riding you like a fever.'

'Is for your sake I doing it, man. For your sake and the children sake. And I doing it to help out Mr Harbans here.'

This was too much for Mrs Baksh.

'Oh God, Baksh! You go land me in court before this election over. Oh God! Sweetness! Sourness!'

★

And that was not all. When Harbans went back to his committee he found Harichand the printer with them.

'If Baksh going up, you go want new posters,' Harichand said. 'In all your present posters your symbol is the star and your slogan is "Hitch your wagon to the star". But they does give out the symbols in alphabetical order. Your name was fust and your symbol was the star. Now Baksh name going to be fust and *his* symbol going to be the star. Yours going to be the heart. Preacher going to be the shoes.'

Chittaranjan said, 'We want a new slogan.'

But Harbans had gone absent-minded.

'Do your part and vote the heart,' Foam said.

'Fust-class,' Harichand said.

Harbans was talking to the back of his hands. 'New symbol, eh? New slogan. New posters. What sin I do to get myself in this big big mess in my old old age?'

Chittaranjan saw the danger sign of approaching tears. 'Is nothing, Mr Harbans. Nothing at all if it make you win the election. And Foam here give you a much nicer slogan. Do your part and vote the heart. Is much nicer.'

'He should take up poetry,' Harichand said.

Harbans looked up from his hands to Harichand. 'I know why you so damn glad, Harichand. I ain't got to go to a university to know why you glad.'

'Glad? Me? Me glad? I ain't glad, Mr Harbans.'

'You sorry?'

Mr. Harbans, it have no reason why you should start

getting suckastic and insultive in my pussonal. Is only help I want to help you out.'

When Harbans was leaving Elvira he was stopped by Mahadeo, and lacked spirit even to make his little joke: 'How much Hindu sick today? And what-and-what is the various entrance fee?' Mahadeo offered his list sadly and received the entrance fees a little more sadly.

When Harbans had left Elvira and was in County Caroni, he stopped the lorry and shook his small fist at the dark countryside behind him.

'Elvira!' he shouted. 'You is a bitch! A bitch! A bitch!'

XI

A DEPARTURE

★

Everyone in Elvira now knew about Tiger and almost everyone accepted him as a mascot against future evil and *obeah*. Tiger thrived. His coat became thicker; not that he was a hairy, fluffy puppy, for after all he was only a common mongrel; but his coat became thick enough. His strength increased. He could sit and get up and walk and run and jump without pain and with increasing zest. But no amount of feeding and care could make him put on flesh to hide his ribs. No amount of feeding could make him lose his rangy figure. He looked the sort of puppy who would grow up into the perfect street dog, noisy but discreet, game for anything, from chasing a chicken to nosing about a dustbin at night. Still, he was Tiger and he was healthy and he was friendly. Herbert was pleased. So was Foam. Mrs Baksh was relieved. The growing health of the dog she interpreted as the weakening of any *obeah* and magic against her family.

Tiger still lived in the cocoa-house. In the early days of his recovery he had been anxious to leave it for the wider world; but stern talkings-to, some slaps and finally a length of rope had taught him that the cocoa-house was home. In time he appreciated his position. He had all the freedom of the freelance with none of the anxieties. But he never tired of reproaching Herbert and Foam. When they were leaving him for the night he would look at them and whine, softly, almost apologetically; and when they came to him in the morning he would wag his tail at first, then lie down and whine, loudly this time, looking away from them.

And now Tiger had to have his first bath. It couldn't be hidden from anyone, not even Herbert, that Tiger was full of fleas. You had only to pass a finger down Tiger's back to see whole platoons of fleas dispersing and taking cover.

Bathing Tiger was no easy business. First Foam and Herbert had to steal a block of Mrs Baksh's strong blue soap. Then they changed into old trousers and shirts because they were going to bath Tiger at the stand-pipe in the main road.

They went to the cocoa-house.

Outside the cocoa-house they saw Lorkhoor's van parked on the wide verge. The grass went up to the hubs of the wheels.

'Hope he not interfering with Tiger,' Herbert said.

On a signal from Foam Herbert fell silent and both boys made their way through the intricate bush to the cocoa-house. They heard Tiger bark. A little snap of a sound, high-pitched but ambitious. They heard someone muttering and then they saw Lorkhoor and the girl. Apparently they had been there some time because Tiger had grown used to their presence and had barked, not at them, but at Foam and Herbert.

The girl said, 'Oh God!' pulled her veil over her face and ran out of sight, through the bush, behind the cocoa-house and then, as Foam imagined, to the road.

Lorkhoor remained behind to brazen it out.

In his excitement he dropped his educated tone and vocabulary and slipped into the dialect. 'Eh, Foreman! You take up *maquereau*ing now?'

'You ain't got no shame, Lorkhoor. Using words like that in front of a little boy.'

Herbert pretended he hadn't heard anything.

Lorkhoor turned vicious. 'You tell anything, and see if I don't cripple you.'

'I is not a tell-tale. And at the same time I is not a hide-and-seek man.'

'Go ahead. Open your mouth once, and I'll have the police on your tail, you hear.'

'Police?'

'Yes, police. You drive a van. You have a driving licence? If I lay one report against you, I would cripple you for life, you hear.'

Foam laughed. 'Eh, but this is a funny world, man. Whenever people wrong, they start playing strong.'

Lorkhoor didn't stay to reply.

'Eh!' Herbert shouted after him. 'But he too bold.'

Tiger, wagging his tail at Foam's feet, barked continually at Lorkhoor. Every now and then he made abortive rushes at him, but he never seriously courted danger.

Foam pursued Lorkhoor with his words. 'You disappoint me, Lorkhoor. For all the educated you say you educated, you ain't got no mind at all. You disappoint me, man.'

They heard Lorkhoor drive off.

Foam said, 'You see the girl who was with him, Herbert?'

'Didn't exactly see she. But . . .'

'All right. You ain't see nothing, remember. We don't want to start another bacchanal in Elvira now. Catch this dog.'

But Tiger wasn't going to be caught without making a game of it. He seemed to sense too that something disagreeable was in store for him. He ran off and barked. Herbert chased. Tiger ran off a little further and barked again.

'Stop, Herbert. Let him come to we.'

Foam put his hand in his pockets. Herbert whistled. Tiger advanced cautiously. When he was a little distance away—a safe distance—he gave his snapping little bark, stood still, cocked his head to one side and waited. Herbert and Foam were not interested. Tiger pressed down his fore-paws and began to bark again.

'Don't do nothing, Herbert.'

Hearing Foam, Tiger stopped barking and listened. He ran off a little, stopped and looked back, perplexed by their indifference. He ran up to Herbert, barking around his ankles. Herbert bent down and caught him. Tiger squirmed and used an affectionate tongue as a means of attack. Herbert leaned backwards, closing his eyes and frowning. Tiger almost wriggled out of his hands and ran up his sloping chest.

'Take him quick, Foam.'

Foam took Tiger. Tiger recognized the stronger grasp and resigned himself.

They took him to the stand-pipe in the main road. To get a running flow from it you had to press down all the time on the brass knob at the top. Herbert was to do the pressing down, Foam the bathing and soaping of Tiger.

'It will drown the fleas,' Herbert said.

Foam wasn't so sure. 'These fleas is like hell to kill.'

'I don't think Tiger going to like this, you know, Foam.'

Tiger hated it. As soon as he felt the water he started to cry and whine. He shivered and squirmed. From time to time he forgot himself and tried to bite, but never did. The water soaked through his coat until Foam and Herbert could see his pink pimply skin. He looked tiny and weak still. Then the blue soap was rubbed over him.

'Careful, Foam. Mustn't let the soap get in his eye.'

The fleas hopped about in the lather, a little less nimble than usual.

Before they could dry him, Tiger slipped out of Foam's hands and ran dripping wet down the Elvira main road.

Water had given him a strong attachment to dry land, the dustier the better. He rolled in the warm sand and dirt of the main road and shook himself vigorously on passers-by. Dirt stuck to his damp coat and he looked more of a wreck than he had before his bath.

Foam and Herbert chased him.

The patch of dirt before Mr Cuffy's house appealed to Tiger. He flung himself on it and rolled over and over. Mr Cuffy stood up to watch. Tiger rose from the dirt, ran up to Mr Cuffy, gave himself a good shake, spattering Mr Cuffy with water and pellets of dirt, and tried to rub against Mr Cuffy's trousers.

Mr Cuffy raised his boot and kicked Tiger away. And for a kick on a thin dog it made a lot of noise. A hollow noise, a *dup!* the noise you would expect from a slack drum. Tiger ran off whining. He didn't run far. He ran into the main road, turned around when he judged it safe to do so; then, taking a precautionary step backwards, let out a sharp snap of a bark. He turned away again, shook himself and ambled easily off.

Herbert, running up, saw everything.

'God go pay you for that, Mr Cawfee,' Herbert said. 'He go make you dead like a cockroach, throwing up your foot straight and stiff in the air. God go pay you.'

'Dirty little puppy dog,' said Mr Cuffy.

Foam came up. 'Yes, God go pay you back, Cawfee. All you Christians always hot with God name in your mouth as though all-you spend a week-end with Him. But He go pay you back.'

'Puppy dog,' Mr Cuffy said.

'He go make you dead like a cockroach,' Herbert said. 'Just watch and see.'

★

Nomination day came. The three candidates filled forms and paid deposits. There were only two surprises. Preacher supplied both. The first was his name, Nathaniel Anaclitus Thomas. Some people knew about the Nathaniel, but no one suspected Anaclitus. Even more surprising was Preacher's occupation, which was given on the nomination blank as simply, 'Proprietor'.

Harbans described himself as a 'Transport Contractor', Baksh as a 'Merchant Tailor'.

The night before, Pundit Dhaniram had suggested a plan to prevent the nomination of the other candidates.

'Get in fust,' he told Harbans. 'And pay them your two hundred and fifty dollars in coppers. Only in coppers. And make them check it.'

'You go want a salt bag to carry all that,' Foam said.

For an absurd moment Harbans had taken the idea seriously. 'But suppose they tell me wait, while they attend to Preacher and Baksh?'

Dhaniram shook his legs and sucked at his cigarette. 'Can't tell you wait. You go fust, they got to attend to you fust. Facts is facts and fair is fair.'

Chittaranjan squashed the discussion by saying drily, 'You can't give nobody more than twelve coppers. More than that is not legal tender.'

Harbans paid in notes.

He paid Baksh his two thousand dollars election expenses only after the nominations had been filed.

'Like I did tell you, boss, can't give you much of a fight with this alone,' Baksh said ungraciously. 'I is a man with a big family.'

That evening Baksh went to Ramlogan's rumshop to celebrate his new triumph. They treated him like a hero. He talked.

★

At the end of that week, the last in July, the Elvira Government School closed for the holidays and Teacher Francis was glad to get away to Port of Spain. Elvira had become insupportable to him. Lorkhoor's behaviour was one thing; and then, as he had feared, most of the Elvira parents had followed Chittaranjan's example and stopped sending their children to him for private lessons.

The children were now free to give more of their time to the election. In their tattered vests and shirts and jerseys they ran wild over Elvira, tormenting all three candidates with their encouragements; impartially they scrawled new slogans and defaced old ones; they escorted Preacher on his house-to-house visits until Mr Cuffy frightened them off.

And the campaigns grew hot.

Lorkhoor roared into the attack, slandering Baksh, slandering Harbans. He spent the whole of one steamy afternoon telling Elvira what Elvira knew: that Harbans had induced Baksh to stand as a candidate.

'A man who gives bribes,' Lorkhoor said, 'is also capable of taking bribes.'

'This Lorkhoor is a real jackass,' Chittaranjan commented, 'if he think that by saying that he going to make Harbans lose. People *like* to know that they could get a man to do little things for them every now and then.'

Lorkhoor turned to Baksh. 'A man who takes bribes,' Lorkhoor said, 'is also capable of giving them.'

'*Give?*' Chittaranjan said. '*Baksh* give anything? He ain't know Baksh.'

Photographs of Baksh and Harbans sprang up everywhere, on houses, telegraph-poles, trees and culverts; they were promptly invested with moustaches, whiskers, spectacles and pipes.

'Making you famous, girl,' Baksh told Mrs Baksh. 'Pictures all over the place. Mazurus Baksh. Hitch your wagon to the star. Mazurus Baksh, husband of Mrs Baksh. Mazurus Baksh, the poor man friend. Mazurus Baksh, everybody friend.'

'Mazurus Baksh,' Mrs Baksh said, 'the big big ass.'

But he could tell that she was pleased.

Harbans's new slogan caught on. When Harbans came to Elvira children shouted at him, 'Do your part, man!' And Harbans, his shyness gone, as Foam had prophesied, replied, 'Vote the heart!'

Foam was always coming up with fresh slogans. 'The Heart for a start.' 'Harbans, the man with the Big Heart.' 'You can't live without the Heart. You can't live without Harbans.' He got hold of a gramophone record and played it so often, it became Harbans's campaign song:

And oh, my darling,
Should we ever say goodbye,
I know we both should die,
My heart and I.

Every day Chittaranjan put on his visiting outfit and campaigned; Dhaniram campaigned, in a less spectacular way; and Mahadeo entered the names of sick Hindus in his red notebook.

For some time Preacher stuck to his old method, the energetic walking tour. But one day he appeared on the Elvira main road with a large stone in his hand. He stopped Mahadeo.

'Who you voting for?'

'Preacher? You know I campaigning for Harbans . . .'

'Good. Take this stone and kill me one time.'

Mahadeo managed to escape. But Preacher stopped him again two days later. Preacher had a Bible in his right hand and a stone—the same stone—in his left hand.

'Answer me straight: who you voting for?'

'*Every*body know I voting for you, Preacher.'

Preacher dropped the stone and gave Mahadeo the Bible. 'Swear!'

Mahadeo hesitated.

Preacher stooped and picked up the stone. He handed it to Mahadeo. 'Kill me.'

'I can't swear on the Bible, Preacher. I is not a Christian.'

And Mahadeo escaped again.

Lorkhoor, copying Foam, gave Preacher a campaign song which featured Preacher's symbol, the shoe:

I got a shoe, you got a shoe,
All God's chillun got a shoe.
When I go to heaven,
Going to put on my shoe
And walk all over God's heaven.

Baksh, whose symbol was the star, went up to Harbans one day and said, 'I want a song too. Everybody having song.'

'Ooh, Baksh. You want song too? Why, man?'

'Everybody laughing at me. Is as though I ain't fighting this election at all.'

In the end Harbans allowed Foam to play a song for Baksh:

How would you like to swing on a star?
Carry moonbeams home in a jar?
You could be better off than you are.
You could be swinging on a star.

Rum flowed in Ramlogan's rumshop. Everyone who drank it knew it was Harbans's rum.

Dhaniram, exultant, consoled Harbans. 'The main thing is to *pay* the entrance fee. Now is your chance.'

And Ramlogan encouraged the drinkers, saying, inconsequentially and unwisely, 'Case of whisky for winning committee. Whole case of whisky.'

And in the meantime Harbans's committee did solid work, Foam and Chittaranjan in particular. They canvassed, they publicized; they chose agents for polling day and checked their loyalty; they chose taxi-drivers and checked their loyalty. They visited warden, returning officer, poll clerks, policemen: a pertinacious but delicate generosity rendered these officials impartial.

With all this doing Harbans, with his moods, his exultations, depressions and rages, was an embarrassment to his committee. They wished him out of the way and tried, without being rude, to tell him so.

'You could stay in Port of Spain and win your election in Elvira,' Pundit Dhaniram told him. 'Easy easy. Just leave everything to your party machine,' he added, savouring the words. 'Party machine.'

At his meetings on the terrace of Chittaranjan's shop Harbans gave out bagfuls of sweets to children; and talked little. It was Foam and Chittaranjan and Dhaniram and Mahadeo who did most of the talking.

First Foam introduced Mahadeo; then Mahadeo introduced Dhaniram; and Dhaniram introduced Chittaranjan. By the time Chittaranjan introduced Harbans the meeting was practically over and Harbans could only receive deputations.

'Boss, the boys from Pueblo Road can't play no football this season. Goalpost fall down. Football bust.'

Harbans would write out a cheque.

'Boss, we having a little sports meeting and it would look nice if you could give a few of the prizes. No, boss, not give them out. Give.'

Another cheque.

It was Harbans, Harbans all the way. There could be no doubt of that.

Dhaniram repeatedly calculated: 'Three thousand Hindu votes and one thousand Spanish make four thousand. Preacher getting three thousand for the most. Baksh getting the thousand Muslim votes.'

Harbans didn't like this sort of talk. He said it gave people wrong ideas, encouraged them not to vote; and when he made a personal plea to some voter for the fourth or fifth time and the voter said, 'But Mr Harbans, you *know* I promise you,' Harbans would say, 'This democracy is a strange thing. It does make the great poor and the poor great. It make me a beggar—yes, don't stop me, I *is* a beggar—and I *begging* for your vote.'

Rumours began to fly. Mr Cuffy had deserted Preacher. Preacher was selling out to Baksh, but was going to do so only on the day before the election. Baksh was selling out to Preacher. Mahadeo was selling out to Preacher. Chittaranjan was selling out to Baksh. Everybody, it seemed, was selling out to somebody. Elvira thrilled to rumour and counter-rumour. Voters ran after candidates and their agents and warned that so-and-so had to be watched. It was agreed on all sides that Dhaniram had to be watched; he was interested only in his tractor and was just waiting to see which side was going to win before throwing in his full weight with it. The most persistent rumour was that Lorkhoor wanted to leave Preacher. That rumour Chittaranjan took seriously.

He said, 'I did always have a feeling that Lorkhoor

wanted something big outa this election, but I couldn't rightly make out what it was.'

★

Chittaranjan was rocking in his veranda late one evening, thinking about going to bed, when he heard someone whisper from the terrace. He got up and looked down.

It was Dhaniram. He held a hurricane lantern that lit up his pundit's regalia. 'Message, Goldsmith,' Dhaniram whispered, barely controlling his excitement.

Chittaranjan whispered back. 'From Baksh?'

'Lorkhoor, Goldsmith. He say he have a matter of importance—said words he use—matter of importance to discuss with you.'

'Wait.'

Dhaniram stood on the terrace, swinging the lantern, humming:

So he called the multitude,
Turned the water into wine.
Jesus calls you. Come and dine!

Presently Chittaranjan came down. In his visiting outfit.

They went to Dhaniram's house.

Lorkhoor was waiting for them. He sat on the balustrade of the veranda, smoking and swinging his legs, not looking in the least like a perplexed traitor. He said, 'Ah, Goldsmith. Sorry to get you up.'

'Yes, man,' Dhaniram said. 'It give me a big big surprise. I was just coming back from Etwariah place—Rampiari mother, you know: she was having a little *kattha*: I was the pundit—and I see Lorkhoor van outside.'

Lorkhoor said, 'Goldsmith, I'm tired of talking.'

Dhaniram was beside himself with delight. He lit a cigarette and smoked noisily.

'I could give you eight hundred votes,' Lorkhoor said. 'If I keep my mouth shut. Worth anything?'

Chittaranjan took off his hat and considered it in the light of the hurricane lantern. 'I don't know if it worth anything at all.'

Lorkhoor laughed. 'Silence is golden, Goldsmith.'

Dhaniram said tremulously, 'Eight hundred more for we and eight hundred less for Preacher. Is a sure sure win, Goldsmith.' He wanted the deal to go through; it would be dramatically proper.

Chittaranjan said, 'You did always think of selling out in the end, not so?'

'That's right.' Lorkhoor didn't sound abashed. 'I have no daughter to marry off.'

Dhaniram gave a nervous giggle.

'And I have no tractor.'

Dhaniram pulled at his cigarette.

Lorkhoor took out some typewritten electoral lists from his hip pocket. 'Eight hundred votes. Checked and signed and sealed. You can check up on them yourself, if you wish. A dollar a vote?'

Dhaniram shouted, '*Doolahin*, bring the Petromax.'

Inside, Dhaniram's wife woke up, complained and fell silent again.

Chittaranjan examined his hat. 'You think you could live in Elvira after the elections?'

Lorkhoor changed his position on the balustrade. 'I was thinking of leaving Elvira altogether.'

'Oh?' Dhaniram shook his legs. 'Where you was thinking of going?'

The *doolahin* brought the Petromax and blew out the hurricane lantern. She behaved with much modesty and Dhaniram was pleased. No pert remarks, no stamping on the shaky floor. She pulled her veil over her forehead and hung up the Petromax.

Lorkhoor watched her walk off with the hurricane lantern. Watching her, he said, 'I was thinking of going to Port of Spain. Get a job on a paper. The *Guardian* or the *Sentinel* or the *Gazette*.'

Chittaranjan stood with his back to the Petromax and studied the lists Lorkhoor gave him. 'How we know these eight hundred Hindus going to do what you say?'

'You will see for yourself. But if I tell them that Preacher has betrayed me, and if I tell them to vote for a Hindu like Harbans, who do you think they'll vote for? Baksh?'

'How we know you not going to change your mind?'

Lorkhoor shrugged. 'I will leave on the Saturday before the elections.'

'Five hundred dollars,' Chittaranjan said.

'Splendid,' said Lorkhoor. 'That suits me fine.'

XII

MORE DEPARTURES

★

That happened one week before polling day. Harbans and Chittaranjan were confident but didn't show it. Dhaniram was shamelessly exultant. Mahadeo was beyond caring. He still had to endure Mr Cuffy's watchful eye, and still had to keep his own vigil over Old Sebastian. And there was his eternal anxiety that some other negro might fall ill. Hindus were falling ill by the score every day now; Muslims had begun to join them, and even a few Spaniards. But no negro became infirm. Mahadeo didn't have time to be thankful.

★

And then Baksh began to play the fool again.

'Bribe number three coming up,' Chittaranjan said.

Baksh told Ramlogan and Ramlogan told Chittaranjan. Baksh told Foam and Foam told Chittaranjan. Baksh told Harichand and Harichand told Chittaranjan.

'Say he ain't got a chance,' Harichand said. 'Not a chance in hell. Say, by asking Muslim people to vote for him, he wasting good good votes. Say it ain't fair to the Muslim to ask them to waste their good good votes. Say that it would look to a lot of people like a Hindu trick to waste good good Muslim votes. Say he thinking that, weighing up everything and balancing it, Preacher is still the better man. Say he thinking of selling out to Preacher. Say is the only thing to give back the Muslim their pride. Say . . .'

'Say he could kiss my arse,' Harbans said. 'Say he could go to hell afterwards.'

'Say,' Harichand went on unperturbed, 'that he willing to talk things over fust.'

'Give them the Muslim vote,' Dhaniram said. 'With the Spanish voting and with Lorkhoor telling the other Hindus not to vote for Preacher, we could give them the Muslim vote.'

Harbans paced about Chittaranjan's veranda with his jerky clockwork steps. 'It go against my heart to give that man another penny. Against my heart, man.'

Chittaranjan said, 'Harichand, tell Baksh we not going to see him until Saturday night.'

'But election is on Monday,' Harichand said.

'We know that,' Chittaranjan said. 'We don't want Baksh to tired out hisself changing his mind *four* times. Three times in one election is enough for one man.'

'Is your election, pappa.' Harichand shook his head, laughed and left.

Harbans fell into one of his unsettling depressive moods. He continued to walk up and down Chittaranjan's tiled veranda, muttering to himself, cracking his fingers.

'It don't matter who the Muslims vote for now,' Dhaniram said. 'Work it out for yourself, Mr Harbans. We getting *all* the Hindu votes and the Spanish vote. Five thousand. If the worst come to the worst and Baksh sell out to Preacher, Preacher could still only get three thousand. Two thousand negro and a thousand Muslim.'

Harbans refused to be comforted.

And Chittaranjan rocking, rocking in his morris chair, wasn't as cool as he looked. It wasn't Baksh's message. He had expected that. And, as Dhaniram had said, Baksh wasn't important now anyway; though it would have been worthwhile, just to make absolutely sure, to see that the

Muslims didn't vote for Preacher. But the message had come at a bad time. Chittaranjan had called Harbans to the committee meeting that Wednesday evening to tell him all about the big motor-car parade on Sunday, the eve of polling day.

Harbans knew nothing about the parade. Chittaranjan, Foam and Dhaniram had planned it among themselves. They were afraid that if Harbans got to know about it too early he might object: the parade was going to be a grand, expensive thing. But the committee wanted it—a final flourish to an impressive campaign.

Big motor-car parades were not new to Trinidad. Up to 1946, however, they had been used only for weddings and funerals. At weddings the decorated cars raced through the main roads with streamers flying and horns blaring. In their sombre way funeral processions were equally impressive; they always had right of way and often dislocated traffic; an important man could paralyse it. In 1946 the political possibilities of the motor-car parade were exploited for the first time by the P.P.U., the Party for Progress and Unity. On the day before the first general election the P.P.U. hired five hundred cars and toured the island. It was the P.P.U.'s finest moment. The party had been founded two months before the parade; it died two days after it. It won one seat out of twelve; ten of the candidates lost their deposits; the President and the funds disappeared. But Trinidad had been impressed by the parade and after that no election, whether for city council, county council or local road board, was complete without a parade.

But parades were expensive.

Chittaranjan, seeing Harbans work his way back and forth across the veranda, wished once again he could manage the campaign without having to manage the candidate as well.

He thought he would be casual. He said, 'You doing anything on Sunday, Mr Harbans?'

Harbans didn't reply.

Chittaranjan said, 'I hope you not doing anything, because we having a little parade for you.'

Harbans stopped walking.

'Small parade really.'

Harbans locked his fingers, looked at them and then at his shoes, cracked his fingers, and continued to walk.

'Motorcade,' Dhaniram said.

'About fifty cars.' Chittaranjan began to write. 'Fifteen dollars a car. And you could give them a few gallons of gas. You got to have food to give the people. And you have to have music.'

Harbans, still jerking about the veranda, only cracked his fingers.

'You can't disappoint the people, Mr Harbans,' Chittaranjan said. 'It go cost you about fifteen hundred dollars, but at the same time it going to make the people who want to vote for you feel good, seeing their candidate at the head of a big big parade.'

'Must have a motorcade,' Dhaniram said. 'Must must. Keep up with the times.' He laughed. '*Pay* the entrance fee.'

Harbans sat down.

When Foam came in they worked out details.

★

The only member of the committee who didn't turn up for that meeting was Mahadeo. Of late he had begun to stay away from committee meetings. It embarrassed him to be continually offering up lists of sick Hindus; much of Harbans's anger had been directed against him and he had had to defend himself more than once: '*I* didn't start up this democracy business, Mr Harbans.'

Old Sebastian was getting more difficult too. Concurrently with a series of unexpected ailments Sebastian had developed a sprightliness that should have heartened Mahadeo. It sickened him with worry. He could no longer rely on Sebastian to stay at home and make fish-pots. He often found him now in Ramlogan's rumshop, drinking free rum with the rest. Mahadeo didn't know where Sebastian got his rum vouchers. (He got them from Harichand, who had printed the vouchers and kept a few.) It didn't take much to get Sebastian drunk. He had lived for too long on an old age pension that had cramped his drinking style.

Mahadeo said, 'This democracy ain't a good thing for a man like Sebastian, you hear.'

And Mr Cuffy said, 'Mahadeo, I ain't know what sort of magic you working on Sebastian, but he acting damn funny. A candle does burn bright bright before it go out, remember. And Sebastian burning it at both ends.'

Sebastian's behaviour also distressed his drinking companion, Haq. Haq had with relief sacrificed his religious scruples so far as to drink in public. It wasn't the drink, he said; he wanted to be in a crowd, otherwise Foam would beat him up. He and Sebastian sat silently side by side on the bench against one wall of Ramlogan's rumshop and drank. They looked curiously alike; only, Sebastian smiled all the time, while Haq looked grumpy and uncompromising behind his spectacles; and Haq's bristle of white beard and whiskers was more impressive than the stray kinky brownish-grey hairs on Sebastian's chin that looked as though they had been despairingly planted by someone who hadn't enough seed to go round.

Mahadeo did his best. He bribed Sebastian to stay home; but Sebastian insisted that one bribe was good enough for only one day; and the days he stayed away from the rumshop he was very ill and alarmed Mahadeo more. He gave

Sebastian money to go to the D.M.O. for a check-up. Sebastian said he went but Mahadeo didn't believe him. He bribed the D.M.O. to go to Sebastian. The D.M.O. reported, 'He'll last for a bit,' and left Mahadeo just as worried. 'A candle does burn bright bright before it go out,' he thought, and remembered Mr Cuffy and the whitewash brush on his face.

Mahadeo was a devout Hindu. He did his *puja* every morning and evening. In all his prayers now, and through all the ritual, the *arti* and bell-ringing and conch-blowing—which seemed in the most discouraging way to have nothing to do with what went on in Elvira—Mahadeo had one thought: Sebastian's health.

★

On the evening of the Saturday before the election Mahadeo noted that Sebastian was not at home. His vigil would be over in two days; he couldn't risk anything happening now. He went straight to Ramlogan's rumshop. It was full of the Saturday night crowd, merrier than usual because they still had rum vouchers; in two days they would have to start paying for their rum again. The floor was wet—the floors of rumshops are always wet. Ramlogan was busy, happy. Mahadeo forced his way through to the bench where Haq and Sebastian normally sat. He caught bits of election gossip.

'The British Government don't want Harbans to win this election.'

'They going to spoil all the poor people votes once they get them inside the Warden Office. Lights going out all over the place.'

'No, I not going to bet you, but I still have a funny feeling that Baksh going to win.'

'When Harbans done with this election, he done with Elvira, I telling all-you.'

'Chittaranjan in for one big shock when this election over, you hear.'

Mahadeo saw Haq, overshadowed by the standing drinkers and looking lost, fierce, but content.

'Where Sebastian?'

Rampiari's husband, his right foot emphatically bandaged, put his big hand on Mahadeo's shoulder. 'Sebastian! I never see a old man get so young so quick.'

Somebody else said, 'Take my word. Sebastian going to dead in harness.'

'Haq, you see Sebastian?'

'Nasty old man. Don't want to see him.'

Rampiari's husband said, 'Yes. In harness.'

'This ain't no joke, you know. Where Sebastian?'

'At home. By you. Go back and see after your wife, Mahadeo boy.'

'Two three years from now some negro child running down Elvira main road calling Mahadeo Pa.'

'All-you ain't see Sebastian? Ramlogan!'

'Mahadeo, who the arse you think you is to shout at me like that? A man only got two hands.'

'Where Sebastian?'

'He take up a little drink and he gone long time.'

'For oysters.'

Mahadeo ran out of the shop, dazed by worry and the smell of rum. He ran back to Sebastian's hut. It was dead, lightless. No Sebastian. He made his way in the dark through the high grass to the latrine at the back of the yard. The heavy grey door—it came from one of the dismantled American Army buildings at Docksite in Port of Spain and heaven knows how Sebastian had got hold of it—the door was open. In the dark the latrine smell seemed to have grown in strength many times over. Mahadeo lit a match.

No Sebastian. The hole was too small for Sebastian to have fallen in. He ran back to the road.

'Mahadeo, choose.'

It was Preacher, smelling of sweat and looking somewhat bedraggled.

'You see Sebastian?'

'The stone or the Bible?'

'The stone, man. The Bible. Anything. You see Sebastian?'

'Take the stone and kill me one time.'

'Let me go, man, Preacher. I got one dead on my hands already.' Then Mahadeo paused. 'Sebastian choose tonight?'

'Like Cawfee.'

'Aha! I did always believe that Cawfee was putting him up to everything. Let me *go*, man, Preacher, otherwise I going to hit you for true with the stone, you know.'

Mahadeo was released. On his way to Mr Cuffy's he passed a crowd on Chittaranjan's terrace, taxi-drivers waiting for instructions about the motorcade tomorrow. They were drinking and getting noisy. Mahadeo looked up and saw the light from Chittaranjan's drawing-room. He knew he should have been there, discussing the final election plans with Harbans and the rest of the committee. Guiltily he hurried away.

There was no light in Mr Cuffy's house. Normally at this time Mr Cuffy sat in his small veranda reading the Bible by the light of an oil-lamp, ready to say 'Good night' to disciples who greeted him from the road.

Mahadeo passed and repassed the house.

'Mr Mahadeo.'

It was Lutchman. Mahadeo couldn't make him out right away because Lutchman wore a hat with the brim most decidedly turned down, as protection against the dew. Lutchman lived in the house with six votes. He was one of the earliest Hindus to report sick to Mahadeo. He had been succoured.

Mahadeo remembered. 'How the pain in your belly?'

'A lil bit better, Mr Mahadeo. One of the boys gone and fall sick now.'

'He fall sick a lil too late. Election is the day after tomorrow.'

Lutchman laughed, but didn't give up. 'You waiting for somebody, Mr Mahadeo?'

'You see Sebastian?'

Lutchman buttoned up his shirt and screwed down his hat more firmly. He held the brim over his ears. 'He sick too?'

'You meet anybody these days who *ain't* sick?'

'Is a sort of flu,' Lutchman said.

There was a coughing and a spluttering behind them.

Mahadeo started, ready to move off.

Lutchman said, 'Look him there.'

A cigarette glowed in Mr Cuffy's dark veranda.

Mahadeo whispered, 'Sebastian, is you?'

There was some more coughing.

'He smoking,' Mahadeo said angrily. 'Picking up all sort of vice in his old age.'

Lutchman said, 'He can't be all that sick if he smoking. Is a funny thing, you know, Mr Mahadeo, but I could always tell when *I* going to fall sick. I does find it hard to smoke. The moment that happen I does say, "Lutchman, boy, it look like you going to fall sick soon." True, you know, Mr Mahadeo.'

'Sebastian!'

'These days I can't even take a tiny little pull at a cigarette, man.'

Sebastian came into the road and Mahadeo knocked the cigarette from his hand.

Then Sebastian spoke.

'Dead,' Sebastian said. 'Dead as a cockroach.' He said it with a sort of neutral relish.

Mahadeo was confused by fear and joy.

'Dead?' Lutchman uncorked his hat.

Sebastian spoke again. 'Put back your hat on. You going to catch cold.'

'As a cockroach?' Mahadeo said.

'As a cockroach.'

The three men went into the lightless house. Mahadeo lit a match and they found the oil-lamp on a corner shelf. They lit that. The floorboards were worm-eaten and unreliable, patched here and there with the boards from a Red Cow condensed milk box. The pea-green walls were hung with framed religious pictures and requests to God, in Gothic letters, to look after the house.

Mr Cuffy sat in a morris chair as though he were posing for a photographer who specialized in relaxed attitudes. His head was slightly thrown back, his eyes were open but unstaring, his knees far apart, his right hand in his lap, his left on the arm of the chair.

'As a cockroach,' Sebastian said. He lifted the left hand and let it drop.

Lutchman, his hat in his hand, wandered about the tiny drawing-room like a tourist in a church. 'Old Cawfee Bible, man. Eh! Mr Mahadeo, look. Cawfee in technicolour, man.' He pointed to a framed photograph of a young negro boy looking a little lost among a multitude of potted palms and fluted columns. It was a tinted black and white photograph. The palms were all tinted green; the columns were each a different colour; the boy's suit was brown, the tie red; and the face, untinted, black.

Mahadeo wasn't looking. It overwhelmed him just to be in Mr Cuffy's house. He felt triumph, shame, relief and awe. Then the shame and the awe went, leaving him exhausted but cool.

'Lutchman.'

'Mr Mahadeo.'

'Stay here with Sebastian. Don't let him go nowhere. Preacher mustn't get to know about Cawfee right now.'

He hurried over to Chittaranjan's, pushed his way through the drunken taxi-drivers on the terrace and went up the red steps. He saw Baksh at the top. Baksh was saying, with unconvincing dignity, 'Is not *you* I come to see, Goldsmith, but Mr Harbans.'

Mahadeo followed Baksh and Chittaranjan into the drawing-room. Harbans was there with his committee. Foam was sitting at the polished cedar table, looking at a very wide sheet which contained all the committee's dispositions for polling day: the names of agents and their polling stations, agents inside the stations and agents outside; taxis, their owners, their drivers, their stations.

Mahadeo said, 'Goldsmith, I have to see you right away.'

Chittaranjan, honouring the occasion by wearing his visiting outfit (minus the hat) at home, looked at Mahadeo with surprise and some contempt.

'Pussonal,' Mahadeo insisted.

Chittaranjan felt the force of Mahadeo's eyes. He led him to the back veranda.

Baksh said, 'Mr Harbans, answer me this frank: if I go up, ain't I just making the Muslims and them waste their good good vote?'

Dhaniram said, 'Ach! You could keep the Muslim vote.'

'I know,' Baksh said. 'You ain't want the Muslim vote *now*. But you think it would look nice? When next election come round, and you *ain't* want the Muslim to waste their vote, what you going to do then?'

Harbans said, '*Next* election? This is the fust and last election I fighting in Elvira.'

Foam studied his chart. He wasn't going to take any part in the discussion.

Baksh knew he was pushing things too far. But he knew he was safe because Foam was there. Otherwise he stood a good chance of being beaten up. Not by Harbans or Dhaniram or Chittaranjan, but by helpers. He could hear the din from Ramlogan's shop next door: the curses and the quarrels, swift to flare up, swift to die down. He could hear the taxi-drivers downstairs, drunk and getting drunker; they were making a row about petrol for the motorcade tomorrow.

Baksh said, 'If the Muslims vote for Preacher, it going to make a little trouble for you, Mr Harbans. You is a old man and I ain't want to trouble you. But is the only proper thing to do.'

'And the only proper thing for *you* to do is to make haste and haul your tail away.' It was Chittaranjan, returning to the drawing-room. 'Dhaniram, at long last we could use your plan. Cawfee dead.'

'Aha! What I did tell you?' Dhaniram was so excited he lit a cigarette. 'One negro was bound to dead before elections. You in luck, Mr Harbans. Lorkhoor going away tonight. And tonight self you get a chance to start paying the negroes *their* entrance fee.'

Harbans was too stupefied by his good fortune to react.

'Wake,' Dhaniram said. 'Coffee. *We* coffee. Ha! Coffee for Cawfee. Coffee, rum, biscuits.'

Chittaranjan remained poised. 'Foam, take the van and run down to Chaguanas and get Tanwing to come up here with a nice coffin and a icebox and everything else. And telephone Radio Trinidad so they could have the news out at ten o'clock. You could make up the wordings yourself.

Dhaniram, go home and get your daughter-in-law to make a lot of coffee and bring it back here.'

'How I go *bring* back a lot of coffee here?'

'Is a point. Foam, when you come back, go and pick up the coffee from Dhaniram place. Nelly mother going to make some more.'

Baksh saw it was no use threatening to sell out to Preacher now. He said, 'Funny how people does sit down and dead, eh? Since I was a boy so high in short pants I seeing Cawfee sitting down in his house, repairing shoe. All sorta shoe. Black shoe, brown shoe, two-tone shoe, high-heel, wedge-heel.' Baksh became elegiac: 'I remember one day, when I was a boy, taking a shoe to Cawfee. Heel was dropping off. One of those rubber heels. I take it to Cawfee and he tack back the heel for me. I offer him six cents but he ain't take it.'

No one listened. Foam was folding up his election chart in a business-like way. Dhaniram was buckling his belt, ready to go and see about the coffee. Harbans was still bemused. Mahadeo, relieved, exhausted, didn't care.

'He ain't take it,' Baksh repeated.

Chittaranjan said, 'Mahadeo, you better go and keep a sharp eye on the house. I going to talk to those taxi-drivers. We go want them for the funeral. I think it would be better to have the funeral before the motorcade.'

Mahadeo went back to Mr Cuffy's house.

Sebastian was sitting in a morris chair, leaning forward and grimacing.

Lutchman said, 'Sebastian ain't too well, Mr Mahadeo. Just now, just before you come, he take in with one belly pain. He sick.'

'Serve him damn right. And let me tell you one thing, Sebastian. If *you* dead, nobody not going to bury you, you hear.'

Sebastian only grimaced.

Lutchman said, 'Food and everything spread out in the kitchen, you know, Mr Mahadeo. Nothing ain't touch. Mr Cawfee,' Lutchman said, feeling for the words, 'get call away rather sudden.'

Sebastian straightened his face and got up. He stood in front of the tinted photograph. He said, 'I did know Cawfee when he take out that photo. Always going to Sunday School.' Abruptly his voice was touched with pathos. 'They use to give out cakes and sweet drinks. Then he get take up with this shoemaking.'

They sat and waited until they heard a van stop outside. Foam, Chittaranjan, the D.M.O. and Tanwing came in. The D.M.O. was a young Indian with a handsome dissipated face. He hadn't forgotten his association with England and continued to wear a Harris tweed jacket, despite the heat.

Foam asked, 'You going to cut him up, Doctor?'

The D.M.O. pursed his lips and didn't reply. He did two things. He took off Mr Cuffy's stout black boots, said, 'Good boots,' turned up Mr Cuffy's right eye-lid, then closed both eyes.

'Heart,' he said, and filled the form.

'Was that self I did think,' Lutchman said.

Tanwing, the undertaker, was pleased by the D.M.O.'s dispatch, though nothing showed on his face. Tanwing was an effervescent little Chinese who had revolutionized burial in Central Trinidad. He had a big bright shop in Chaguanas with a bright show window. In the window he had coffins of many sizes and many woods, plain and polished, with silver handles or without any handles at all, with glass windows on the lid through which you could look at the face of the deceased, or without these windows. Every coffin had its price tag, sometimes with a hint like: 'The same in cyp, $73.00.' There were also tombstones, with tags like this: 'The same with kerbs, $127.00.' The slogan of Tanwing's was Economy with Refinement; because of the former he had abandoned horse-drawn hearses for motor ones. Refined economy paid. Tanwing was able to sponsor a weekly fifteen-minute programme on Radio Trinidad. The other programme of this sort was a hushed, reverent thing called 'The Sunshine Hour'. Tanwing gave his audience fifteen lively minutes of songs from many lands on gramophone records, and called his programme 'Faraway Places'.

Tanwing fell to work at once. He wasted no time sympathizing with anybody. But he was anxious to do his best; Mr Cuffy was being laid out in one of his more expensive coffins.

By now it could no longer be hidden from Elvira that something had happened to Mr Cuffy.

Shortly after the D.M.O. had signed the death certificate, Foam and Chittaranjan had taken over quantities of rum, coffee and biscuits to the house; and the news was broken. People began to gather, solemn at first, but when the rum started to flow all was well. Harbans mingled with the mourners as though they were his guests; and everyone knew, and was grateful, that Harbans had taken all the expenses of the wake upon himself. Some of Mr Cuffy's women disciples turned up in white dresses and hats, and sat in the drawing-room, singing hymns. The men preferred to remain in the yard. They sat on benches and chairs under Mr Cuffy's big almond tree and talked and drank by the light of flambeaux.

Baksh came, rebuffed but unhumbled. He said nothing about the election and was full of stories about the goodness of Mr Cuffy. The mourners weren't interested. Baksh was still officially a candidate and still the controller of the thousand Muslim votes; but politically he was a failure and everybody knew it. He knew it himself. He drank cup after cup of Harbans's weak black coffee and maintained a strenuous sort of gaiety that fooled no one.

He felt out of everything and ran from group to group in the yard, trying to say something of interest. 'But I telling all-you, man,' he said over and over. 'I see old Cawfee good good just last night. I pass by his house and I give him a right and he give me back a right.'

Baksh was romancing and no one paid attention. Besides, too many people had seen Mr Cuffy the day before.

Baksh drank. Soon the rum worked on him. It made him forget electioneering strategy and increased his loquaciousness. It also gave him an inspiration. 'All-you know why Cawfee dead so sudden?' he asked. 'Come on, guess why he dead so sudden.'

Lutchman said, 'When your time come, your time come, that is all.'

Harichand the printer was also there. He said, 'The way Cawfee dead remind me of the way Talmaso dead. Any of all-you here remember old Talmaso? Talmaso had the laziest horse in the whole wide world . . .'

'So none of all-you ain't going to guess why Cawfee dead?' Baksh said angrily. Then he relented. 'All right, I go tell you. Was because of that dog.'

Harichand pricked up his ears. 'That said dog?'

Baksh emptied his glass and rocked on his heels. 'Said said dog.' When Baksh drank his full face lost its hardness; his moustache lost its bristliness and drooped; his eyebrows drooped; his eyelids hung wearily over reddened eyes; his cheeks sagged. And the man spoke with a lot of conviction. 'Said dog. Cawfee run the dog down and give the poor little thing five six kicks. Herbert did warn him that if he kick the dog he was going to dead. But you know how Cawfee was own way and harden, never listening to anybody. Well, he kick the dog and he dead.'

Rampiari's husband, heavy with drink, said, 'Still, the man dead and I ain't want to hear nobody bad-talking him.'

'True,' Harichand said. 'But the way Cawfee just sit down and dead remind me of how Talmaso dead. Talmaso was a grass-cutter. Eh, but I wonder where the hell Talmaso did get that horse he had. Laziest horse in the world. Lazy lazy. Tock. Tock. Tock.' Harichand clacked his tongue to imitate the horse's hoofbeats. 'Tock. Tock. So it uses to walk. As if it was in a funeral. Lifting up his foot as though they was make of lead: one today, one tomorrow. Tock. Tock. Tock. And then Talmaso uses to take his whip and lash out *Pai! Pai! Pai!* And horse uses to go: tocktocktock-tock-tock-tock-tock. Tock. Tock. Tock. *Pai!* Tocktocktock-tock-tock. Tock. Tock. But you couldn't laugh at Talmaso horse. Talmaso run you all over the place. Every morning horse uses to neigh. As if it did want to wake up Talmaso. Horse neigh. Talmaso get up. One morning horse neigh. Talmaso *ain't* get up. Only Talmaso wife get up. Talmaso wife uses to give Talmaso hell, you know. Horse neigh again. Still, Talmaso sleeping. Sound sound. Like a top. Wife start one cussing-off. In Hindi. She shake up Talmaso. Horse neigh. Still, Talmaso sleeping. Like a baby. Wife push Talmaso. Talmaso roll off the bed. Stiff. Wife start one bawling. Horse neighing. Wife bawling. Talmaso dead. Horse never move again.'

'What happen to it?'

'Horse? Like Talmaso. Sit down and dead.'

Rampiari's husband exclaimed, 'Look! Preacher coming. All three candidates here now.'

Preacher didn't bustle in. He came into the yard with a solemn shuffle, kissing his right hand and waving languid benedictions to the crowd. They looked upon him with affection as a defeated candidate. His long white robe was sweat-stained and dusty; but there was nothing in his expression to show regret, either at the election or at Mr Cuffy's death: his tolerant eyes still had their bloodshot faraway look.

In the interest which greeted Preacher's arrival there was more than the interest which greets the newly defeated. Preacher was without staff, stone or Bible. And he was not alone. He had his left arm around Pundit Dhaniram, who was in tears and apparently inconsolable.

Mahadeo said, 'I know this wake was Dhaniram idea. But he taking this crying too damn far, you hear.'

Foam followed. 'No coffee from Dhaniram,' he announced.

'Dhaniram wife dead too?' Harichand asked, and got a laugh.

Chittaranjan staggered in with a large five-valve radio. It was his own and he didn't trust anyone else with it.

The women sang hymns in the drawing-room. In the yard some men were singing a calypso:

O'Reilly dead!
O'Reilly dead and he left money,
Left money, left money.
O'Reilly dead and he left money
To buy rum for we.

Chittaranjan and Foam fiddled with wires from the loud-speaker van, attaching them to the radio. The radio squawked and crackled.

'Shh!'

The hymn-singers fell silent. The calypsonians fell silent. Only Dhaniram sobbed.

The radio was on. A woman sang slowly, hoarsely:

I've found my man,
I've found my man.

Then an awed chorus of men and women sang:

She's in love:
She's lovely:
She uses Ponds.

There was a murmur of disappointment among the mourners, which was silenced by the radio announcer. '*This is Radio Trinidad and the Rediffusion Golden Network.*' He gave the time. Some trumpets blared.

'Shh!'

A fresh blare.

'Listen.'

Time for a Carib!
Time for a Carib
La-ger!

The mourners became restless. Chittaranjan, responsible for the radio, felt responsible for what came out of it. He looked appeasingly at everybody.

Solemn organ music oozed out of the radio.

'Aah.'

The announcer was as solemn as the music. '*We have been asked to announce the death . . .*'

Rampiari's husband had to be restrained from giving a shout.

But the first announcement was of no interest to Elvira.

The organ music drew Tanwing out of the bedroom where he had been busy on Mr Cuffy. The hymn-singers made room for him and looked at him with respect. He held his hands together and looked down at his shoes.

The organ music swelled again.

'Now.'

'*We have also been asked to announce the death of Joseph Cuffy . . .*'

There was a long, satisfied sigh. Rampiari's husband had to be restrained again.

'*. . . which occurred this evening at The Elvira in County Naparoni. The funeral of the late Joseph Cuffy takes place tomorrow morning, through the courtesy of Mr Surujpat Harbans, from the house of mourning, near Chittaranjan's Jewellery Establishment, Elvira main road, and thence to the Elvira Cemetery. Friends and relations are kindly asked to accept this intimation.*' Then there was some more music.

As soon as the music was over Tanwing unclasped his hands and disappeared into the bedroom and set to work on Mr Cuffy again.

A woman sang:

Brush your teeth with Colgate,
Colgate Dental Cream.

'Take the damn thing off,' Rampiari's husband shouted.

It cleans your breath
(One, two),
While it guards your teeth.

The radio was turned off. The hymn-singers sang hymns.

Pundit Dhaniram's grief was beginning to be noticed. A lot of people felt he was showing off: 'After all, Cawfee was Preacher best friend, and Preacher ain't crying.' Preacher was still consoling Dhaniram, patting the distraught pundit; while the announcement was coming over the radio Preacher had held on to him with extra firmness and affection. Now he took him to the bedroom.

It was close in the bedroom. The window was shut, the jalousies blocked up. The pictures had been turned to the wall and a towel thrown over the mirror. Tanwing and his assistants worked by the light of an acetylene lamp which was part of the equipment they had brought; candles burned impractically at the head of the bulky bed. The assistants, noiseless, were preparing the icebox for Mr Cuffy. Mr Cuffy's corpse was without dignity. The man's grumpiness, his fierce brows—all had gone for good. He just looked very dead and very old. The body had already been washed and dressed, with a curious clumsiness, in the shiny blue serge suit Elvira had seen on so many Friday evenings.

Preacher released Pundit Dhaniram and looked at Mr Cuffy as though he were looking at a picture. He put his hand to his chin, held his head back and moved it slowly up and down.

Dhaniram still sobbed.

This didn't perturb Tanwing. He looked once at Dhaniram and looked no more. He was still fussing about the body, putting on the finishing touches. He was trying to place camphor balls in the nostrils and the job was proving a little awkward. Mr Cuffy had enormous nostrils. Tanwing had to wrap the camphor balls in cotton wool before they would stay in. Tanwing had the disquieting habit of constantly passing a finger under his own nostrils as though he had a runny nose, or as though he could smell something nobody else could.

When Dhaniram and Preacher left the room they were met by Chittaranjan. Dhaniram almost fell on Chittaranjan's shoulder, because he had to stoop to embrace him.

'You overdoing this thing, you know, Dhaniram,' Chittaranjan said. 'You ain't fooling nobody.'

'She gone, Goldsmith,' Dhaniram sobbed. 'She gone.'

'Who gone, Dhaniram?'

'The *doolahin* gone, Goldsmith. She run away with Lorkhoor.'

'Come, sit down and drink some coffee.'

'She take up she clothes and she jewellery and she gone.

She gone, Goldsmith. Now it ain't have nobody to look after me or the old lady.'

Outside the men were singing a calypso about the election:

And I tell my gal,
Keep the thing in place.
And when they come for the vote,
Just wash down their face.

The drinking and singing continued all that night and into the morning. Then they buried Mr Cuffy. Preacher did the preaching.

XIII

DEMOCRACY TAKES ROOT IN ELVIRA

★

In Mr Cuffy's yard the flambeaux had burned themselves out and were beaded with dew. The smell of stale rum hung in the still morning air. Under the almond trees benches lay in disorder. Many were overturned; all were wet with dew and coffee or rum. Around the benches, amid the old, trampled almond leaves, there were empty bottles and glasses, and enamel cups half full of coffee; there were many more in the dust under the low floor of Mr Cuffy's house. The house was empty. The windows and doors were wide open.

It was time for the motorcade.

Outside Chittaranjan's the taxis were parked in jaunty confusion, banners on their radiators and backs, their doors covered with posters still tacky with paste. The taxi-drivers too had a jaunty air. They were all wearing cardboard eye-shades, printed on one side, in red, DO YOUR PART, and on the reverse, VOTE THE HEART.

Some taxis grew restless in the heat and prowled about looking for more advantageous parking places. Disputes followed. The air rang with inventive obscenities.

Then a voice approached, booming with all the authority of the loudspeaker: 'Order, my good people! My good people, keep good order! I am begging you and beseeching you.'

It was Baksh.

Without formal negotiation or notification he was campaigning for Harbans. In the loudspeaker van he ran up and down the line of taxis, directing, rebuking, encouraging: 'The eyes of the world is on you, my good people. Get into line, get into line. Keep the road clear. Don't disgrace yourself in the eyes of the world, my good people.'

His admonitions had their effect. Soon the motorcade was ready to start.

Harbans, Chittaranjan, Dhaniram and Mahadeo sat in the first car. Dhaniram was too depressed, Mahadeo too exhausted, to respond with enthusiasm to the people who ran to the roadside and shouted, 'Do your part, man! Vote the heart!'

Mrs Baksh and the young Bakshes had a car to themselves. Mrs Baksh was not only reconciled to the election, she was actually enjoying it, though she pretended to be indifferent. She had decked out the young Bakshes. Carol and Zilla had ribbons in their hair, carried small white handbags which contained nothing, and small paper fans from Hong-Kong. The boys wore socks and ties. Herbert and Rafiq waved to the children of poorer people until Zilla said, 'Herbert and Rafiq, stop low-rating yourself.'

Baksh was with Foam in the loudspeaker van. He did his best to make up to Harbans for all the damage and distress he had caused him. He said, 'This is the voice of . . . Baksh. Mazurus Baksh here. This is the voice of . . . Baksh, asking each and every one of you, the good people of Elvira, to vote for your popular candidate, Mr Surujpat Harbans. Remember, good people of Elvira, I, Mazurus Baksh, not fighting the election again. I giving my support to Mr Surujpat Harbans. For the sake of unity, my good people. This is the voice of . . . Baksh.'

Then Foam played the Richard Tauber record of the campaign song:

And oh, my darling,
Should we ever say goodbye,
I know we both should die,
My heart and I.

And Baksh added, 'Don't let nobody fool you, my good people. Vote the heart. Make your X with a black lead pencil, my good people. A black lead pencil. Not a red pencil or a pen. Do your part. This is the voice of . . . Baksh.'

The motorcade was well organized. One van alone carried food—*roti, dalpuri* and curried goat. Another carried hard liquor and soft drinks. There were small mishaps. Two or three cars broke down and had to be pushed out of the way. Once the motorcade enthusiastically went beyond Elvira, snarled with the motorcades of other candidates in the next constituency, and when the dust settled Chittaranjan saw that the first half of the motorcade, which contained the candidate, the committee and the loudspeaker van, had got detached from the second half, which carried the food and the liquor.

A long grey van pulled up. It belonged to the Trinidad Film Board, who were shooting scenes for a Colonial Office documentary film about political progress in the colonies, the script of which was to be written, poetically, in London, by a minor British poet. Apart from the driver and an impressive tangle of equipment behind the front seat, the van carried a negro cameraman dressed for the job: green eyeshade, unlit cigar, wide, brilliant tie, broad-collared shirt open at the neck, sleeves neatly rolled up to mid-forearms. The cameraman chewed his cigar, sizing up Harbans's diminished motorcade.

Chittaranjan went to him. 'You drawing photo?'

The cameraman chewed.

'If is photo you drawing, well, draw out a photo of *we* candidate.'

Harbans smiled wanly at the cameraman.

The cameraman chewed, nodded to his driver and the van moved off.

'Everybody want bribe these days,' Chittaranjan said.

He sent Foam off in the loudspeaker van to look for the rest of the motorcade. Foam came upon them parked not far off in a side road near Piarco Airport. The food van had been plundered; the liquor van was being noisily besieged. Harichand was there, Lutchman, Sebastian, Haq, and Rampiari's husband, moving about easily on a bandaged foot.

Foam broke the party up. All went smoothly after that.

★

Baksh made one last attempt to cause trouble.

It happened after the motorcade, early in the evening, when Harbans was sitting in Chittaranjan's drawing-room, signing voucher after petrol voucher. He was giving each car six gallons for polling day. Baksh said it wasn't enough.

Harbans said, 'Ooh. When that finish, Baksh, come back to me and I go give you another voucher.'

Baksh snorted. 'Ha! Is *so* you want to fight elections? You mean, when my gas finish, I must put down whatever I doing? Put it down and come running about looking for you? Look for you, for you to give me another voucher? Another voucher for me to go and get more gas? Get gas to go back and take up whatever it was I was doing before I put it down to come running about looking for you . . .' He completed the argument again.

The taxi-drivers were drunk and not paying too much attention, and nothing would have come of Baksh's protests but for a small accident.

Chittaranjan had, at his own expense, got his workmen

to make heart-shaped buttons for Harbans's agents and taxi-drivers to wear on polling day. Shortly after the motorcade Foam came downstairs to distribute the buttons. They were in a shoebox. A taxi-driver at the bottom of the steps tried to grab a handful. The man was drunk and his action was high-spirited, nothing more. But Foam turned nasty; he was thoroughly tired out by all the festivities, first Mr Cuffy's wake, then the motorcade.

He said, 'Take your thiefing hand away!' That was bad enough, but as Foam spoke his temper rose, and he added, 'I going to make you wait till last for your button.'

When he finally offered, the man declined. 'I don't want none.'

'Come on. Ain't you was grabbing just now? Take the button.'

'Not going to take no damn button. All you people running about behaving like some damn civil servant, pushing away people hand as if people hand dirty.' He raised his voice: 'My hand ain't dirty, you hear. You hearing me good? I is a taxi-driver, but I does bathe every day, you hear. My hand ain't dirty, you hear.'

A crowd began to gather.

Foam said, 'Take your button, man.'

The other taxi-drivers were already sporting theirs.

Foam tried to pin the button on the driver's shirt.

The driver pushed him away and Foam almost fell.

The taxi-driver addressed his audience: 'They want to use people car, but they don't want to give people no button. I ask for one little button and the man push away my hand and practically threaten to beat me up. Giving button to everybody. Everybody. And when he come to me, passing me. I is a dog? My name is Rex? I does go bow-wow-wow? Well, I is *not* a dog, and my name *ain't* Rex, and I ain't taking no damn button.'

Foam's tactics were wrong. He tried to be reasonable. He said, 'I threaten to beat you up? Or you mean that you try to grab the whole shoebox of button?'

The driver laughed. He turned his back on Foam and walked away, the taxi-drivers making a path for him; then he turned and walked back to Foam and the ring of taxi-drivers closed again. 'Is so all you people does get on. So much money all-you spend for this election and now, on the second-to-last night, all-you start offending people and start getting insultive and pussonal.'

Foam continued to be reasonable. 'I was insultive?'

But nobody was listening.

Another taxi-driver was saying, 'And today, when they was sharing out food, I ain't even get a little smell. When I go and ask, they tell me it finish. When I go and ask for a little shot of grog, they drive me away. Harbans spending a lot of money, but is the people that helping him out who going to be responsible if he lose the election. I mean, man, no food, no grog. Things like that don't sound nice when you say it outside.'

And then came this talk about petrol.

'Six gallons ain't enough,' Baksh said.

Somebody else said, 'You know how much they giving taxi-drivers in Port of Spain? Thirty dollars a day. And then in addition too besides, they fulling up your tank for you, you hear. And it have good good roads in Port of Spain that not going to lick up your car.'

That at once made matters worse.

Chittaranjan, Mahadeo and Harbans were upstairs, besieged by more taxi-drivers. Harbans was filling in petrol vouchers as Chittaranjan called out the amount, the number of the taxi, the name of the driver. They were not using the cedar dining-table; it was too good for that; Chittaranjan had brought out the large kitchen table, spread it over with newspapers and jammed it, like a counter, in the doorway between the drawing-room and the veranda. The drivers pressed around the table, waiting for Harbans to fill in and sign their vouchers. Mahadeo was trying to keep some order among the drivers, fruitlessly. They shouted, they cursed, laughed, complained; their shoes grated and screeched on the tiled floor. Harbans filled in and signed, filled in and signed, in a daze, not looking up.

Through all the press Chittaranjan sensed that something was wrong downstairs, and he sent Mahadeo to see what was happening. Mahadeo came back with the news that unless the men were given at least ten gallons of petrol they were going to go on strike the next day.

The taxi-drivers around the table took up the cry.

'Ten gallons, man. I got a big American car. No English matchbox. I does only do fifteen miles to the gallon. Six gallons is like nothing to my car, man.'

'In Port of Spain they fulling up your tank for you.'

'Let Harbans watch out. He think he only saving two gallons of gas. If he ain't careful he saving hisself the trouble of going up to Port of Spain every Friday afternoon to sit down in that Legislative Council.'

Not even Chittaranjan's authority could quell the unrest.

'Mahadeo,' Chittaranjan called. 'Go down and tell them that they going to get their ten gallons. Those that get six, tell them to come up for another voucher.'

Harbans didn't stop to think.

Chittaranjan just whispered to him, 'Ten gallons. Driver name Rapooch. He taxi number is HT 3217.'

An Harbans wrote, and wrote. If he stopped to think he felt he would break down and cry. His wrinkled hand perspired and shook; it had never done so much writing at one time.

Mahadeo went downstairs and spread the healing word.

★

Elvira was stirring before dawn. A fine low mist lay over the hills, promising a hot, thundery day. As the darkness waned the mist lifted, copying the contours of the land, and thinned, layer by layer. Every tree was distinct. Soon the sun would be out, the mist would go, the trees would become an opaque green tangle, and polling would begin.

Polling was to begin at seven; but the fun began before that. The Elvira Estate had given its workers the day off; so had the Public Works Department. Chittaranjan gave his two workmen the day off and put on a clean shirt. Baksh gave himself the day off. He rose early and went straight off to start celebrating with Rampiari's husband and the others. As soon as he was up Foam went over to Chittaranjan's. Harbans was there already. Harbans had wanted to spend the night in Elvira, but Chittaranjan had advised him not to, considering the irreverent mood of the taxi-drivers.

Mahadeo, according to Chittaranjan, was behaving even at that early hour in an entirely shameless way. He was drunk and, what was worse, drinking with the enemy.

Chittaranjan, his hat on, his shirt hanging nice and clean on him, said, 'I did feel like lifting up my hand and giving Mahadeo one good clout with my elbow. I meet him drinking with some good-for-nothing and I say, "Why for you drinking with these good-for-nothing, Mahadeo?" I did expect a straight answer. But the man drunk too bad, man. He tell me he drinking with them because he want to find out which way the wind blowing.'

At seven, or thereabouts, the polling stations opened. Presently there were queues. Agents sat on the roots of trees still cool with dew, ticking off names on duplicated electoral lists, giving cards to voters, instructing the forgetful in the art of making an X. 'No, old man, they ain't want two X.' 'Ah, *maharajin*, it ain't a scorpion they want you to draw. Is a X. Look . . .' 'No, man. They ain't want you to vote for *everybody*. You just put your little X by the heart. Do your part, man.' 'You want to kill him or what? Not *inside* the heart, man.'

Foam's job was to see that the organization worked smoothly. He had to see that the food van made regular rounds; officially, this was to feed agents and other accredited representatives, but many other people were to benefit. He had to make periodic tours of the polling stations to see that no one played the fool.

At ten o'clock Foam reported: 'They staggering the voting at the school.'

'Staggering?'

'Taking six seven minutes over one vote.'

Chittaranjan said, 'I did always feel that man was going to make trouble. You better go and see him, Mr Harbans.'

Harbans knew what that meant.

He went to the school, Teacher Francis's domain, but now in the holidays without Teacher Francis, who was in Port of Spain.

There was a long complaining queue.

Foam said, 'A lot of people leave because they didn't want to stand up all this time.'

The clerk, a cheerful young negro, greeted Harbans with unabashed warmth. 'Is a big big day for you today, Mr Harbans.'

'Ooh, I hear you having a little trouble here.'

'People ain't even know their own name, Mr Harbans.'

'But ain't they got a number?'

The clerk didn't stop smiling. 'I ain't want to know their number. Want to know their name.'

'Ooh. And when they tell you their name, you spend a long long time finding out whether they on the list, and then sometimes you does ask them to spell out their name? Let we look at the election regulations together.'

The clerk brightened.

From his hip pocket Harbans pulled out an orange pamphlet folded in two. He opened it so that only he and the clerk could see what was inside. It was a ten-dollar note.

The clerk said, "Hm. I see what you mean. My mistake. Just leave these regulations here, Mr Harbans.'

Foam was still anxious. 'You can't be too careful in this place. In Trinidad you can't say anybody win election until they draw their first pay. We have to follow the ballot-boxes back to the Warden Office, otherwise you don't know what sort of chicanery they not going to try.'

For that task he and Chittaranjan had chosen men of tried criminality.

One man asked, 'You want me take my cutlass, Goldsmith?'

'I don't want you to land yourself in the Supreme Court again,' Chittaranjan said. 'Just take a good stick.'

Dhaniram stayed at home all morning. With no *doolahin* about, he had to empty his wife's spitting-cup; he had to cook for her; he had to lift her from her bed, make the bed, and put her back on it. He had no time to think about the election, yet when he went to Chittaranjan's he announced, 'Things going good good for you up Cordoba way, Mr Harbans. I spend the whole morning there.'

Chittaranjan barely widened his smile. 'Is a funny thing that you didn't see Foam. Foam going around everywhere all morning.'

Dhaniram changed the subject. 'I too break up by the *doolahin* and Lorkhoor.' He did indeed look ravaged; his skin was yellower, his eyes smaller, redder, without a twinkle.

But he was going to get no sympathy from Harbans. Foam's reports from the polling stations had convinced Harbans that he had practically won the election.

He kept making little jokes with Chittaranjan and Dhaniram.

'I wonder what colour the cheque going to be.'

Chittaranjan couldn't enter into the spirit of the game. 'I don't think they does pay members of the Legislative Council by cheque. I think you does get a sorta voucher. You got to cash it at the Treasury.'

'But what colour you think *that* is?'

'All government voucher white,' Chittaranjan said.

'Ooh, ooh. Least I did expect it woulda be pink or green or something nice like that. Eh, Goldsmith? Ooh, ooh. Just white, eh?' He laughed and slapped Chittaranjan on the back.

Chittaranjan preserved his gravity.

'The thing to make sure you win now,' he said, 'is rain.'

'Ooh, ooh.' Harbans poked Dhaniram in the ribs. Dhaniram laughed painfully. 'Listen to the goldsmith, Pundit. Rain! Ooh, ooh.'

'Rain,' Chittaranjan explained, 'going to keep back all those people who going to vote for Preacher. Preacher ain't got cars to take them to the polling station. We got all the cars.'

'Ooh, Goldsmith, how you could wish that for the poor man? I ain't have nothing against Preacher, man. Eh, Dhaniram?'

'I ain't got nothing against him neither,' Dhaniram said.

Chittaranjan said, 'Talking about taxi remind that the

ringleader last night ain't even turn out this morning.' He consulted his chart. 'Oumadh. HV 5736.'

'Ooh. HV 5736, eh?' Harbans laughingly noted the number in a small notebook. 'We go fix him up, Goldsmith. Going to put the police on his tail. Parking. Speeding. Overloading. From now on he going to spend more time in court than driving taxi. Eh, Goldsmith? Eh, Dhaniram?'

Baksh spent the morning drinking with Mahadeo and Rampiari's husband and Harichand. Mahadeo didn't even vote. He had clean forgotten.

At noon Ramlogan closed his shop and came across.

'Ooh, Ramlogan, man,' Harbans greeted him. 'Look out, man!' Ramlogan roared with laughter.

'Look out, man, Ramlogan. Ooh, you getting fat as a balloon. Ooh, he go bust. Ooh.' Harbans poked Ramlogan in the belly.

Ramlogan laughed even louder. 'You done win already, Mr Harbans.'

Harbans showed his neat false teeth and dug Dhaniram in the ribs. 'How he could say so, eh, Pundit? How he could say so? Ooh, Ramlogan!'

'But you done win, man.'

'Ooh, Ramlogan, you mustn't talk like that, man. You putting goat-mouth on me.'

And many more people kept coming to congratulate Harbans that afternoon. Even people who had announced that they were going to vote for Preacher and had in fact voted for Preacher, even they came and hung around Chittaranjan's shop. One man said, to nobody in particular, 'I is a kyarpenter. Preacher can't afford to give me no kyarpentering work. Preacher and people who voting for Preacher don't build house.'

The attitude of the policemen changed. In the morning they had been cautious and reserved: most of them had come from outside districts and didn't know much about the prospects of the candidates. In the afternoon they began to treat Harbans and his agents with respect. They waved and smiled and tried to keep their batons out of sight.

And then Chittaranjan had his wish. It rained. The roads became muddy and slippery; agents had to leave their positions under trees and move under houses; taxis, their windows up and misted over, steamed inside.

By three o'clock nearly everyone who was going to vote had voted. It was a fantastically high poll, more than eighty-three per cent. The fact was noted with approval in official reports.

★

Foam's last duty was to keep an eye on the ballot-box at the polling station in the school. At five o'clock he went with a taxi-driver and waited. Through the open door he could see the poll clerk, the staggerer of the morning's vote, sitting at Teacher Francis's own table, flanked by Harbans's agent and a negro girl, one of Preacher's few agents. The ballot-box looked old and brown and unimportant. Foam could see the clerk taking out the ballot-papers and counting them.

Harbans's agent came to the door and waved to Foam.

Foam shouted, 'You is a ass. Go back and see what they doing.'

The agent was a slim young man, almost a boy, with a waist that looked dangerously narrow. He said, 'Everything under control, man,' but he went back to the table.

The watch lasted until dark.

The policeman who had been hanging about outside the school went up the concrete steps. The clerk said something to him. The policeman came down the steps, went across the road and called, 'Bellman!' He spoke with a strong Barbadian accent.

A middle-aged negro in washed-out khaki trousers and a thick flannel vest came out into his veranda.

'Bellman, you got a lamp? They want it borrow over here.'

Bellman brought out an oil lamp. Unprotected, the flame swayed and rose high, smoking thickly.

Bellman said, 'I sending in my account to the Warden.'

The policeman laughed and took the lamp to the school. The checking was still going on. Apparently there had been some mistake in the checking because the ballot-box had been emptied again and the ballot-papers lay in a jagged white pile on the table.

The taxi-driver said, 'If that agent don't look out, they work some big big sort of trick here, you know.'

The policeman looked at Foam and the taxi-driver and swung his long baton, a casual warning.

Another of Harbans's taxis came up. The driver leaned out and asked, 'You got the score here yet?'

Harbans's agent, hearing the noise, came out with a sheet of paper. 'Preliminary,' he said, smiling, handing it over.

'Haul your tail back quick,' Foam said. 'See what they doing.'

The agent smiled and ran back up the steps.

Foam's taxi-driver said, 'What you want for elections is strong agents. Strong strong agents.'

They looked at the paper.

Foam read: 'Harbans 325, Thomas 57, Baksh 2.'

The other taxi-driver whistled. 'We giving them licks on all fronts. But some people don't listen at all, man. Baksh get two votes after the man ask them not to vote for him.' Then he delivered his own news: 'At Cordoba, Harbans 375, Thomas 19, Baksh 0. At Cordoba again, the second polling station, is Harbans 345, Thomas 21, Baksh 0.'

Foam's taxi-driver said, 'Yaah!' and took a drink of rum from the bottle on the dashboard shelf.

The other taxi-driver drove away.

The box was being sealed and signed.

Foam couldn't help feeling sorry for Preacher's agent. She was one of those who had sung the hymns at Mr Cuffy's wake. She sat unflinchingly at the table, being brave and unconcerned; while Harbans's agent, to the disgust of Foam and the taxi-driver, was jumping about here and there, doing goodness knows what.

Bellman pushed his head through his window curtain and said, 'Look, all-you finish with my lamp? That costing the Warden six cents, you know. I sure all-you done burn six cents' pitch-oil already.'

They were finished. The box was sealed, signed and brought out to the steps. The policeman took the lamp back to Bellman; then he rejoined the girl, Harbans's agent and the ballot-box. The clerk was padlocking the school door.

Foam shouted, 'What the hell all-you waiting for?'

Harbans's agent smiled.

They waited for about twenty minutes.

The clerk went home. The girl, Preacher's agent, went home. Harbans's agent said, 'This is a lot of arseness. Foreman, you could look after the ballot-box now yourself. I hungry like hell.'

Foam said, 'Good. Go. But I marking you for this. You hungry? You ain't eat? The food van ain't bring you nothing?'

'What food van? I ain't even see the food van. Everybody did tell me about this famous food van, but I ain't see nothing.' And he went home.

Foam said to his taxi-driver, 'Let that teach you a lesson. Never pay people in advance.'

The policeman kept on coughing in the darkness.

'Put on your lights,' Foam said.

When the lights went on, the policeman stopped coughing.

The taxi-driver went for a little walk. Then Foam went for a little walk. The policeman was still waiting.

When it was nearly half-past seven and it seemed that no one had even honourable designs on the ballot-box, Foam lost his patience.

He went to the policeman. 'What you waiting for?'

The policeman said, 'I ain't know. They did just tell me to wait.'

'You want a lift to the Warden Office?'

'You going there?'

They took the policeman and the ballot-box to the Warden's Office.

In the asphalt yard next to the Warden's Office Foam heard the loudspeaker—his father's voice; and he heard the enthusiastic shouts of the crowd. Apparently some results had already been rechecked and given out as official.

They delivered the policeman and the ballot-box; then they drove through the crowd to a free place in the yard.

Baksh was announcing: 'Kindly corporate with the police. Keep death off the roads. Beware of the Highway Code. This is the voice of Baksh telling you to beware of the Highway Code and keep death off the roads. Come in a lil bit more, ladies and gentlemen. Come in a lil bit. Another result just come in. But come in a lil bit more fust. This is the voice of Baksh begging you and beseeching you to corporate with the Highway Code and keep death off the roads. Another result. From Cordoba, station number one. Another result. From Cordoba One. Final result. Baksh nought. Baksh nought.'

The crowd appreciated the joke.

'Harbans 364, Harbans 364.'

Clamour.

'Come in a lil bit, ladies and gentlemen. Be aware of the Highway Code. Beware of the Highway Code. Thomas 45.'

Shouts of 'Yaah!' Spontaneous drumming on car bonnets.

Baksh took advantage of the pause to have another drink. The gurgling noises were magnified by the loudspeaker. Someone was heard saying, 'Give *me* a chance at the loud-peaker. Beware of the Highway Code, ladies and gentle-men. Beware . . .' Baksh's voice broke in, conversationally, Is for the government I working tonight, you know. Not or any-and everybody. But for the government.' Then officially: 'Thomas 45. Thomas 45.'

What Baksh said was true. He was working for the government, as an official announcer; he had paid well to get the job.

The loudspeaker was silent for some time.

Then there was a shout, and sustained frenzied cheering. Harbans had appeared. In his moment of triumph he man-ged to look sad and absent-minded. The crowd didn't mind. They rushed to him and lifted him on their shoulders nd they took him to the loudspeaker van and made him tand on one of the wings and then they grabbed the micro-hone from Baksh and thrust it into Harbans's hands and shouted, 'Speech!'

Baksh tried to get the microphone back.

'This is government business, man. All-you want me to et in trouble or what?'

Harbans didn't object. 'Is true, eh, Baksh?' and he passed he microphone back.

'Ladies and gentlemen, corporate with the police. Beware f the Highway Code. Be aware of the Highway Code, adies and gentlemen.'

The crowd shouted obscene abuse at Baksh. Some of it was picked up by the loudspeaker.

'Ladies and gentlemen, unless you corporate with the

government and unless and until you corporate with the police and start bewaring of the Highway Code, I cannot give out the last and final result which I have at this very present moment in my own own hand. Ladies and gentlemen, come in a lil bit fust, ladies and gentlemen. Keep the road clear. Keep death off the roads. Think before you drink. Drive slowly. 'Rrive safely. Come in a lil bit fust. Last result. Last result. Corporate with the police. Last result. Final grand total. Ladies and gentlemen, come in a lil bit.'

Harbans remained on the wing of the van, almost forgotten.

'Baksh 56. Baksh 56.'

Boos. Ironical cheers. Laughter.

'Repeat. Final result. Baksh 56. Harbans five thousand . . .'

Tumult.

'Beware of the Highway Code. Harbans five thousand, three hundred and thirty-six. Five three three six.'

The crowd swarmed around the van, grabbed at Harbans's ankles, knees. Some offered up hands. Harbans grabbed them with astonishing vigour and shook them fervently.

Baksh tried to carry on calmly, like a man on government business. 'Thomas seven hundred . . .'

They wanted to hear no more.

Baksh shouted at them without effect. He shouted and shouted and then waited for them to calm down.

'Ladies and gentlemen, you is *not* corporating. Thomas seven hundred and sixteen. Seven one six. And so, ladies and gentlemen, I give you your new Onble Member of the Leglisative Council, Mr Surujpat Harbans. But before I give him to you, let me make a final appeal to corporate with the police. Beware of the Highway Code.'

Harbans, on the wing, was in tears when he took the microphone. His voice, coming over the loudspeaker, was a magnified coo. 'I want to thank everybody. I want to thank you and you and you . . .'

Somebody whispered, 'The police.'

'. . . and I want to thank the police and the Warden and the clerks and I want to thank everybody who vote for me and even people who ain't vote for me. I want to thank . . .' Tears prevented him from going on.

Baksh recovered the microphone. 'Corporate, ladies and gentlemen. That was your new Onble Member of the Legislative Council, Mr Surujpat Harbans.'

Foam wandered among the crowd looking for members of the committee. Mahadeo was drunk and useless. Dhaniram he couldn't see. At the edge of the yard, in the darkness, he saw Chittaranjan, leaning against the radiator of a car.

'Well, Goldsmith, we do it. We win.'

Chittaranjan pressed down his hat and folded his arms. 'What else you did expect?'

At that moment Preacher was going around briskly from house to house, thanking the people.

And so democracy took root in Elvira.

EPILOGUE

THE CASE OF WHISKY

★

Harbans spent the rest of that night settling his bills. The taxi-drivers had to be paid off, Ramlogan's rum-account settled, petrol vouchers honoured, agents given bonuses. And when all that was done, Harbans left Elvira, intending never to return.

But he did return, once.

It was because of that case of whisky Ramlogan had promised the committee of the winning candidate. Ramlogan wanted the presentation to be made in style, by the new Member of the Legislative Council. Chittaranjan thought it was fitting. He hadn't always approved of the publicity Ramlogan gave the case of whisky; but now he was glad of the excuse to get Harbans back in Elvira. Harbans hadn't dropped a word about marrying his son to Nelly. Chittaranjan knew the rumours that had been going around Elvira during the campaign, knew that people were laughing at him behind his back. But that had only encouraged him to work harder for Harbans. He had made those heart-shaped buttons at his own expense. He had worn his visiting outfit nearly every day; he had used up one shirt; his shoes needed half-soling. Harbans had taken it all for granted.

The presentation was fixed for the Friday after polling day; it was to take place outside Chittaranjan's shop. Benches and chairs were brought over from the school. Dhaniram lent his Petromax. Chittaranjan lent a small table and a clean tablecloth. On the tablecloth they placed the case of whisky stencilled WHITE HORSE WHISKY PRODUCE OF SCOTLAND 12 BOTTLES. On the case of whisky they placed a small Union Jack—Ramlogan's idea: he wanted to make the whole thing legal and respectable.

Haq and Sebastian came early and sat side by side on the bench against Chittaranjan's shop. Harichand came, Rampiari's husband, Lutchman. Tiger came and sniffed at the table legs. Haq shooed him off, but Tiger stayed to chase imaginary scents all over Chittaranjan's terrace.

Foam dressed for the occasion as though he were going to Port of Spain.

Mrs Baksh asked, 'And what you going to do with the three bottle of whisky? Drink it?'

'Nah,' Foam said. 'Keeping it. Until Christmas. Then going to sell it in Chaguanas. You could get anything up to eight dollars for a bottle of White Horse at Christmas.'

'You say that. But I don't think it would please your father heart to see three bottle of whisky remaining quiet in the house all the time until Christmas.'

'Well, you better tell him not to touch them. Otherwise it going to have big big trouble between me and he.'

Mrs Baksh sighed. Only three months ago, if Foam had talked like that, she could have slapped him. But the election had somehow changed Foam; he was no longer a boy.

Ramlogan prepared with the utmost elaborateness. He rubbed himself down with coconut oil; then he had a bath in lukewarm water impregnated with leaves of the *neem* tree; then he rubbed himself down with Canadian Healing Oil and put on his striped blue three-piece suit. A handkerchief hung rather than peeped from his breast pocket. His enormous brown shoes were highly polished; he had even bought a pair of laces for them. He wore no socks and no tie.

Chittaranjan put on his visiting outfit, Mahadeo his khaki uniform.

Dhaniram wasn't going to be there. He was so distressed by the loss of the *doolahin* that he had lost interest even in his tractor. He didn't see how he could replace the girl. He was a fussy Brahmin; he couldn't just get an ordinary servant to look after his food. Ideally, he would have liked another daughter-in-law.

Outside Chittaranjan's shop the crowd thickened. People were coming from as far as Cordoba and Pueblo Road. It was like Mr Cuffy's wake all over again.

Foam told the other members of the committee, sitting in Chittaranjan's drawing-room, 'I feel it going to have some trouble tonight.'

Chittaranjan felt that himself, and despite his friendship with Ramlogan, snapped out, 'Well, if people must show off . . .'

Ramlogan took it well. He laughed, took out his handkerchief and fanned his face. 'Gosh, but these three-piece suit hot, man. What trouble it could have? Whisky is for the committee, not for everybody in Elvira. Election over, and they know that.'

It was Friday evening; the people downstairs were in the week-end mood. Talk and laughter and argument floated up to the drawing-room.

'They could say what they want to say. But I know that Baksh coulda win that election easy easy.'

'What I want to know is, who put Harbans in the Council? Committee or the people?'

'No, man. Is not *one* case of whisky. Is twelve case.'

'Hear what I say. Preacher lose the election the night Cawfee dead. I was backing the man strong, man. Had two dollars on him.'

'That one case under the Union Jack is just a sort of *sign* for all the twelve case.'

'If Cawfee didn't throw up his four foot and dead, you think Harbans coulda win?'

'Yes, twelve case of whisky on one small table wouldn't look nice.'

Then Harbans came.

'Pappa! Eh, but what happen to the old Dodge lorry?'

Harbans had come in a brand-new blue-and-black Jaguar.

'Lorry! What happen to Harbans?'

He wasn't the candidate they knew. Gone was the informality of dress, the loose trousers, the tie around the waist, the open shirt. He was in a double-breasted grey suit. The coat was a little too wide and a little too long; but that was the tailor's fault. Harbans didn't wave. He looked preoccupied, kept his eye on the ground, and when he hawked and spat in the gutter, pulled out an ironed handkerchief and wiped his lips—not wiped even, patted them—in the fussiest way.

The people of Elvira were hurt.

He didn't coo at anybody, didn't look at anybody. He made his way silently through the silent crowd and went straight up the steps into Chittaranjan's drawing-room. The crowd watched him go up and then they heard him talking and they heard Ramlogan talking and laughing.

They didn't like it at all.

Presently the committee appeared on the veranda. Foam looked down and waved. Mahadeo looked down and waved. Harbans didn't look down; Chittaranjan didn't look down; and Ramlogan, for a man who had just been heard laughing loudly, looked ridiculously solemn.

The walk down the polished red stairs became a grave procession. Foam and Mahadeo, at the back, had to clip their steps.

'Tock. Tock. Tock,' Harichand said. '*Pai! Pai! Pai!* Tocktocktocktocktock.'

The crowd laughed. Tiger barked.

Chittaranjan frowned for silence, and got it.

Harbans looked down at his shoes all the time, looking as miserable as if he had lost the election. Ramlogan would have liked to match Harbans's dignity, but he wanted to look at the crowd, and whenever he looked at the crowd he found it hard not to smile.

The chairs and benches had been disarrayed. The crowd had spread out into the road and formed a solid semicircle around the case of whisky draped with the Union Jack.

Harbans sat directly in front of the whisky. Ramlogan was on his right, Chittaranjan on his left. Foam was next to Ramlogan, Mahadeo next to Chittaranjan. Not far from Foam, on his right, Haq and Sebastian sat.

As soon as the committee had settled down a man ran out from the crowd and whispered to Harbans.

It was Baksh.

He whispered, urgently, 'Jordan can't come tonight. He sick.'

The word aroused bitter memories.

'Jordan?' Harbans whispered.

'Sick?' Mahadeo said.

Baksh ran back, on tiptoe, to the crowd.

Sebastian looked on smiling. Haq sucked his teeth and spat.

Chittaranjan stood up. 'Ladies and gentlemen'—there were no ladies present—'tonight Mr Harbans come back to Elvira, and we glad to welcome him again. Mr Harbans is a good friend. And Mr Harbans could see, by just looking at the amount of people it have here tonight, how much all-you think of him in Elvira.'

Harbans was whispering to Ramlogan, 'Jordan sick? Who is Jordan? He fall sick too late.'

Ramlogan roared, for the audience.

Chittaranjan shot him a look and went on, 'I want to see the man who could come up to me and tell me to my face that is only because Mr Harbans win a election that everybody come to see him. I know, speaking in my own pussonal, that even if Mr Harbans *didn't* win *no* election, Mr Harbans woulda *want* to come back to Elvira, and all-you woulda *want* to come and see him.'

There was some polite clapping.

'And so, ladies and gentlemen, without further ado, let me introduce Mr Foreman Baksh.'

Foam said, 'Ladies and gentlemen, it nice to see so much of all-you here. Tonight Mr Ramlogan'—he nodded towards Ramlogan, but Ramlogan was too busy talking to Harbans to notice—'Mr Ramlogan going to present a case of whisky to the committee. The committee, ladies and gentlemen, of which I am proud and happy to be a member. Ladies and gentlemen, times changing. People do the voting, is true. But is the committee that do the organizing. In this modern world, you can't get nowhere if you don't organize. And now let me introduce Mr Mahadeo.'

Foam's references to the whisky and the committee caused so much buzzing that Mahadeo couldn't begin.

Baksh used the interval to run forward again.

'Don't forget,' he whispered to Harbans. 'Jordan ain't here. He sick.'

Chittaranjan stood up and said sternly, 'Ladies and gentlemen, Mr Mahadeo want to say a few words.'

Mahadeo said, 'Well, all-you must remember . . .'

Chittaranjan pulled at Mahadeo's trousers.

Mahadeo broke off, confused, 'I sorry, Goldsmith.' He coughed. 'Ladies and gentlemen.' He swallowed. 'Ladies and gentlemen, Mr Harbans ain't have nothing to do with the whisky. I ain't really know how the rumour get around, but this case of whisky'—he patted the Union Jack—'is for the committee, of which I am proud and happy to be a member. The whisky ain't for nobody else. Is not Mr Harbans whisky. Is Mr Ramlogan whisky.'

The buzzing rose again.

Mahadeo looked at Ramlogan. 'Ain't is your whisky, Mr Ramlogan?'

Ramlogan stood up and straightened his striped blue jacket. 'Ladies and gentlemen, what Mr Mahadeo say is the gospel truth, as the saying goes. Is my whisky. Is my idea.' He sat down and immediately began to talk to Harbans again.

The murmurings of the crowd couldn't be ignored. Mahadeo remained standing, not saying anything.

Rampiari's husband, bandageless, came out from the crowd. 'Wasn't what *we* hear. We didn't hear nothing about no whisky for no committee. And I think I must say right here and now that Elvira people ain't liking this bacchanal at all. Look at these poor people! They come from all over the place. You think a man go put on his clothes, take up his good good self and walk from Cordoba to Elvira in the night-time with all this dew falling, just to see committee get a case of whisky?'

Harichand said, 'Everybody think they could kick poor people around. Let them take back their whisky. The people of Elvira ain't got their tongue hanging out like dog for nobody whisky, you hear. The people of Elvira still got their pride. Take back the damn whisky, man!'

The people of Elvira cheered Harichand.

Ramlogan stopped talking to Harbans. Harbans's hands were tapping on his knees.

Mahadeo, still standing, saying nothing, saw the crowd break up into agitated groups. He sat down.

Ramlogan didn't smile when he looked at the crowd.

Suddenly he sprang up and said, 'I have a damn good mind to mash up the whole blasted case of whisky.' He grabbed the case and the Union Jack slipped off. 'Go ahead. Provoke me. See if I don't throw it down.'

The silence was abrupt.

Ramlogan scowled, the case of whisky in his hands.

Rampiari's husband walked up to him and said amiably, 'Throw it down.'

The crowd chanted, '*Throw it down! Throw it down!*' Tiger barked.

Chittaranjan said, 'Sit down, bruds.'

Ramlogan replaced the case of whisky and picked up the Union Jack.

Baksh ran to Harbans. He didn't whisper this time. 'Don't say I didn't tell you. Jordan sick. Remember that.'

Harbans was puzzled.

'Why Jordan sick?' he asked Ramlogan.

Ramlogan didn't laugh.

The crowd became one again. Harichand and Rampiari's husband came to the front.

Harichand said, 'Mr Harbans, I think I should tell you that the people of Elvira not going to take this insult lying down. They work hard for you, they waste their good good time and they go and mark X on ballot-paper for your sake.'

Rampiari's husband tightened his broad leather belt. 'They putting money in your pocket, Mr Harbans. Five years' regular pay. And the committee get pay for what they do. But look at these poor people. You drag them out from Cordoba and Ravine Road and Pueblo Road. I can't hold back the people, Mr Harbans.'

Harbans yielded. He rose, held his hands together, cracked his fingers, shifted his gaze from his feet to his hands and said, cooing like the old Harbans, 'The good people of Elvira work hard for me and I going to give Ramlogan a order to give ten case of whisky to the committee to give you.' It would cost him about four hundred dollars, but it seemed the only way out. He couldn't make a run for his Jaguar. 'Ten case of whisky. Good whisky.' He gave a little coo and showed his false teeth. 'Not White Horse, though. You can't get that every day.'

Almost miraculously, the crowd was appeased. They laughed at Harbans's little joke and chattered happily among themselves.

But Chittaranjan was in the devil of a temper. He was annoyed with the crowd; annoyed with Harbans for giving in so easily to them; annoyed because he knew for sure now that Harbans never had any intention of marrying his son to Nelly; annoyed with Ramlogan for offering the whisky and making so much noise about it.

He jumped up and shouted, 'No!' It was his firm fighting voice. It stilled the crowd. 'You people ain't got no shame at all. Instead of Mr Harbans giving you anything more, you should be giving *him* something, for a change.'

The crowd was taken by surprise.

'Most of you is Hindus. Mr Harbans is a Hindu. He win a election. *You* should be giving him something. You should be saying prayers for him.'

There was a murmur. Not of annoyance, but incomprehension.

'Say a *kattha* for him. Get Pundit Dhaniram to read from the Hindu scriptures.'

The effect was wonderful. Even Rampiari's husband was shamed. He took off his hat and came a step or two nearer the case of whisky. 'But Goldsmith, a *kattha* going to cost a lot of money.'

'Course it going to cost money!'

Rampiari's husband withdrew.

Harbans got up, cooing. 'Ooh, Goldsmith. If they want

to honour me with a *kattha*, we must let them honour me with a *kattha*. Ooh. Tell you what, eh, good people of Elvira. Make a little collection among yourself fust.'

The crowd was too astonished to protest.

Only Haq staggered up and said, 'Why for we should make a collection for a Hindu *kattha*? We is Muslims.'

But no one heard him. Harbans was still speaking: 'Make your collection fust.' He flashed the false teeth again. 'And for every dollar you collect, I go put a dollar, and with the money *all* of we put up, we go have the *kattha*.' Harbans had heard Haq though; so he turned to Foam, as a Muslim, for support. 'Eh, Foreman? You don't think is the best idea?'

Foam rose. 'Is the best thing. And I agree with the goldsmith that the people of Elvira should give something to their own Onble Member.'

That really caused the trouble.

Rampiari's husband didn't mind when Chittaranjan had said it. Everyone respected Chittaranjan as an honourable man, and everyone knew that he hadn't got a penny from Harbans. But when Foam said it, that was different.

'Is all right for *you* to talk, Foreman Baksh,' Rampiari's husband said. 'Your pocket full. You get your two hundred dollars a month campaign-managing for Harbans.'

'And your father get a whole loudspeaking van,' Harichand chipped in. 'And everybody in Elvira damn well know that out of the fifty-six votes your father get, your father vote was one.'

Baksh danced to the front of the crowd.

'What loudspeaking van?' he asked.

Chittaranjan was on his feet again. 'And we, the members of the committee, going to give back the case of whisky to Mr Ramlogan.'

This made Mahadeo lose his temper.

'Why? Why for we must give back the case of whisky?'

'And how the hell you know I ain't vote for Harbans, Harichand?'

'The clerk tell me,' Harichand said.

For a moment Baksh was nonplussed. Then he shouted, 'Harbans, if you going to give money for a Hindu *kattha*, you damn well got to give the Muslims a *kitab*.'

Mahadeo said, 'Goldsmith, why for we must give back the whisky?'

'Hush your mouth, you damn fool,' Chittaranjan whispered. 'We not giving it back really.'

Haq had limped right up to the whisky and was saying, 'Muslim vote for Harbans too. What happen? They stop counting Muslim vote these days?'

'All right,' Harbans cooed. 'All you Muslim make your collection for your *kitab*. And for every dollar you put, I go put one. Eh?'

Then somebody else leapt up and asked what about the Christians.

Rampiari's husband shouted, 'Haq, what the hell you doing there? You vote for Harbans?'

'Who I vote for is my business. Nobody ain't make you a policeman yet.'

Then it was chaos. Rampiari's husband switched his attack to Baksh. Baksh was attacking Harbans. Foam was being attacked by innumerable anonymous people. Mahadeo was being attacked by people whose illnesses he had spurned. Haq was poking questions directly under Harbans's nose. Harbans was saying, 'Ooh, ooh,' and trying to pacify everybody. Only two objects remained immovable and constant: Chittaranjan and the case of whisky.

Somehow, after minutes of tortuous altercation, something was decided. The committee were to give back the case of whisky. The people of Elvira were to get religious consolation. The Muslims were to get their *kitab*, the Hindus their *kattha*, the Christians their service.

But nobody was really pleased.

Ramlogan insisted that Harbans should give him back the case of whisky ceremonially.

Harbans said, 'Ladies and gentlemen, was nice of all-you to ask me down here today to give away this whisky. But I can't tell you how happy and proud it make me to see that the committee ain't want it. Committee do their duty, and duty is their reward.'

There was some derisory cheering.

'So, Mr Ramlogan, I give you back your whisky. And I glad to see that at this moment the people of Elvira putting God in their heart.'

Foam said, 'Three cheers for the Onble Surujpat Harbans. Hip-hip.'

He got no response.

Only, Baksh ran up.

'Jordan sick, Mr Harbans.'

'I hope he get better.'

'For the last time, Mr Harbans. Jordan sick.'

The crowd pressed forward silently around the committee.

Harbans buttoned his over-large coat and prepared to leave. He put his hand on the arm of Rampiari's husband, to show that he wasn't cowed. 'Give me a little break. Let me get through.'

Rampiari's husband folded his arms.

'Give me a break, man. Last time I come to Elvira, I telling you. All you people driving me away.'

Rampiari's husband said, 'We know you is a Onble and thing now, but you deaf? You ain't hear what the man saying? Jordan sick.' Rampiari's husband turned his back to Harbans and addressed the crowd. 'All-you see Jordan tonight?'

The reply came in chorus: '*No, we ain't see Jordan.*'

'What happen to Jordan?' Rampiari's husband asked.

'*Jordan sick*,' the crowd replied.

Harbans looked at Chittaranjan.

Chittaranjan said, 'You better go.'

Jordan lived in one of the many traces off the main road. It was a moonless night and the occasional oil lamps in the houses far back from the trace only made the darkness more terrible. At the heels of Harbans and his committee there was nearly half the crowd that had gathered outside Chittaranjan's shop. Tiger ran yapping in and out of the procession. One horrible young labourer with glasses, gold teeth and a flowerpot hat pushed his face close to Harbans and said, 'Don't worry with the old generation. Is the young generation like me you got to worry about.'

Jordan was waiting for them, reclined on a couch in his front room, a plump sleepy-faced young negro with a pile of stiff kinky hair. He wore pyjamas that looked suspiciously new. Chittaranjan was surprised. Nobody in Elvira wore pyjamas.

'Jordan,' Harbans called. 'You sick?'

'Yes, man,' Jordan said. 'Stroke. Hit me all down here.' He ran his hand along his left side.

'The man break up bad,' Rampiari's husband said. 'He can't do no more work for a long time to come.'

'It come sudden sudden,' Jordan said. 'I was drinking a cup of water and it come. Bam! Just like that.'

An old woman, a young woman and a boy came into the room.

'Mother, wife, brother,' Baksh explained.

'Jordan supporting all of them,' Harichand said.

Chittaranjan regarded Jordan and Jordan's family with contempt. He said, 'Give him ten dollars and let we go.'

'Ten!' Jordan exclaimed acidly. 'Fifty.'

'Fifty at least,' Baksh said.

'At least,' said Rampiari's husband.

'Is not something just for Jordan,' Baksh said. 'You could say is a sort of thank-you present for everybody in Elvira.'

'Exactly,' Harichand said. 'Can't just come to a place and collect people good good vote and walk away. Don't look nice. Don't sound nice.'

Harbans said, 'This election making me a pauper. They should pass some sort of law to prevent candidates spending too much money.' But he pulled out his wallet.

Jordan said, 'God go bless you, boss.'

Harbans took two twenty-dollar notes and one ten-dollar note, crackled them separately and handed them to Jordan.

Without warning Tiger sprang on the couch, trampled over Jordan's new pyjamas, put his front paws on the window-sill and barked.

Almost immediately there was a loud explosion from the main road. Seconds later there were more explosions.

The crowd in the trace shouted, 'Fire!'

Jordan's stroke was forgotten. Everybody scrambled outside, committee, mother, wife, brother. Jordan himself forgot about his stroke and knelt on his couch to look out of the window. In the direction of the main road the sky was bright; the glare teased out houses and trees from the darkness.

Somebody cried, 'Mr Harbans! Goldsmith!'

But Harbans was already in the trace and running, awkwardly, like a woman in a tight skirt.

He found the crowd standing in a wide silent circle around the burning Jaguar. It was a safe spectacle now; the petrol tanks had blown up. The firelight reddened unsmiling, almost contemplative, faces.

Harbans stopped too, to watch the car burn. The fire had

done its work swiftly and well, thanks to the Jaguar's reserve petrol tank, which Harbans liked to keep full. There was little smoke now; the flames burned pure. Behind the heat waves faces were distorted.

The people from the trace ran up in joyful agitation, flowed around the car, settled, and became silent. Harbans was wedged among them.

Foam acted with firmness.

He beat his way through to Harbans.

'Mr Harbans, come.'

Harbans followed without thinking. They got into the loudspeaker van. It wasn't until Foam drove off that the people of Elvira turned to look. They didn't cheer or boo or do anything. Only Tiger, missing Foam, ran barking after the van.

'Is okay now, Mr Harbans,' Foam said. 'If you did stay you woulda want to start asking questions. If you did start asking questions you woulda only cause more trouble.'

'Elvira, Elvira.' Harbans shook his head and spoke to the back of his hands, covered almost up to the knuckles by the sleeves of his big grey coat. 'Elvira, you is a bitch.'

And he came to Elvira no more.

The Jaguar was less than a week old. The insurance company bought him a new one.

★

It made Lorkhoor's reputation. He was living with the *doolahin* in a dingy furnished room in Henry Street in Port of Spain. He had already applied, without success, for jobs on the *Trinidad Guardian* and the *Port of Spain Gazette* when, on Saturday, the news of the burning Jaguar broke. Lorkhoor took a taxi down to Harichand's printery in Couva and got the facts from Harichand. That, and his own inside knowledge, gave him material for a splendid follow-up story which he submitted to the *Trinidad Sentinel.* It appeared in the Sunday issue. Lorkhoor wrote the headline himself: 'A Case of Whisky, the New Jaguar and the Suffrage of Elvira'. He had fallen under the influence of William Saroyan.

On Monday Lorkhoor was on the staff of the *Sentinel.* He began to contribute a regular Sunday piece for the *Sentinel*'s magazine section, *Lorkhoor's Log.*

★

Foam had his wish. He got Lorkhoor's old job, announcing for the cinemas in Caroni. In addition, he had earned two hundred and twenty-five dollars as Harbans's campaign manager; and he had been able to snub Teacher Francis.

Teacher Francis deteriorated rapidly. In the Christmas holidays he married into one of the best coloured families in Port of Spain, the Smiths. He renounced all intellectual aspirations, won the approval of the Education Department and an appointment as Schools Inspector.

And Ramlogan. He had won his largest rum-account. He could buy that refrigerator now. Now, too, he could pick his own flowers and eat his own breadfruit and zaboca.

And Dhaniram. He had some luck. His brother-in-law died in September, and his sister came to live with him.

And Tiger. He had won a reprieve. He was to live long and querulously.

And Chittaranjan. But he had lost. He sent many messages to Harbans but got no reply. At last he went to see Harbans in Port of Spain; but Harbans kept him waiting so long in the veranda and greeted him so coldly, he couldn't bring himself to ask about the marriage. It was Harbans who brought the point up. Harbans said, 'Chittaranjan, the Hindus in Trinidad going downhill fast. I say, let those who want to go, go quick. If only one hundred good Hindu families remain, well, all right. But we can't let our children marry people who does run about late at night with Muslim boys.' Chittaranjan accepted the justice of the argument. And that was that.

But if Chittaranjan had lost, Nelly had won. In September of that year she went to London and joined the Regent Street Polytechnic. She went to all the dances and enjoyed them. She sent home presents that Christmas, an umbrella for her father, and a set of four china birds for her mother. The birds flew on the wall next to the picture of Mahatma Gandhi and King George V. The umbrella became part of Chittaranjan's visiting outfit.

★

So, Harbans won the election and the insurance company lost a Jaguar. Chittaranjan lost a son-in-law and Dhaniram lost a daughter-in-law. Elvira lost Lorkhoor and Lorkhoor won a reputation. Elvira lost Mr Cuffy. And Preacher lost his deposit.